NEVER
Make You Cry

Also by Geneva Lee

THE ROYALS SAGA

Command Me

Conquer Me

Crown Me

Crave Me

Covet Me

Capture Me

Complete Me

Cross Me

Claim Me

Consume Me

Breathe Me

Break Me

X: Command Me Retold

THE DYNASTIES SAGA

London Dynasty

Cruel Dynasty

Secret Dynasty

THE RIVALS SAGA

Blacklist

Backlash

Bombshell

OLYMPIC FALLS

Never Give You Up

Never Let You Down

Never Make You Cry

Never Say Goodbye : A Liam Novella

THE SINNERS SAGA

Beautiful Criminal

Beautiful Sinner

Beautiful Forever

FILTHY RICH VAMPIRES

Filthy Rich Vampire

Filthy Rich Vampires: Second Rite

STANDALONE

The Sins That Bind Us

Two Week Turnaround

NEVER
Make You Cry

GENEVA LEE

ESTATE

To every girl who has every cried over a man.
Don't settle for a knock-off.

One

SEATTLE, WASHINGTON WAS A VERITABLE minefield of ex-boyfriends. Turn a corner. Step out of a building. Grab a quick bite to eat. And boom!

I had found myself face-to-face with three already, and I hadn't even finished the first day of my internship. I was beginning to wonder if the university had started a male consignment program, loaning out every eligible bachelor on campus to the greater metropolitan area. Not that all of them were still eligible—and none of them were available, according to my standards.

My day started with running into Luka, a.k.a. Mr. Freshman Year, while trying to pay for parking. As if paying twenty-five dollars for the privilege to leave my car wasn't bad enough, the machine wouldn't take my card. When the man behind me kept persistently clearing his throat, I'd finally lost my cool and spun around. "Do you need a cough drop, jacka...?"

The words died on my lips when I saw those familiar blue

eyes. I'd peered into them enough a few years back to have each fleck in his irises memorized. If only I'd bothered to look a little deeper. That had been hard given his off-the-charts hotness. I'd been taken in by his unruly blond hair and square jaw. The two hours a day he spent in the gym hadn't hurt either. Not initially. It probably should have clued me in that he was a Grade A narcissist.

"Cassie?" He sounded as surprised as I felt, which was a much-needed boost to my confidence. Maybe he hadn't expected to run into anyone he knew, or maybe—just maybe —I'd come a long way from the nineteen-year-old girl he'd known. I'd traded in my yoga pants and Uggs for Jimmy Choos and pencil skirts. I was well past my basic bitch stage. Now, I was a badass bitch.

"The machine is broken." As far as I was concerned that was the only explanation. I'd tried for five minutes to get it to accept payment.

"Let me try." Luka's lips quirked into the arrogant smirk I'd once found so charming. Back then it had won him an all-access pass to my panties. Now, I fought the urge to slap him. Did he not recognize my new status as a badass bitch?

Obviously not, because he swiped the Visa from my hand. Stepping forward, he flipped it over and swiped it. The payment processed instantly.

Life must be easier for the really, truly stupid. They probably weren't aware when they did something really, truly idiotic. Though I was not really, truly stupid, I was now *very* well-aware that I'd done something really, truly idiotic.

A string of curses slipped from my mouth that would have made a sailor blush.

He handed the card back to me. My parking spot was secured, but my dignity was in shambles.

"Thanks." I stuffed the card in my purse and avoided eye contact. Why couldn't it have been a stranger behind me? A soccer mom or a wizened old executive? Someone who wouldn't have noticed I didn't know how to use a credit card machine.

"What are you doing here?" he asked, as he punched in the number of his parking spot and paid for it.

"Internship," I bit out, eyeing the exit. "Actually, I need to go or I'll be late."

He pocketed his receipt. Turning to face me, his eyes swept over my body, paying extra attention to my chest. "We should hang out sometime. God, you haven't changed a bit."

I couldn't stop myself. If Luka didn't think I'd changed, he had another thing coming. "Me or my tits?" I spat. "It's you who haven't changed." I didn't wait to see if I'd wiped the smug grin off his face. I was out of the parking garage instantly.

Yes, I still had the same body—thanks to five hours a week at the gym. But equating me with my breasts was exactly why my relationship with Luka hadn't worked out. His attention didn't extend postcoitus. I'd wanted a commitment and all he could offer was orgasms. That had been enough for a while. But when the eyes that wandered over my body started to wander in other directions, I'd kicked him to the curb.

I made a mental note to park in another—less convenient —parking garage and moved on with my life.

The trouble was that my life was following the cues of a

Dickens novel, complete with the ghosts of boyfriends past. When I popped into the coffee shop on the corner, the brown eyes accompanying the barista were all too familiar. It was Mr. Nice Guy himself. Danny lit up when he saw me, which made me feel two inches tall despite my five-inch heels. He was the definition of a nice guy. Too nice. We'd dated after a string of bad decisions and a tequila-induced vow to give up bad boys.

He was writing my name on a cup before I could back out the door I'd just entered.

"On the house!" he called cheerfully, starting to make my drink without waiting for my order. Danny remembered how I took my coffee. Because Danny was an honest-to-god, good person—and I was dirt.

"Are you sure?" I asked, shifting back and forth on my heels. If he let me pay for it, I would have something to do besides stare at his angelic face beaming back at me. It's important to note that Danny was smoking hot in a sorta boy-next-door way. Even in the requisite Sound Coffee t-shirt he wore, his muscular upper body was on display—a body he'd gotten from rock-climbing, biking, and volunteering at the local animal shelter. As he finished up my drink, a thick lock of brown hair fell into his eyes. He pushed it behind his ear. I'd seen him do it a million times. In a way, it was comforting. And therein lied the problem with Danny. He was comfortable and safe. Everything I had thought I wanted.

No matter how hard I'd tried—and we'd dated for months—it had been like kissing my brother. We'd never even made it past second base. I'd broken up with him over text because ending it to his face would have been worse than kicking a puppy.

Naturally, he'd taken it well and judging from the genuine happiness radiating from him, I hadn't done any long-term damage. So why did I still feel so awful?

"How are you?" he asked as he slid a cardboard sleeve over my cup.

"Good." I accepted the free drink. After all, it was a big day. A free drink was like a little karmic good luck charm. Maybe I hadn't been so terrible to Danny after all. Maybe I wasn't a garbage person. Maybe I was being given the chance to see how much I'd changed. "How are you?"

I took a tentative sip of the drink he'd handed me. Three shots of espresso, skim milk, and the tiniest pump of mocha. It was exactly how I liked it.

"Great." He leaned forward so we could talk over the clatter of the coffee shop. "I've been working here since my dad died. I'm trying to save up tuition for one more year, so my mom doesn't have to help me with a student loan."

The coffee turned to ash in my mouth and I nearly dropped the cup. "Oh my god. I'm so sorry, Danny. I hadn't heard!"

"It's okay." He dismissed my shock with a wave of his hand. "It's been two years. I miss him, but I know he's watching out for me."

Two years? It didn't take much mental arithmetic to recount where I'd been two years ago. I'd been fresh off my text break-up with Danny and hitting the bars with my best friends and a couple of fake IDs. As much as I wanted to ask him why he hadn't told me, I knew the answer. Why update an ex-girlfriend who couldn't even break up with you in person?

"We should get together sometime," I said guiltily, thanking him one more time for the drink as I took off. I dumped it in the first garbage can I saw. That was where I belonged: in the garbage. Now I had to find a new drink, so I wouldn't have to repeat that interaction every time I went for coffee—if I could bear to face him again.

Maybe I could face Danny again if I was clear that I wasn't interested in anything more than friendship. Then we could hang out. A friend might be exactly what he needed. Not that he didn't have any. He'd always been the guy surrounded by buddies. Probably because he was the guy you could call to help you move or paint a room or mow your lawn. Danny was possibly the world's last nice guy. I was still considering how I could make it up to him when I entered the lobby of NorthWest Investments for the first time.

I had completed my interviews over the phone and on campus, which meant I'd never seen the offices before. Given what I knew about the business, I'd expected a cramped, cubicle-ridden studio. The owners of the group weren't much older than me. The CEO wasn't even thirty. Despite the fact they'd been buying up neglected Seattle landmarks and restoring them, I hadn't expected there to be real money behind the operation. Everything from the floor-to-ceiling windows, polished marble floors, and the gleaming bank of elevators proved me wrong. I'd been excited to cut my teeth working in public relations for a start-up. Standing here, I was elated—and nervous. This internship was obviously a much bigger deal than I had thought. I allowed myself a moment to let it soak in. It wasn't a real job—not yet. But it was the closest I'd ever come to one.

Shouldering my bag, I started toward the reception desk before skidding gracelessly to a halt as a man stepped into my path. Running into Luka had felt like a bad omen. Catching up with Danny had left me reeling. But the last person I wanted to see, in the last place I wanted to see him, waited for me inside the NorthWest Investments lobby.

Trevor, the most recent catch that I'd released, held up his hands in surrender. He'd made a similar gesture when I'd caught him with another woman last Christmas. The vulnerability didn't jibe with the rest of him. He'd talked a big game and his ability to romance had completely blinded me to his bad behavior. In my book, he would always be Señor Douchebag.

My mind began to race. What was he doing here? Had he followed me? Maybe I'd gone to the wrong place. I double checked the door and saw that I was exactly where I was supposed to be. Then the pieces began to click into place. I'd applied for this summer internship last fall during the dark period when we'd still been dating. Fury burned through me as I realized what had happened.

He'd applied for the same internship. I didn't remember there being two openings, which meant he'd purposefully put himself in direct competition with me—while we were still dating. I'd thought his cheating was bad, but apparently, he could, and did sink lower.

"Let me explain," he began, but I walked past him. Trevor followed me to the reception desk.

I did my best to block out his lame excuses as I checked in with the man behind the counter.

"Hi George," I said, reading the nameplate on the desk. "I'm here for the internship program."

George's lips twitched as he assessed the situation. We had to look pretty ridiculous: a slimy dude throwing out every clichéd excuse in the book and the ex-girlfriend trying to ignore him. I probably had steam coming out of my ears. "What's your name?"

"Cassandra Hart," I said sweetly.

"Mr. North will be here for the intern orientation in a moment. If you'd like to take a seat..." he trailed away. No doubt, he knew that I'd rather spend that time skewering my fellow intern.

Turning, I calmly walked toward a sitting area, but before I could take a seat, Trevor hit me with, "We need to clear the air."

"Really?" I whirled on him. Dropping my voice to a low hiss, I decided to do just that. "You are unbelievable. You stole this internship from me."

"You're here, too. I hardly stole anything."

He had a point, but I wasn't about to concede that. "You did this deliberately. I have no idea why—and God help you —if it's to try to win me back. Let me be clear. You and me? We're over. So, if this is a pathetic attempt—"

"It's not," he stopped me.

That threw me. "Well....good. Because if you screw this up for me, I will cut off your balls and feed them to the seagulls."

Trevor's face darkened, but before he could respond, we were interrupted by a polite cough.

"I guess we'll start with the sexual harassment policy."

We both turned to the source of the low, masculine voice. I squared my shoulders in a bid to look confident, but my cheeks burned. The heat ratcheted to an inferno when my eyes landed on him: Mr. Tall, Dark, and Handsome in a tailored suit. His black hair was tucked behind his ears and his electric, blue eyes studied me. Judging by his scowl—the only thing marring his gorgeous face—he didn't like what he saw.

My knees buckled slightly and I took a swift step forward to catch myself. It took me a second to find my voice, but when I did, it was strong and clear. "Mr. North?"

He tilted his head in acknowledgment and my heart sank. Given his age, he couldn't be more than a few years older than I was. I'd hoped he might be another intern. Or a secretary. Or a bizarrely nosy stranger. Anyone but the CEO of the company.

"Call me Gavin," he offered. "I assume you two know each other."

I nodded and caught Trevor doing the same.

"We're old friends." The lie slid easily out of Trevor, and Gavin's eyebrows shot up. Gavin North obviously had a more finely tuned bullshit detector than I did. Still, he didn't call him out. Trevor stepped forward before I could recover. "I'm Trevor."

I hated that he introduced himself first. Thrusting my hand out before Trevor could, I said, "Cassie. I mean, Cassandra."

Gavin looked back and forth between us before shaking my hand as if making a decision. Two overly eager interns determined to best the other. He chose me, grabbing my hand in a firm grip. Sparks flew the second our skin touched, and I stifled a gasp. He was hot and I was wound tight, it was a terrible combination. I drew away, hoping he didn't see how flustered the contact had made me. But when our eyes locked, his were stone cold. Too cold. Either he already hated me or he'd decided to keep his distance. Maybe I wasn't the chosen one after all. Considering the threat I'd been leveling at Trevor when he walked in, I wouldn't blame him on either count. The butterflies in my stomach turned into a swarm of pissed-off bees.

"If you two are finished"—he didn't wait for us to respond—"allow me to welcome you to your first day at NorthwestNorthWest Investments."

The chill in his voice did nothing to stem the sickening anxiety I felt over my actions. I forced a smile, wondering if my first day would also be my last. By the time I got home that evening, I wished it had been.

Two

My current boyfriend was reliable, attentive, and battery-operated. So what if my longest lasting relationship had variable speeds and pulsating action? Mr. Dependable, my vibrator, had never let me down. It was also sitting in the middle of the floor in my new condo. My roommate's cat dozing lazily next to it.

"Seriously!" I grabbed it from the cat who batted at my hands as if put out by the theft. "It's mine, you know. How did you even get into my underwear drawer?"

Great. Now I was talking to a cat. Further proof that today had nearly broken me. When she tried to follow me into my bedroom, I slammed the door before she made it inside. She responded with a frustrated meow. At least, the cat was talking back. I plucked a few of her hairs off the vibrator and returned it to its resting place among my unmentionables, then kicked off my heels. I'd thought the last couple of years walking a college campus would have prepared me for being on my feet all day, but Seattle's terrain was hilly and prone to cracked sidewalks. I'd also quickly learned that despite the bank of elevators at NWI, I could wait my whole life for one to come, so I'd made myself acquainted with the stairs as I delivered files from office to office in an effort to get to know the building better.

I didn't bother to undress before flopping gracelessly onto my bed. I was too exhausted from the potent combination of nerves, excitement, and annoyance that had held me for most of the day. My phone showed a dozen missed texts from my best friends, Jillian and Jess. Ones wishing me luck and checking in on me. The messages had gotten progressively more anxious when I hadn't responded. I heaved a sigh and sent one back.

Cassie: Chat?

Jess: I think it's like 1 AM in Scotland. Jillian might be asleep.

I kept forgetting to check the time difference. She'd only been gone for a few weeks. Not long enough to process her absence fully. Even during summer vacations when I headed home to Texas, we hadn't really been that far away from one another. But before I could backtrack, she responded.

Jillian: I'm up!

Of course, she was up. She'd probably been having toe-curling sex with her boyfriend, Liam. He was the reason she was halfway across the world. In fact, both of my best friends were out of the country, thanks to the men in their lives. Jillian in Scotland with her boyfriend and Jess in Mexico with her *husband*. Another change I hadn't fully processed yet.

It took a few minutes to get both of them on the screen. Jess was lounging in a hammock, sunlight haloing her face and highlighting her honey blonde hair. She was tanner than I'd ever seen her and thanks to her lack of make-up, I noticed she had a few more freckles speckling her nose than she usually did in rainy Washington. It was dark in Scotland and Jillian had clearly snuck off to have this chat without waking up Liam or his family. I could barely make out her dark hair piled into a messy crown atop her head. Her mascara was slightly smeared and she had a glow radiating from her that wasn't courtesy of cosmetics. I'd been right about why she was still up.

"You look gorgeous!" Jillian sang, no doubt referencing the fierce color palate of sharply lined eyes and classic red lipstick I'd chosen in an effort to look less like the baby intern I was. "Very boss babe."

"I don't think I fooled anyone into thinking that," I said with a roll of the eyes.

"I bet they had a ton of applicants and they chose you," Jess reminded me, her image swaying slightly on the screen as if she was being rocked by a gentle, invisible breeze.

"There are two interns," I said in a measured tone, meant to sound casual. Both my friends visibly tensed, but waited for me to continue. "It wasn't what I expected."

"Tell us about it," Jess said, moving the screen closer to her face as if to show her genuine interest.

That was the amazing thing about best friends. They knew exactly when to listen, even when the sad single of the lot wanted to cry about ex-boyfriends and rough days at work. I hadn't been too busy to notice that both of them had started calling less frequently for venting sessions of their own. Now they had their own significant others to cry to, which, if I was being honest, made me a little jealous. Not that I was losing them—I knew that I'd never really lose either of them—but because part of me wanted what they had. For the moment, they were stuck dealing with listening to my life's little curveballs.

"Yeah, spill it," Jillian encouraged as if she could read my mind. She had an uncanny knack for knowing how to say just what I needed to hear. She was here for me. Jess was here for me. Regardless of their relationship statuses.

"I ran into Luka," I started, deciding to make the day's events a slow burn. At least today had the makings of a helluva story.

"Wait, freshman year Luka? The Italian sex god who spent all day in the gym?" Jillian clarified.

"It seems like you remember him fine," I said with a shake of my head. Maybe I didn't want to relive today or all the memories it dredged up.

"There was a one-month period where you only left your room for classes—and don't get me started on how loud you two were." Jess's lips pursed as if recalling an unsavory smell.

"You're one to talk. I spent my last vacation listening to you and Roman bang," I reminded her. I was teasing, especially since she had a point. At least, she'd been discreet with Roman. Luka and I had been caught in the men's restroom by the dormitory advisor and been cited on several occasions for noise violations. Yeah, my relationship with him was memorable.

I filled them in on that awkward, chance encounter, even admitting to my idiocy with the credit card machine.

"That was a real crappy start to your day," Jillian said with sympathy.

"At least, it could only get better, right?" Jess chimed in.

Such wishful thinking. If she only knew. "Actually, then I ran into Danny."

"Danny?" They both repeated in unison with blank faces.

"The nice guy who kissed me like he was my brother."

That jogged their memories.

"Oh, he was super nice. I liked him! I don't even really remember you two breaking up," Jess said. She was a big fan of nice guys. She'd always dated them. She'd nearly wound up getting engaged to her own yawn-inducing boyfriend because of it.

Jillian for her part giggled. "He was boring."

"But nice," Jess appended as if offended on his behalf.

"He was nice," I agreed, before tacking on, "and boring. He remembered how I took my coffee."

Both my best friends visibly cringed, their discomfort growing as I recounted the rest of that spontaneous reunion.

"Wow," was all Jillian said when I finished. If she only knew.

"Just wait. It gets better," I muttered. "Guess who the other intern is?"

Jess's mouth dropped open mirroring the expression of horror on Jillian's face. My girls knew me too well. Or maybe they'd always seen Trevor for the scum bucket he was and had expected something like this to happen.

"No!" Jillian vocalized her disbelief.

"Señor Douchebag," I confirmed, satisfied by their reaction even if I was still pissed at his behavior.

"I can't believe he did that," Jess said after a few moments of silence. "Who does that?"

"I mean, he knew you applied for that position!" Now Jillian was getting riled up.

It was as though they'd lived through the waking nightmare of this morning, too. In a way, they had. They'd been present for every poor choice and resulting heartbreak I'd made over the years. They'd met all of these guys. It wouldn't be hard for them to sympathize with my plight.

"All these boys stacking up. It's like a none-too-subtle reminder of every bad choice I ever made dating," I admitted in a low voice.

"Think of it like a path," Jess said. "They're just a reminder of how far you've come."

"And where you're headed," Jillian added.

I wasn't sure when my best friends had gotten so wise, but I suspected it was when they had found their own forevers. I wanted to believe them.

"I think maybe I took a wrong turn or two," I said dryly. I was done looking for love in all the wrong places and falling in love with all the wrong faces. Dating, men—they were bad habits that I had kicked thanks to heartbreak, romance novels, and my trusty vibrator.

"Nah." Jillian shook her head. "You're just not there yet.

"Where?" I asked, my eyebrow curving up.

"You'll know when you reach it," she said simply.

"Seriously, when did you two turn into freaking gurus?" I couldn't help having a little fun at their expense.

"How was the rest of your day?" Jess asked, bypassing the good-natured taunt altogether.

"I broke the copy machine, except I didn't. I just pressed the wrong button, so I looked like a jerk when I told my new boss I did."

"The same boss that overheard you threatening Trevor?" Jillian asked.

"Mr. Tall, Dark, and Handsome himself." I sighed at the memory. "Then he got on me for not being at my desk when I was out making the rounds and meeting people."

Jess's eyes narrowed. "I hate him already."

"We hate him," Jillian chimed in.

"Meanwhile, Trevor practically glued his lips to this guy's ass. You've never seen such a sycophant."

"Were you jealous?" Jess asked.

"I mean, sure, he's insanely hot. But he gets this weird look on his face every time he sees me. I guess he is the boss, but that doesn't mean I'm beneath him."

"I meant about Trevor," Jess said."

"Oh."

"She thought you were talking about the boss," Jillian said with a touch too much enthusiasm. I braced myself for the inevitable peer pressuring that followed.

"It's been six months," Jess said as if she'd been keeping a calendar of my break-ups.

"I told you that I'm done with men. Or really, boys. Basically, anything with a penis."

"Thanks for the clarification." Sarcasm dripped from Jillian's voice. "It's okay to date again."

"Just take it slow," Jess advised.

"I'm hanging up," I warned them. My finger hovered over the disconnect button.

"I'm sure he doesn't think you're beneath him," Jillian said.

"He just wants you *beneath* him." Jess grinned wickedly.

"Isn't marriage supposed to make you settle down? You're shameless."

"Speaking of, my husband is calling me into dinner, so I need to run." The grin morphed into a full-blown smile that lit up her whole face. Even thinking about him had that affect on her. I couldn't remember ever feeling something so strongly that it radiated from me like the sun.

Jealous. Table for one.

"I should get some sleep. We're driving up to Inverness tomorrow." Jillian yawned, and I realized it was now after two in the morning in her part of the world.

"Tell my sister hi," Jess said as we began our goodbyes.

"I'm going to tell her that you're love crazy and acting like a damn fool." I would do no such thing, but Jess had been my straight-laced, good girl friend for too long to not revel in the insane 180 degree turn she'd made that had ended only a month ago in her elopement.

"I worry about her," Jess said. "I think we may lose her to Scotland."

"I'll call her mother," I threatened, only half joking. I wanted my best friends to find their happily-ever-afters. I just wanted them to do it closer to home.

"DOES your cat know how to open drawers?" I asked as soon as Lillian got in from the office hours later.

She startled at the sound of my voice but recovered quickly as she dropped her purse and briefcase on to the dining table. "Not that I know of."

Lillian and I were still growing accustomed to each other's presence. Since I'd spent my last three years living in a dormitory it was a bit easier on me. She still seemed surprised to find me there every night. It had only been two weeks since I'd moved in with Jess's older sister for the summer. Since Lillian was a high-profile lawyer she worked late. Really, really late. She pretty much used her condo for the bed and shower, even going into the office on weekends.

That was one of the reasons she had agreed to let me stay with her when I landed the internship at NorthWest Investments. There had been stipulations, of course. No partying. No boys. Since I wasn't in the market for either, I'd agreed. Seattle was an expensive city and I knew I wouldn't find cheaper rent anywhere. Okay, *free* rent. I hadn't figured out yet whether I should stay in my room and out of sight, or if she wanted company.

Tonight, she smiled blearily as she dug through the fridge and came out with a takeout container. She didn't bother to reheat the noodles. Instead, she grabbed a fork and sat on the opposite end of the couch.

"How was the first day?"

I shrugged, not ready to share the details after my hour-long conversation with Jess and Jillian. Lillian didn't pry. We weren't exactly close. Given her insane workload, she'd only visited Jess in Olympic Falls a few times. We'd been out to dinner or come to the city to see her, but we didn't know one another that well.

"That good, huh?" She slurped down a long, greasy noodle.

"You can tell?"

"Lawyers know how to read people," she explained. Her cat jumped into her lap and glared at me as if to say this was her time with her.

"It was just stupid first day stuff." I closed the book I'd been reading and decided to slip back to my quarters, so she could relax in her own home.

"I spilled coffee on one of the partners at my first internship. A steaming hot, vanilla latte. Gave him second degree burns. Did you do that?" she asked, her lips tugging up as if the memory amused her. Maybe now that she was successful, she could see past the mortification. I laughed a little, which startled the cat and she ran off. Lillian stretched her legs now that she'd abandoned her lap.

"I didn't." Yet. I sensed this situation was doomed somehow. I'd probably drop my mocha on Gavin tomorrow and ruin his expensive suit. Then he really would hate me. That was if I didn't dump it over Trevor's stupid head first.

"Then you'll be fine," she promised.

"I'm heading to bed," I told her. Pausing at my door, I called back, "What did he do? Your boss?"

So, I hadn't spilled burning hot coffee on Gavin North, but he didn't like me. I wondered how her boss had reacted when she'd doused him with a latte.

"He fired me," she said, "so I went across the street and got an internship at their rival firm."

"Nicely played." Somehow it didn't surprise me that Lillian had the moxie to march up to another law firm and ask for an internship. Her sister had always called her a workaholic. It seemed she had always been that way. "Good night."

Going to the rival of NorthWest Investments? That wasn't going to be an option for me. Besides which, I hadn't been fired. I just needed to prove that I could cut it, and I would without groveling to the higher up, especially Gavin. That man wasn't going to bring me to my knees.

I did my best to ignore the faint ember that thought stoked inside me. Getting involved with someone wasn't going to happen anytime soon. Getting involved with my boss wasn't going to happen *ever*. The growing beat between my legs suggested my body was considering mutiny.

The truth was that what I missed most about being in a relationship was the sex. I'd never admit that to anyone. It made me sound easy. But that wasn't it. I'd worked hard to get where I was: landing a full-ride scholarship to Olympic Falls University, keeping my grades up so I didn't lose it, building my resume. On a daily basis the stress of it wound around me until I was a ball of anxiety. Sex had been my release. The trouble was that sex came with emotional baggage I didn't have room in my life for anymore. I needed to find new ways to relieve that stress. For now, I turned to my dresser.

And found the damn cat sitting in the open drawer.

"How do you do that?" I asked, before scooping her up and depositing her back into the hall. The last thing I needed was anyone—even a cat— trying to get into my panties.

Three

Being five minutes late on my second day— especially after my emotionally traumatizing first day—felt like as bad an omen as the gray sky above. Seattle was usually sunny in the summer, offering a brief reprieve from the nine months of drizzle it was known for, but today was the exception. I dashed into the lobby as the first soft droplets hit the pavement. George, the receptionist, looked up and shook his head.

"I know, I know." I dug into my purse to fish out my brand-new employee ID card. Somehow I've already managed to lose it. I found it at the very bottom, it having worked its way down to the bowels of my bag like all important objects usually do. I held it up triumphantly.

George leaned toward the counter and lowered his voice conspiratorially. "Mr. North is on a tear. I'd head straight to the sixth floor. He hasn't made it there yet."

"Thanks," I said gratefully even as my stomach took a

nosedive. Not only was I late, but if I wasn't careful, I risked angering my already annoyed boss.

"Look busy!" he called after me.

The elevator took the length of a Bible to arrive after I hit the button, my stress level ratcheting up with each second that passed until I'd hit a level of anxiety previously unheard of in a human being. I could be studied for science. When it finally came I breathed a sigh of relief, stepped in, and hit the button for the sixth floor.

I wasn't certain what Gavin North's problem was exactly. At the first opportunity, he'd passed me off to another associate for the tour. Then he'd shown Trevor around himself. Maybe he was a chauvinist, another white guy holding on to an old boys club mentality. It hadn't been what I expected to encounter when I came to work here. Not after my numerous phone interviews and not after the research I'd done on the company. To be fair, there'd been a lot less information on Gavin North available. Most news outlets preferred to focus on the scandalous life of his late, silent partner Nathaniel West. Reporters were obsessed with figuring out why the real estate investor had chosen to get into business with a relative novice in his industry. Part of me was curious as well. I'd have to actually spend some time with him to find out, which would be difficult if he continued his preference for Trevor's company.

I needed a plan. I would head to the sixth floor, drop my bag at my desk, and then latch onto the nearest friendly face. It was my best option, considering that on day two I didn't really have a routine or a workload.

Fate had different ideas. The elevator stopped on floor

three and I wanted to scream. Halfway to safety, the doors slid open and Gavin North got in. He stepped to one side, his gaze traveling over me and stopping at the purse on my shoulder.

"Just getting in, Miss Hart?" he asked conversationally.

Was it a trick question? If I said yes, would he morph into the terrifying boss monster George had just warned me about? I considered lying—a bad precedent to set this early on.

"Yes," I admitted after an uncomfortably long pause. Best to stick to the truth. "I'm not used to Seattle. I get lost a lot."

"An honest answer." There seemed to a genuine note of surprise in his voice and something else. Interest maybe?

"Would you rather I lied?"

He raised a shocked eyebrow and I realized what I'd done. My Cassie filter had been off. I'd yet to activate it this morning. It had taken years for me to cultivate the presence of mind not to curse like a sailor. Mostly because I didn't hear myself cursing. My best friends had spent the better part of our first years of college repeating what I'd just said back to me. But before coffee, I wasn't fully present—at least not mentally—to put the bad habit in check.

I didn't need to look in the mirrored walls of the elevator to know I'd turned the color of a freshly cooked lobster.

"I'm so sorry," I blurted out, carefully annunciating each word to avoid doing it again. "I speak sailor—literally. I haven't had my coffee yet, so I don't know what I said."

"You don't know what you said?" he repeated. Yes, it was clearly interest coloring his voice now. The elevator came to a halt on the sixth floor, but he hit the stop button before the doors could open. I was trapped with a god in a three-piece suit, who—rumor had it—was in a very bad mood. Except he didn't seem like he was grumpy.

Gavin turned to face me and for the first time I saw how young he really was. I mean, he was older than me by several years, but the confidence he exuded made him seem older. My confession had stripped that away, leaving only the man behind. A slight smirk had crept onto his lips but it never became a full-blown smile. I swallowed hard as he unbuttoned his jacket and then smoothly slid his hands in the pockets of his slacks. Even with the arrogant, bossy veneer temporarily lifted, he moved with ease and the air of a man who wasn't often caught off-guard.

"I suggest you work on that," he advised. It took a second for me to process the soft words. At first, I thought he was being kind, a move which felt seriously against his nature. Then, I realized he was holding back.

"Are you laughing at me?" I took a step toward the elevator's control panel, but he moved in front of it.

"I've never met anyone with swearing induced amnesia before."

"It's not amnesia." I darted closer to the buttons again, which also took me a step closer to him—close enough that I could smell the expensive cologne he was wearing, a heady mixture of leather and bergamot that rattled me. I closed my eyes for a second to collect myself. "It's more like a filter."

"So your own language offends you?" The smirk had turned into a grin. It wasn't the panty-dropping smile that usually caught my attention. No, Gavin's smile lit his whole face and radiated out from him. I might as well have been made out of ice cream because I practically melted.

"I don't find curse words offensive," I admitted. "I just think of them as words. Maybe that's why I don't hear them. Are you aware of every time you say 'the' or '"and'?"

"You're actually making a compelling argument." Finally, a laugh. Somehow it felt better to hear it than to know he was holding it back. Maybe because it was as warm and genuine as his smile.

"Once I have coffee, I promise I'll be in better control of it." I eyed the big red button that would deliver me from the incredible awareness of this moment and into a shame spiral that would probably force me into hyperventilating in the bathroom.

"Coffee it is." He hit the panel and the elevator dinged, announcing our arrival. With one fluid motion, he stepped to the side and gestured for me to go first.

Gavin North was a gentleman. I'd barely processed that thought when he added, "We wouldn't want you to lose control at work."

I'D BEEN around the block with more than one guy, and I didn't mean that sexually. I'd been cheated on, lied to, worshipped, stalked. Basically, I'd endured the full gamut of romantic relationships. That meant I was also an expert on picking up on double meanings. Like when Gavin had tacked 'at work' onto that final thought before we'd parted ways at the coffee station.

But Gavin North was not my boyfriend or my ex-boyfriend or boyfriend material. And I was not in the market for one either. Which made me wonder why I was suddenly so obsessed with the topic of boyfriends anyway. Because I knew myself well-enough to know that once I started down that line of thought, I was screwed—figuratively and often literally. I needed caffeine and a clear head. But as I waited for the automatic espresso machine to warm up, Trevor joined me. It was pretty hard to clear my head when he usually induced a fog of war.

I considered what my best friends would do in this situation. I could almost hear Jess's calm, soothing voice walking me through a list of steps: place your cup under the spout, hit the button, keep your eyes on the machine, take your cup, and walk away. By some miracle, George, the receptionist, joined us. He glanced at both of us as he took a cup, not too subtly studying the situation.

"Terrible coffee, but what are you going to do?" he asked as he waited for me to make my own.

I smiled in welcome and he winked as if he understood exactly what was going on. He was stepping into the role of buffer. I owed him good coffee later, even if it meant facing another ex.

My salvation was short lived.

I got to step two as Trevor leaned casually against the wall.

I got to step three before he cleared his throat meaningfully.

I was getting a little worried about what I would do when I got to step four and had a boiling hot coffee in my hands. Better not to risk it, I decided.

"Can I help you?" I kept my eyes on the machine. I'd never been so dedicated to going through a series of motions before in my life.

"Making coffee?" he asked.

I couldn't keep my eyes from rolling, but I managed to refocus them as a stream of espresso filled my cup. "No, I'm studying particle physics."

A small laugh escaped George, earning him a sharp glare from Trevor. He met it with a snort. At least, I had one ally in this office.

"You want to make me one?" Trevor asked. The edge of laughter in his voice betrayed that he was enjoying this. Not only had he stolen my internship, now he was going to spend the entire summer trying to get a rise out of me.

I didn't bother to respond. Even leveling another threat at him seemed like a waste of breath. He didn't deserve anymore of my attention. I refrained from sighing with relief when the machine switched off and I grabbed my cup with a to-go lid. Shifting to George, I asked him sweetly. "Can I make that for you?"

His lips formed a thin line to repress laughter as he shook his head. "I've got it."

"Shouldn't you be at the front desk?" Trevor drawled in a bored voice. If he wasn't going to get me to bite on a fight maybe he could start one I couldn't ignore.

George got there before I could. "Someone loosened my chains, so I escaped."

I giggled, earning me an approving smile from George and a contemptuous glare from Trevor. It was like winning the lottery twice.

"I'll see you later," George said to me, pointedly ignoring Trevor, as he waved goodbye.

With my buffer gone, I decided to follow suit and get out before Trevor could engage me in battle again.

"Are you going to the meeting now?" he asked as I stepped away.

Too late. He'd launched a new counter-strike when my defenses were lowered.

What meeting?

I paused and made a split-second decision. If I'd missed a memo or email in my frantic dash into the office, it was better to hear it from anyone—even a snake like Trevor—than miss it. I gathered up as much pride as I could muster and turned to face him. "I just got here. What meeting?"

"Oh, never mind. Mr. North asked me to sit in on a meeting about their plans for the old Majestic Theatre in Capitol Hill. I think it's just for the steering committee. I thought I would see if you were heading that way." His beatific face didn't hide the self-satisfaction in his words. He had been invited to the steering committee meeting and I hadn't. He relished that fact and I wanted to kick him in the junk.

I'd be doing the female species a favor.

"Enjoy. I'm heading over to..." I stumbled in my search for something important sounding. The truth was that it was my second day—our second day—and I wasn't really clear on what I was supposed to do. For that matter, I didn't really know where to go. There was no work waiting at my desk. As interns we didn't really have assigned tasks. Yesterday, we'd done tours and introductions. I'd expected the work to start today, and for Trevor, it had.

"Don't worry about it. I'm sure they have something planned for you." He waved a dismissive hand before strutting off.

Hate wasn't a strong enough word for how I felt about him. I loathed Trevor. I disdained him. I abhorred him. I despised him. Where he got off being the dick was impossible for me to fathom. He had cheated on me. He'd lied to me. He'd led me on.

I dialed Jess, who was at least in the same time zone as me and ducked into a quiet room.

I didn't expect her to pick up. Mostly because I envisioned her sunning herself on a Mexican beach while her shiny, new husband fanned her with palm leaves. Still, she answered on the second ring, sounding mildly breathless.

I ignored the fact that I'd probably interrupted a honeymoon moment and jumped right into the sordid story. "Trevor is a dick of spectacular proportion—and I mean that figuratively. Because he definitely doesn't have a dick that fits that description."

"What did he do?" she asked.

I filled her in, this time fully aware of how many expletives were filtering through. I was averaging an F-bomb every other word.

"Why is he so intent on making my life miserable? He's the one who cheated."

"Didn't you charge a $10,000 vacation to his credit card?" It was more of a statement than a question.

She had me there. I had done that, and I'd enjoyed said

vacation all the more. She had been present for that monetary revenge scheme. Hell, she was enjoying her own honeymoon because of it. "That was damages for the emotional trauma of finding him with that girl from his business class."

Jess wisely didn't respond.

"Okay," I conceded, "so he can hate me, but why does he get to be the chosen one?"

"Screw him. Go to that meeting."

"I wasn't invited to it."

"Better to ask forgiveness than permission," she advised. "He stole this internship from you. Take it back."

"You might have a point." She did have a point. I'd only needed her to say it out loud. I needed to hear it. There had been bad behavior on both our sides following our break-up, but that was then, this was now.

"Let me know how it goes," she said.

I promised I would before hanging up. Was I really going to sit around and let Trevor seize another one of my opportunities? I charged off in the direction he had headed before my courage faltered. It didn't matter if I knew where the meeting was being held. I'd given my conscious thought over to my inner tigress and she was on the hunt. All I had to do was follow the trail of bullshit Trevor had left behind.

Four

I'D JUST PROWLED THROUGH THE MAZE OF cubicles when I ran into him and a whole bunch of people I hadn't actually met yet. Trevor raised an eyebrow in surprise, but I forced a confident smile.

"Sorry, I'm late. I forgot to ask where the meeting was. New intern. Second day," I added by way of explanation.

No one batted an eye at my uninvited presence, although Trevor looked like he had swallowed a lemon. I chose a seat as far from his as possible. Glancing around, I realized with a sinking feeling that everyone around me had iPads or note-books. A quick search of my purse yielded me some Post-Its and a pen. My only other options were the backs of receipts. Post-Its it was. I set my phone next to the meager prepara-tions and hoped I didn't look as unprofessional as I felt. Trevor had worn a suit into the office today, no doubt in attempt to emulate our young boss. I wondered if I looked similarly overdressed in my wrap dress and heels. Most of the other employees had stuck to business casual. A few were in jeans. It was going to take some getting used to the Seattle vibe. I'd thought the tendency toward casual on my college campus was just that—a college thing. The more time I spent in the city, the more I began to suspect it was a Pacific North-West thing.

Gavin appeared after most of the chairs were taken. In a room full of his employees, most of whom were much older than he was, he stood out. But not because he seemed so much younger. He exuded an energy and confidence that had nothing to do with his three-piece suit or power tie. He walked into the room like he owned it. He did, of course, but there was no doubt that he knew that. I wasn't sure I'd ever had that much conviction in anything. It was why the whole room fell silent as he crossed to the head of the table—and the chair right next to mine.

I had not intentionally placed myself at the right hand of the CEO. I'd just chosen a chair based on its distance from certain undesirables. Judging from the amount of side-eye I was getting, that choice had been interpreted differently. I plastered an indifferent mask on my face and turned my attention to Gavin.

"Glad to see our new interns here," he said, his gaze lingering on me before he redirected it to the group. "I'm sure you've all met Cassandra and Trevor. They are the poor, unpaid workers we'll be taking advantage of this summer. Go easy on them."

The joke was met with easy laughter. If I'd questioned how his age affected his rapport with his colleagues, I had my answer. Other than my seating faux pas, people seemed relaxed. Happy even. I wondered what had upset him this morning when George had warned me away. I'd always imagined a big city business, especially one in real estate development, to be a bit more on edge. Stock market crashes, federal regulations, homeowners associations – they could all conspire to make these people's lives a living hell. Still, everyone here was in good spirits, except Trevor, who was looking a little green.

"And since Becky just went on maternity leave, these interns are pretty much our entire PR department."

I sat up a bit straighter in my seat, feeling the burden of new responsibility light upon my shoulders. It felt better than a perfect purse.

"We won't let you down," Trevor called from the back of the room. A few of the older workers shot each other looks. It was a bit over eager. And I was glad I hadn't let myself jump in with a similar exclamation. I made a mental note to toe the line between head cheerleader and anarchist.

"That's good to know, because we have a bit of a PR situation," Gavin said, turning toward the whiteboard behind him. He pulled down a screen and clicked a handheld remote. A PowerPoint presentation began. "This is the Majestic Theater in Capitol Hill."

The picture on the screen was of a ramshackle, worn down building that had clearly been beautiful once. The now darkened marquee was fading and drooping with years of disuse. Grass and weeds had clogged up the sidewalk and begun to grow along the walls and up toward the vacant ticket office. Still, underneath the ravages of time, I could see the life it once had. I could almost imagine the sign lit up displaying this week's feature film. We had a similar theater in Abilene, but it had been kept up. I'd gone there almost every weekend with my parents. In high school, my friends and I had hung out there, paying for one ticket and then spending the whole day theater hopping or just waiting for the next show to start. The management hadn't minded. It was just the way things were in a small town with not much to do. I supposed that in a big city where there was lots of opportunity to go see movies and new theaters opening all the time, it was easy to let something like this fall to disrepair. It was a crying shame.

"Gee boss," a redhead piped up from across the table, "maybe you want to run it by us before you buy these things."

Gavin enjoyed a laugh at his own expense while everyone else snickered. "I know, I know. I'm an old softy. But this building has an amazing history. And the city was about to tear it down. Forgive me, Agnes."

I was a bit surprised that a twenty-something was named Agnes, but now I had the redhead's name burned indelibly into my brain. At least, I knew one other person besides Trevor and George.

He hit a button on the remote and a new picture popped up. This time of the interior. It wasn't any better. In fact, it might be worse. While a set of ornate, golden carvings were still intact on either side of the screen, the curtains that should have hung near them were half torn down and one was missing altogether. The screen had a giant rip through the center. Those weren't the biggest problems though. It was obvious a few seats had disappeared over the years. I imagined they'd found their way into hipster living rooms. In their place, sleeping bags and abandoned trash littered the floor.

"It looks like we have some tenants already," someone else said from the back of the table.

"The locks have been changed and the entrances secured. I don't imagine we'll have much more problems with squatters. But we did leave a number of posters for the local shelters and rehabilitation centers, for those seeking a warm, dry place to sleep."

My heart fluttered a little at the thoughtfulness. He didn't have to do that. It was going to be important to take care of the uninvited guests before we could move forward with any type of restoration. The corporate thing to do was to change the locks and scare them off. Gavin was worried about where those people had to go. He had a heart and movie star looks. My attraction to him ballooned. I could only hope he'd put his foot in his mouth and provide the proverbial pen to pop my burgeoning intrigue.

"Well, a new curtain is going to set you back a pretty penny and it looks like most of those chairs won't be of any use. Do you want to keep it a theater?" Agnes, the redhead, asked, pointing to the various eyesores on the screen.

"That's the plan. It's also going to be our biggest line of defense with the preservation committee."

There was a cacophony of groans. I looked around waiting for someone to explain. My eyes fell on Gavin and he rolled his eyes like we were in on a private joke. This obviously wasn't his first rodeo, but it was mine. "We run into this a lot," he explained. "A number of Seattle neighborhoods are experiencing rapid development and growth with all the big companies setting up shop in the city. That means that a lot of historic buildings are being repurposed or torn down."

"Which means preservation committees," I guessed.

Gavin nodded. "In a way, we're on the same side."

"Tell them that," Agnes grumbled.

"They have a reason to be concerned. The building was scheduled for demolition, and they were fighting hard against that. It's one of the reasons we got the building for such a good deal."

"Because it came with a pain in the ass preservation committee?" I piped up, instantly regretting it.

There was a weary round of laughter that stopped the embarrassed blush threatening to appear. It seemed I had hit the nail on the head.

"This is nothing we haven't dealt with before," Gavin reminded us. "And it's the perfect thing for our PR department to cut their teeth on."

Except the PR team hadn't dealt with this before. Or with anything. All the books and essays and presentations and tests weren't the same as facing a pissed-off, antagonistic group dedicated to undermining our work. Most of my professors taught Public Relations with offensive tactics. I'd been told to get out ahead of problems and to control the spin when news broke. The cat was already out of the underwear drawer on this one.

"What you need us to do?" Trevor asked while I was still contemplating the existential crisis between the ivory tower and my first real world job. I imagined squishing Trevor's head between my thumbs, but kept my attention on Gavin.

Gavin looked toward me. "We're going to need to meet them in the middle on this. They'll want things that aren't possible. Like a restoration of the original screen or seats. As you can see, that's not going to happen. If they're reasonable, they'll see that. But we can expect a lot of backlash for going in to do any work at all. We need to show them a plan where we modernize the theater while still maintaining as much of the original history as possible, and we'll need our PR people ready to hit the ground as soon as our permits are approved."

I raised an eyebrow and bit my lip before sharing my concerns. "Honestly, that sounds a little bit more like the work of your building department."

"And it is," Gavin agreed, "but we need a strong presentation with a clear direction that leaves room for their suggestions without leaving room for their protests."

Why didn't he just ask for a unicorn that vomited cupcakes?

He continued with his tall order. "We need a series of press releases that make us look like the good guys and some type of strong community involvement that shows that we're there to help preserve the history of Capitol Hill."

If we were going to do that it should be one step at a time, leaving lots of room for adjustment based on their reactions.

"What about a sponsored community event?" I asked, tapping my pencil on my Post-It notes and thrilling at the quick-fired repartee of the board room.

"We'll need more than that. It will take at least nine

months to finish this project — and that's if we don't run into issues with the permits. We need to be active in the community during that whole time, showing them that they don't have anything to worry about, or we'll start to get protesters, and union workers don't like to cross picket lines."

"Seriously?" It slipped out before I could hold it back.

"You'll have to forgive her. She's from Texas," Trevor added as though begging forgiveness for the alien in the room.

"We have protesters in Texas," I shot back. "I'm just surprised a committee could muster that kind of firepower."

"There's usually someone with money spearheading these campaigns," Agnes started to explain. "Do we know who it is yet?"

Gavin shook his head, but I noticed the corners of his mouth tighten. He was holding something back. I stared at him wondering if he was going to open up, but instead he continued, "I suspect I do. I promise I'll let you know as soon as it's confirmed."

I was no Agatha Christie, but I'd venture to guess he knew exactly who it was and for some reason he was holding this information back from the team. Gavin's mystery deepened.

His politic answer was met by mutterings and the rumblings of fledgling conversations, but Gavin held his hands up and everyone fell silent. It was amazing to watch. Even though he was so much younger than many of the people in the room, they all looked to him for leadership. It was ridiculously hot. This wasn't a college boy in front of me. It was a man, taking charge of the situation and showing that teamwork and responsibility could overcome.

"So, were going to throw the poor, helpless interns into the lion's den on this one?" Agatha asked. She grinned impishly at me from across the table.

"I hope some of you will be helpful. But I think they can handle it. Actually, I imagine that they still have ideas about changing the world. They aren't as cynical as the rest of us. Yet."

Everyone nodded in agreement, smiling, as though self-admitted cynicism was just part of the job. I hoped I never got to that point. I hoped I still cared in five years and ten years and fifteen and twenty. Gavin gave me some hope. He might have lumped himself in with the cynics, but his actions proved otherwise. He still cared. I could see it in the actions he'd taken to help those who were most vulnerable. Then again, I learned that a strong offense was a good defense, maybe it was best to have a little armor when coming up against preservation committees or detractors. There had to be a balance. But whatever gooey, soft interior Gavin was hiding under that three-piece suit, he'd managed to be successful with a beating heart.

"So your only PR person is on maternity leave?" Trevor chimed in from the back, asking a question I wanted the answer to as well. Gavin turned his attention to him and nodded.

"Obviously, we've been growing at a really rapid rate. PR has always been important to us, but as we take on more projects like this, we're going to need a bigger team. We will definitely be looking to expand as soon as Becky's back and can be part of that decision."

My opportunity radar went off and I straightened in my seat. That sounded like in a few months there would be jobs available. I wouldn't be out of school yet. But if I did a good enough job, that would mean more than any resume coming across Gavin or Becky's desk. Suddenly, this wasn't a project.

It was an audition, and I was up for the lead role.

Five

I HAD NOTHING. AS SOON AS THE MEETING HAD adjourned I'd returned to my desk and gotten to work. I sat there for what could've been hours, maybe days, and wound up with diddly-squat to show for it. I didn't even notice that I'd missed my lunch hour. It was amazing considering I'd gotten nothing accomplished.

By hour five of nada, it felt as if the walls of my cubicle were closing in on me, dooming me to an existence of total mediocrity. I was never going to impress the NorthWest Investments team at this rate. The job that Gavin had dangled over my head seemed to be farther and farther out of reach. I'd probably graduate with no job and no prospects and return home to wait tables at one of Abilene's dozen restaurants.

If I couldn't come up with a proposal that would meet the needs of the community and show them what North-West Investments stands for, how could I work on larger projects. How could I be part of a bigger team? How could I ask them to invest in me?

I was getting nowhere and it was wearing down my usual, get-it-girl attitude.

When I stood up from my desk, my back was sore and one of my feet was asleep. I needed to get going, move, get the blood flowing. I decided to run down to the corner for a cup of coffee and whatever carbohydrates they had in their display. I needed sugar and whatever energy—albeit temporary—it provided. The elevator was actually on my floor for once, and I decided to take it lest stairs prove as unmanageable as my own brain. As the doors started to slide closed, a hand reached out to stop them. Trevor got on next to me.

Because this day needed to be any longer.

"Been working on the proposal?" he asked I nodded, keeping my eyes on the buttons as they lit up. At least it wasn't a large building.

"You?"

"Yeah, I'm killing it. I swear the ideas are just flowing."

Just like the bull shit, I added silently. The truth was that Trevor had always been an ideas man. It was the follow-through he lacked. He'd been good at foreplay and bad at sealing the deal. He talked a big game and delivered a C-average. I didn't doubt that he'd already come up with a dozen great proposal ideas. Could he actually make any of them happen?

Not by himself, I realized. Maybe my stubbornness was going to be what got the best of me. Gavin had said they needed a PR team not a PR person. NorthWest Investments touted teamwork and community. I wasn't doing that. I was sitting alone and struggling. All while Trevor was coming up with ideas left and right. Maybe if we played our cards right there would be a job in it for both of us. I ignored the nauseous roll of my stomach at the thought of working with Trevor longer than this summer. The truth was we were both auditioning. We might both be hired. Gavin had said team and there was no I in team, as the saying went.

I wouldn't always get a say in who I had to work with, so now was the time to get used to the idea of working with someone like Trevor. It was hard to imagine a coworker that would grate on me more, but if I could learn to work with him I could work with anyone.

I might even find the secret key to establishing world peace in the process.

"Maybe we could sit down when I get back from grabbing coffee," I suggested. "I could show you what I have. You could show me what you have."

"I think it's better if we keep our eyes on her own papers." Trevor scoffed at my casual suggestion like I just asked him to make up with me and get married.

"I just think that Gavin wants a PR team—"

Trevor cut me off. "We both know that working together isn't part of either one of our long-term plans. Why pretend?"

That's what I got for trying to be the diplomat. I strode past him and up to the receptionist's desk. For all his big talk, Trevor followed behind and continued, "It's nothing against you. I know you're really smart, Cassie. But I need to land a job in Seattle when I'm out of school. You have all sorts of opportunities. You could go back to Texas."

"I could…" No good would come of me acknowledging that suggestions, except the world might have one less Trevor in it. Instead I turned to George and smiled sweetly.

"Would you like a cup of coffee? I'm going down to the corner for some." I spoke in even, measured tones, belying the fact that I was about to blow my top.

"Thank the lord." George said as he took in the afternoon show that had just started. "I'd love an Americano with some cream if it's not too much trouble. Of course, if you need to stay and finish this discussion…"

"This discussion is all wrapped up," I told him.

Trevor wasn't getting the hint. "I suppose if you want me to look over your presentation, that would be okay, but I think it's important—"

He stopped suddenly and his mouth fell open. I looked up to see what had struck him dumb. It wasn't hard to figure out because easily one of the most beautiful women in the world had just walked through the doors to NorthWest Investments. Long, silky black hair fell past her shoulders. It was clearly a shade or two darker than her natural color based on her dusty, olive skin tone. As she whipped off her sunglasses and tucked them into the Chanel bag she was carrying, the bright blue of her eyes was mesmerizing as she passed. Her carefully tailored trousers stopped a few inches above her ankles allowing her long legs to stream into sky high, patent leather heels. Her loose, ivory blouse was sleeveless and skimmed her slender figure, moving softly with each step she took. She was the definition of poise, even I couldn't help staring.

"You might want to close your mouth," I muttered to

Trevor as she passed. I mimed rolling up my tongue. He was so disgusting.

"Who is that?" Trevor asked and I could almost see him mentally putting her on some type of wish list.

"Imogen Sound," George told us from behind the desk. "She must be here to see Gavin. She's—"

"Hot as hell," Trevor jumped in.

George heaved the sigh of someone who'd spent too much time dealing with the younger generation. He didn't bother to continue whatever he'd planned to tell us.

I rolled my eyes and shouldered my purse higher. It felt distinctly less glamorous with her nearby. "I'm off to get you that coffee."

I'd only stepped away from the desk when Gavin appeared out of the elevator and met Imogen. The smile that spread over his face as he saw her was like a fist around my heart. Squeezing and squeezing, it felt like it might pop like a grape under the pressure. In all my concern over not flirting with my boss, I'd never considered that he might not be available. Imogen leaned over and kissed him on the cheek before circling her arms around his shoulders in a tight hug, and I had my answer. Gavin paused and kissed her on the forehead before wrapping an arm around her shoulders and turning back toward the elevator. He looked up and caught sight of me watching them. Gavin opened his mouth as though he was about to call out to me, but I wasn't in the mood to be introduced to his girlfriend. Not today. Not while confusion churned inside me like a tsunami about to hit the shore.

Six

GAVIN HAD A GIRLFRIEND. A FACT MADE ALL THE more annoying by its alliterative qualities. It was also a fact that I shouldn't be annoyed over—forget that, had *no right* to be annoyed over.

I was annoyed.

I was pretty sure I wasn't imagining his subtle insinuations to me, which made him just another wannabe cheater. The rest of the work day went by in a haze of half smiles and wandering thoughts. No matter how hard I tried to redirect my attention away from Gavin and his lunch date, I kept finding myself thinking about him. She was pretty and nice and if a girl like her couldn't keep a guy interested, what hope did a neurotic head-case like me have? And having Trevor around was proving to be a constant reminder that I wasn't the girl that got forever. I was the in-between girl a guy settled on while he waited for a better investment. I was a lost cause. I should have it tattooed on my forehead.

When five o'clock hit I was more than thrilled to stop

phoning it in and go home. I stood a better chance of being able to work there without the possibility of running into the walking distractions that haunted this building.

Today Seattle had given in and conceded to June. The skies were bright blue and cloudless, even Mt. Rainier was visible on the horizon. Back home, we would have been well into the season and preparing for the sweltering stickiness of a Texas summer. Here summer meant perfect 74 degree days and clear skies. Maybe I'd finally venture down to the condo's community pool. I needed sun and a new attitude.

I'd parked in a lot a mile uphill from the office, and by the time I reached it, I was ready to dive into the pool fully clothed. My trusty, old Corolla was parked in the far corner. It was a hand-me-down from my mom who'd driven it halfway across the country so I'd have a car for my big internship. My parents couldn't wrap their head around living somewhere where a car wasn't necessary. Now I felt obliged to drive it, and I would as long as they kept funneling parking money into my bank account. Despite the breezy day, I'd managed to choose the sunniest spot in the lot, and when I opened the driver's side door a wave of heat greeted me. After the hike up the hill, the last thing I felt like doing was waiting for the air conditioner to get going. Instead, I opened the back passenger door and slung my purse inside. Leaning against the car, I closed my eyes and turned my face upward to the sun.

It was the one thing I missed about Texas. Here I might go weeks without enjoying a sunny day. In the winter, it was sometimes months. Everything else about Washington suited me fine. I'd chosen my college based on scholarship funds. I hadn't even bothered to visit before I took them up on their full-ride, but I'd been pretty happy with the hand fate had dealt me. Now that summer was here I could enjoy three months of uninterrupted bliss.

A car horn interrupted the happy thought. Maybe summer would be less chill on this side of the Puget Sound. I cracked one eye warily, unwilling to engage with a stranger, even for small talk, and then heaved a sigh. A stranger I could ignore. An ex-boyfriend I could not. Despite changing lots and parking much farther than necessary—all in an attempt to avoid *him*—Mr. Freshman Year had found me. Luka was overdressed in a suit that didn't match his age or what I knew about his personality. With any luck he was selling used cars. I didn't think to ask. He was really the last person I wanted to run into, especially right now.

"Didn't want to deal with that parking meter?" Luka asked, glancing at my car.

"Lot was full." Who cared if it was a lie. I wasn't about to admit to being bested by a stupid credit card machine. Plus, it would be just like Luka to decide that I was going out of my way to avoid him. Sure, I might have been doing just that, but he didn't need to know. "Good to see you. Gotta run."

"Plans?"

Did he want a printed itinerary or was he calling bullshit on me? Because yeah, my hot date involved sitting by the pool, calling the girls for moral support, and digging into this Majestic Theatre project. It did not include wasting one more second of my life on him. "It was a long day."

"I can tell." His eyebrows knit together in concern that

looked disconcertingly genuine. "Everything okay? You look tired."

That was the last thing any girl wanted to hear. Of course I was tired, I had like decades of patriarchal male crap to move past, a corporate ladder looming overhead, and a starting gun that hadn't gone off. In other words, I was an unpaid intern.

I started to tell him just that when he hit me with, "Actually, you look fantastic. I think catching you with your eyes closed tricked me."

I clamped my mouth shut to keep the rant from spilling out. So here was the thing. Luka was bad news—I knew that. I'd also spent the day competing with Señor Douchebag and being disappointed in Mr. Tall, Dark, and Handsome. I was so not above preening over a compliment regardless of the source. Without my besties around to start my day with compliment showers, I'd been left wondering if I was overdressed at the office where people seemed almost surprised to see a woman in heels—as though I couldn't dismantle the patriarchy in Jimmy Choos. Even secondhand ones.

"You know, I've been hoping to run into you again. It feels like destiny took a hand," he continued, somehow managing to keep his eyes on my face.

If he'd known how far I'd gone to thwart destiny, he might truly believe that. "Really? Why?"

"I was a bit of a jerk the other day. I shouldn't have laughed about the machine. That thing is screwy. But also because I meant what I said. We should hang out sometime. Catch up."

Was Luka asking me on a date? "Maybe you need to check the ferry schedule, because that ship has sailed."

"Not like that," he said quickly before I could climb into my sufficiently cooled down car and drive away. "I was a kid when we dated, so were you. I've always wondered what you were up to since we moved out of the freshman dorm."

He was presenting a compelling argument, and he'd softened me up with a compliment. Maybe I was wrong about him. I would hate it if someone assumed I was still the same person I was at nineteen. A lot had changed. Still, my focus needed to be on the internship. I couldn't afford to divide my attention. "I've got to work tonight."

"That's cool. How about Friday?"

I hesitated just long enough to reveal my weekend was wide open. He'd know if I was lying, which led me to commit girl sin numero uno: agreeing when I wanted to say no. "Okay."

"Here." He grabbed my phone from my hand and began inputting his number. It felt like a violation somehow, but I was too shocked to stop him. "I'll text you."

"Great." I managed a half-hearted goodbye before ducking into the safety of my mom's Toyota. It took a second to adjust the radio and the AC. Luka waved as he pulled out in a BMW. A BMW? Maybe I did want to catch up with him.

"Nooo!" I banged my head on the steering wheel hoping to dislodge the number of terrible ideas that had passed through my brain today. First, I had flirted with Gavin, challenged Trevor, and now I'd agreed to go on a non-date with Luka. The axis of idiocy was complete. Not for the first time I considered how much easier the world would be if it was all women. The trouble was that I cared too much. I'd grown up with overly affectionate parents. I'd watched my best friends find the one. There was far too much proof that true love was real for me to ignore it. I wanted to, because I hated feeling like I was waiting around for some prince to knock at my door. In real life, all the good princes were taken. I just didn't know how to make peace with being single and waiting for Mr. Right. I liked my life. I liked myself. That should be enough, but it clearly wasn't because I'd just agreed to go out on a date with a guy that was a walking mobius strip of hormones. Maybe he wouldn't text and I would stop driving to work and we'd both live happily ever after—without ever seeing one another again.

I let the fantasy unfold as I put the car into drive, just as Luka's first text came through. Or maybe I'd have to slay the ex-boyfriend dragon first.

IT WAS 2 AM in Scotland, and I didn't care. Somehow I managed to dump the entire contents of my closet onto my bed while Face-timing with Jillian over the phone. I'd made a mess of my room, my life, and wrecked her chance to get enough sleep. Dipping my toe into the real world with an internship was proving a complete failure.

"I don't know what I was thinking," I huffed as I dug through a pile of skirts, looking for something professional that wasn't too dressy for tomorrow. "Luka is a first class jerk and I know it. So what if he was nice to me today? That doesn't mean I have to go on a date with him. He banged half the girls in our graduating class while we were dating."

"Did he actually say *date*? Like did he say 'can we go out on a date?'" Jillian yawned, her eyes bleary from the sleep I'd obviously woken her from.

"No. He said we would just go out as friends to catch up, but we all know what that means."

Jillian blinked a few times before shaking her head in confusion. "What if he just wants to catch up?"

Clearly, she was going soft in her new committed relationship, especially if she couldn't remember what "catch up" meant in ex-boyfriend speak. "Catching up is a clear sexual invitation."

And I had RSVPed.

"How is that a sexual invitation?"

"Everyone knows that when a guy asks you out and you've already slept with him, *even* if he says it's to catch up, he's really saying that he wants to sleep with you." I couldn't believe I was actually explaining this to her.

"I must have missed that Cosmo article," she said dryly. At least her sarcasm was awake.

In all fairness, Jillian hadn't been one for serious relationships before she had met Liam. I could spot his head of messy, blond hair on the pillow next to her. A soft snoring came from the other side of the bed. It was just like a man to sleep through anything, even a best friend ranting from the other side of the world. "You're making me feel crazy."

"That's not what I'm trying to do." Jillian shook her head defiantly, as though I had threatened to take away her best friend card. "I'm just tired."

"And I'm the bitch who woke you up in the middle of the night." I really had lost my mind. Why on earth had I thought this couldn't wait until morning? Then I remembered that when it was morning in Scotland, I would be asleep in Seattle.

"It's no big deal," she said with a shrug. "Being so far away is hard for all of us. I'm always here for you though, even when we're not in the same country."

"Or even the same continent," I grumbled. "When are you coming home again?" I put on my best puppy dog eyes. If I had to lure my best friends back through shameless, guilt trips I would.

"I don't know yet." Jillian's eyes darted off-camera, and I couldn't help but think she was dodging the question. Now wasn't the time to call her on that, not when I'd jostled her from a deep sleep next to a hot, Scottish man.

"What do I do? Do I ignore him? He's already texted me, and he put his number in my phone, so I can't pretend it's the wrong number."

Jillian perked up, obviously interested in this info. "He already texted?"

"Yeah. Don't look so happy about it. Whose side are you on anyway?" I was not above reminding her of best friend proclamation number one: chicks before dicks.

"Here's the thing," Jillian began, "you said yourself, you've both changed. How do you know Luka hasn't change for the better?"

" Because he's still breathing. Look, I've kissed a lot of frogs and none of them have turned out to be princes," I reminded her.

"I'm just saying, you wouldn't want him to treat you like you were still the same person. Maybe you need to give him a second chance. What do you have to lose?"

The things I had to lose were far too long to list during a single phone call. Right on top were my dignity and my self-respect. I kept that thought to myself. "What do I have to gain?"

"Maybe you'll learn something," Jillian suggested.

It was is if a lightbulb had gone off over her head. She was absolutely right. There was something I could get out of this. I could learn something from Luka. "Jillian, you're a genius!"

"Tell me something I don't know. But really why am I a genius?" she tacked on, her confusion not diminishing her sly grin.

Liam shifted in his sleep, rolling over to showcase his bare chest. I did my best to not stare at him. It felt a little weird ogling Jillian's boyfriend, but it couldn't be helped. It was more like going to a museum. I could admire a painting in all its glory and still respect that it belonged to someone else. Tearing my eyes away from him, I focused on her. "This date doesn't have to be a total loss. Maybe I can find out from Luka exactly why he cheated on me."

"Because he's a first-class jerk?" she guessed. "You said that yourself."

I'd been telling her that since we got on the phone. Of course, now she would get with the program. "No, there had to have been a reason that he cheated. We were pretty hot and heavy. He was totally getting everything he could possibly want. Why would he go hook up with another girl?"

"Because he's a first-class jerk. But I repeat myself."

"I'm not disagreeing with you, but think of it this way, it's like a progress report at work. Every once in a while you need to review how far you've come. Going out with Luka will give me that chance."

"How far are you going to take this? Are you going to go out with Trevor, too?"

I stuck my tongue out at her. It was a childish gesture, but one that was well-deserved. "Absolutely not!"

"You might be overthinking this."

"Look, there is no need to evaluate my progress with Trevor. Not with him breathing down my neck at the office every day." No, this was a unique opportunity. I just had to make her see that. "A night with Luka might not be fun exactly, but I guess being around him not only shows me where I was, but how far I've come. Maybe it will show me where I'm going wrong, too. One guy cheating is me making a poor choice. Two guys?"

"It's not your fault if a guy cheats," she interjected.

I ignored her and continued thinking out loud, pacing across the room. "Plus, free dinner. It's a win-win. What do I have to lose?"

"Your dignity," she mumbled.

I paused to glare at her. "Not likely."

Suddenly there was a crashing noise followed by a loud, whirring noise. I whipped around to find Lillian's cat jumping out of my underwear drawer with my vibrator in her mouth.

"What are you saying about losing your dignity?" Jillian began laughing hysterically, causing Liam to stir next to her. "How can a cat that tiny even pick up that size of vibrator?"

"You are not being helpful!" I darted towards the cat, but it narrowly escaped my grip. "Here kitty. Come here cat."

The cat backed toward the door, uninterested in my demands.

"I hate you," I added under my breath.

"Do you even know that cat's name?" Jillian managed to ask between a fit of giggles. Liam was now fully awake and trying to catch up on what he had missed.

"What does that cat have in its mouth?" Liam asked in his heavy Scottish accent, wiping sleep from his eyes.

I really wanted to die. Meanwhile, Liam's contribution had sent Jillian over the edge. She had fallen off the bed, leaving her phone propped on the nightstand. Liam was peering over the edge, but all I could see of Jillian were her feet in the air. I hit the end button on the chat and went after the cat. I really was going to have to learn its damn name. I wasn't even sure if cats responded to their names. And what was her obsession with my vibrator? I had just managed to corner the damn thing when the door to the apartment opened.

Lillian was carrying about a million files. Her top knot had started to droop to the side and her dress suit was a wrinkled mess. She took a step inside and stopped, taking in the scene unfolding before her. Her unexpected entrance momentarily distracted me and the cat slipped through my fingers again.

"What is your cat's name?" I asked through gritted teeth.

"Olive," she responded, looking torn as to whether or not to step in and help.

Olive? That was a delicious, Mediterranean snack not a tiny, furry beast from hell.

"What does she have..." she trailed away as realization dawned. She did an amazing job of masking the horror of discovering her cute, little kitten with a purple, vibrating phallus. "How on earth did she get that?"

Now wasn't the time to tell her that her cat had an obsession with my sex toy. I was pretty certain it never was the time to tell your roommate something like that. I finally managed to wrestle it away. Lillian lifted the cat into her arms and nuzzled her in the most affectionate way I'd ever seen her act to a living being before. "Poor girl got fixed, now she wants to get laid. We understand."

We understood? Did I look that desperate to get laid? The vibrator in my hand was probably a dead giveaway.

"Night!" I took off before the situation could get any more awkward. I stopped in the bathroom to give Mr. Dependable a quick wash. I wasn't fixed like poor Olive, but this was still my best option. No wonder I hadn't rejected Luka on the spot.

Maybe I didn't need Mr. Dependable at all, because I was obviously screwed.

Seven

THE WEEK FLEW BY IN THE WAY TIME PASSES WHEN you're dreading something—going to the dentist, a trip to the DMV. In this case, the cherry on top of a craptacular week was a date with Luka. Maybe life wasn't as bad as I thought, but it wasn't going swimmingly exactly. I'd spent the last couple of days trying to find the right approach to the Majestic Theatre presentation. What I'd wound up with was a whole lot of nothing. The always helpful Trevor had offered to give me a hand, but I told him that I'd been sticking to my make shift office , the cubicle walls providing a much-needed barrier from being seen. Maybe if no one knew how much I was struggling, they wouldn't hold it against me. Plus, it meant I wasn't running into Trevor at every turn. Or for that matter, Gavin and his beautiful girlfriend. I needed to focus on work, but as the hours ticked by on Friday afternoon and I couldn't help but watch the clock. Unlike everyone else, my plans for the weekend weren't something I was looking forward to. More and more of my fellow workers logged off early and headed out, ready to go climb mountains or kayak or whatever the hell else the outdoorsy types did on their time off. By 3 o' clock I was dragging, struggling under the weight of my own failure to produce any results as well as the looming dread of my date. I grabbed my purse and decided it was time to turn things around.

George was busy talking with the deliveryman, so I waved at him on my way out the door. There were only a few people in line at Sound Coffee which gave me time to consider exactly how much caffeine I required. I noted that Danny wasn't behind the counter. Thank heaven for small mercies.

I still haven't decided on a drink before it was my turn. The friendly barista at the cash register looked a little less amiable as I stuttered out an order. I grabbed George his customary Americano and asked for a couple extra sugars, just the way he liked it. It was easier to keep him happy than to figure out where my ID card was every morning. Then I glanced off and ordered the first thing on the menu: a Coconut milk latte with extra shots. Whatever. I would try anything once. By the time, I got my order and headed out the door, the sky overhead had darkened in an ominous way. Despite the day being a muggy 80 degrees, clouds were rolling in and although Seattle rarely enjoyed a true thunderstorm, I'd bet money that it was going to rain this evening. Could a date be called on inclement weather?

George was free when I got back to the office, and I handed him his Americano.

He took it with a suspicious frown on his face. "Most people need a coffee run on mid-Monday not mid-Friday."

I pretended to take the cup back. "If you don't want it..."

"I am not most people." He snatched it back and began adjusting the lid. "What are your weekend plans? You look like you have a date with bad news? Balancing the checkbook?"

"If only I was just going to pay my bills." I shook my head, wishing it was something as painless as that. "No, I got roped into having dinner with an old...*friend*."

George raised an eyebrow. He saw right through that little fib.

"Okay, it's an ex-boyfriend," I confessed. "I didn't know how to say no."

"N-O," he spelled it for me with a snap of his fingers.

"It's a bit late now. He's picking me up in four hours."

"Is it a date? "George asked, looking a little more interested.

"Absolutely not! He is on my do-not-date list." I didn't bother to add that every man that was breathing was on my do-not-date list at the moment.

"Then why are you going out with him?"

I leaned in and lowered my voice. Somehow I got the impression that George would understand. "I want to see why he cheated on me."

"Oh honey, there's only one reason a man cheats." He clucked his tongue against the roof of his mouth in a remarkable imitation of my mother.

"And what is that?" I took a tentative sip of my drink. It wasn't bad, but I probably wouldn't order it anymore. Some day I would find my perfect drink again. It seemed more likely than finding my perfect man, even with George's insights.

"Because he's a cheater. You can't change a man that cheats. You can't fix a man that cheats. And it's never *your* fault."

"I know that." I began to study the Sound Coffee label as though it were a piece of fine art. Did I really know that? If I did, then there was no reason to go on this date. I could cancel. I could have canceled already, but I hadn't.

"I can tell you until I'm blue in the face, honey," he said. "But the thing is you're going to have to believe it. So you may as well go on your date, but let me tell you preemptively: I told you so."

I rolled my eyes. "That's very helpful."

"I live to serve."

George was right if I really believed that Luka cheating on me wasn't my fault, I wouldn't be going tonight. I guess I did have something to prove to myself. "I know it's a bad idea, but I have to do it."

He nodded as if this was a dilemma he could relate to just as a fresh wave of corporate evacuees came off the elevator. I caught sight of Gavin and tried to hide behind the fern George kept on the counter. The last thing I needed was a run-in with the boss. Not when I was trying to avoid him, and what had George just said about cheaters? If he was right, and I knew he was, then it was best to keep my distance from Gavin.

"Where you going?" George asked, oblivious to my Houdini antics.

I shrugged, afraid my voice would carry across the lobby.

Luka had texted me the restaurant, but I had never been there. "Some place downtown, near Pike Place Market. Some little French bistro."

"Oh. French food," he said with meaning, adding another motherly cluck of disapproval. "He definitely wants this to be a date."

"Well, I don't." As far as I was concerned, that was my final word on the subject. I would get what I wanted out of Luka, which only seemed fair after he used me for sex our entire freshman year. I deserved answers, and a little bit of French food on the side wouldn't hurt either.

Gavin shot me a tight smile as he strode quickly out of the office building. I'd been spotted! But he didn't stop to chat. My heart did a traitorous flip as I watched him leaving.

"Now that man—" George began, but I cut him off.

"Is definitely off limits."

I was standing firm and leaving no room for arguments. No dates. No romance. George opened his mouth like he was going to try to argue anyway, but before he could Trevor came running up.

"Did you see Mr. North, I mean, Gavin?" He was a little out of breath and red in the face like he'd just raced down the stairs instead of taking the elevator.

I ignored him. George did the same.

"Oh come on, guys! I'm supposed to go to some last-minute meeting."

Why on earth was Trevor getting invited to a last-minute meeting? Maybe Gavin was playing favorites. Or maybe hiding out in my cubicle all week had got me kicked off the invite list. I tried not to look sour about it.

"He just left," I said in a low voice, so he couldn't hear my frustration. Thwarting Trevor, no matter how much he deserved it, wasn't professional and I was determined to take the high road from now on.

"Thanks!" He dashed off to catch up with him.

"I don't think we should have told him" George said with a fair amount of sass.

"He would have found him. In fact, I'm surprised he lost track of him at all. His lips are usually firmly attached to his ass."

"That's your other ex-boyfriend, isn't it?" George chuckled at this and took a sip of his Americano "Girl, you've got a weird love life."

I spun to face him, almost spilling my drink in the process. "Neither of them have anything to do with my love life."

"Sure, sure. Whatever you want to tell yourself." He held up one hand in surrender, the other still clutching his coffee a safe distance from my flailing limbs.

"Good. I'd hate for you to lose your coffee hook up." I was joking. Mostly. George meant well, and like it or not, he was probably right about a few things.

I said goodbye, grabbed my coffee and went back up to work. The next hour and a half would pass whether I was here or at home, but once I got home it would be time to get ready for my date with Luka—and that was the last thing I wanted to do. Staring at my cubicle wall sounded like paradise in comparison. I punched the up button, George clucking his tongue and muttering to himself behind me.

· · ·

NO RAIN MATERIALIZED. Instead, the evening got hotter as though to warn me I was about to enter my own, personal hell. Luka picked me up in the BMW I'd seen him drive off in the other day. He'd been driving a used Honda Accord a few years ago, and like me, he had been a scholarship kid. I didn't think Luka's parents were poor exactly, but they weren't rolling in it. It had been something we had in common when we met. I couldn't help but wonder how much his life had changed since then if he could afford something like this now. I got into the car unable to help admiring the buttery leather and gave him a small smile.

He looked me over and whistled appreciatively. "You look fantastic."

I did look fantastic, in fact. Even though I'd been dreading this date, I decided to make the most of it. For me, that meant a little black dress with criss-crossing straps and a pair of black mesh Jimmy Choos that I had scored from a secondhand fashion site. I'd wanted to feel on equal footing on this date. I might not be driving a BMW, but I'd come a long way since we were nineteen.

"This is a really nice car." A compliment felt in order, but I didn't want to give him the wrong idea by telling him he looked hot. Even though he did. I'd met his parents once. He'd scored his blond hair and blue eyes from his Russian mom and his Italian attitude from his father. It had resulted in a man who knew exactly how good-looking he was.

"Thanks," he said with a grin. "It was a graduation present to myself."

Of course, it was. I glanced down at my shoes and wondered if other people had the same reaction when I said that it was a present to myself. "I guess I didn't realize you graduated."

"Yeah, it was getting harder to keep my scholarship, so I felt like I needed to get out of there. You understand." He shifted gears and zoomed ahead, weaving in and out of the traffic. Nineteen-year-old me would've been impressed with his driving. Current me was terrified. Did he know how crazy traffic was downtown this time of night? Suddenly, an even scarier thought occurred to me. What if Luka hadn't changed at all? Would that wreck my entire experiment? It was too late to back out now. It was probably too late for anything, because Luka was going to kill us. I clutched the armrests and sent a silent prayer to anyone who was listening.

Please if you get me out of this tonight, I promise to not date any more guys like this. Ever.

"You still have another year?" he asked over the roar of the engine.

I managed to nod, which given the speed he was driving felt like it gave me whiplash. "After this summer I have one more semester of classes. Then I need to find a paid internship to round out my degree."

We were in the hell of small talk. The place where people who no longer had anything in common wound up trapped and chatting for all eternity. If this was a first date, I could hope that we would move past it—maybe into the hell of 'tell me about your family' or 'what industry are you going into.' But this far into our relationship—having already slept together—there was no hope. I already knew the next couple of hours were going to be even worse. Ninth Circle of hell stuff.

When we finally reached Pike Place and parked, Luka was out of the car and around to open my door before I'd reached one shaky hand toward the handle. I got out on wobbly feet and considered kissing the blessed concrete beneath my heels.

"Are you okay?" Luka's eyebrows knitted together in concern. He'd asked me this the other day in the parking lot in exactly the same way. Then, it had seemed genuine. Now it felt perfunctory like he'd practiced this, as though he needed to rehearse being a decent human being.

I shook my head emphatically, refraining from lunging at him, even if I did want to strangle him. "You drive like a crazy person."

I was already wondering if I could get away with taking an Uber home. But Ubers were expensive, and I was an unpaid intern. Still, it would cost less than dying.

Luka visibly bristled, but then he smirked. I'd seen this move before. If he acted like he didn't care, then there must not be a problem. I was still fuming when he reached out, in a way-too-friendly fashion, to put one arm around my shoulders. I wasn't sure what to do. I wasn't a big fan of him touching me. Still the gesture wasn't overly intimate. I shrugged it off anyway and gave him a small, conciliatory smile.

"You've just forgotten what it's like to ride with me." I thought I got the edge of a secondary meaning to that, but before I could respond he grabbed my hand and began to walk forward.

Again with the touching! It was pretty clear he thought this was a date. I supposed the fact that he insisted on picking me up should have been a sign. No matter what *I* wanted this to be or what *I* hoped to get out of it, I couldn't ignore what Luka's motives were. This time I let him hold my hand. It didn't feel as bad as I wished it did. There was a comforting familiarity to it. We'd been like that when we were dating — affectionate, overly so sometimes. I remembered both Jillian and Jess complaining about it. Things had been different back then though. I hadn't minded when he drove around town like an insane person in his Accord, acting like he was a cast member from the Fast and the Furious. I'd been too caught up in the hormones of it. Now? It felt kinda nice to hold someone's hand.

Pike Place was crowded enough to make conversation difficult. I wanted to kiss every tourist I passed for being so loud. The white noise kept me from having to confront Luka about the past, about tonight, about any of it. The restaurant itself was tucked on the side of the hill down a narrow alley and mostly out of sight. When we arrived, I discovered it was charming and cozy and a little too intimate. A waitress sat us at a small table in the back—the kind reserved for lovers out for a romantic night.

I almost asked her if she had a booth available.

But I knew it wouldn't do any good. Luka had chosen this place for a reason. From looking around I had to guess it had high ratings for first dates on Yelp. We were presented with menus which were, also charmingly, in French. A language I didn't speak.

Luka leaned over and whispered, "I'll translate for you."

With horror, I remembered that Luka had studied French all through high school. He must've continued to do so in college. He was really pulling out all the stops. Why couldn't a guy I wanted to date do that? I could dig on some cheesy, romantic gestures but not when they were a play by my ex. At least it meant I stood a chance of getting him to open up to me.

Maybe Jillian was right and I wasn't giving him enough credit. I was a different person than when we had dated. I was smarter, savvier, and less likely to put up with his bullshit. Maybe if he was ready for a commitment, things could be different. Then, I remembered how he drove. I wasn't going to make any bets on who Luka had become.

A haggard looking waiter appeared at our table and stared us down while he began rattling off the evening's specials. Most of them I was familiar with. I might not speak French but I had eaten French food before. I didn't need to give Luka the opportunity to show off. Before I could process all my options, Luka began to order, "We'll start with an order of the escargot and also the foie gras. Bring a bottle of the Dom Perignon. The lady will have the veal and I will have the cassoulet."

He closed the menu with satisfaction.

I happened to like veal. It was probably what I would have ordered. But I resented the fact that he had tried to do it for me. I caught the waiter's eye before he could turn away. "Actually the lady will have the filet medium rare." I quickly tacked on a "please."

The waiter looked from Luka to me and back. If he had thoughts on what had just happened, he didn't share them. Instead he nodded and muttered a "very good" before disappearing toward the kitchen. How very French.

"My apologies. They're known for their veal here. I wanted you to try something new."

"I grew up on a Texas ranch. I've tried every kind of meat there is." I wished I could swallow the last part back down. It had much too strong a whiff of double entendre.

Luka must have noticed because he tried to hide a smile, turning his head to look out the window. "This place is lovely. I haven't been here before."

Now it felt like he was baiting me, as though my correcting him on the veal issue meant that I was somehow more worldly than him. Apparently, this evening was going to turn into a pissing contest. Well, I might not be able to pee standing up, but I could hold my own.

"I've been really busy at work," I said sweetly.

"An internship, right?"

I nodded. I already didn't like where this line of questioning was going.

"Paid?" he asked.

"No, it's a fantastic opportunity though. The investment group is doing really good work. In fact, it might turn into a job when I graduate."

"Is it a nonprofit?" he spit the question out like it tasted bad in his mouth.

Yes, companies working for the betterment of society were to be looked down upon. The reasons why Luka and I were incompatible were stacking up higher than the ivory tower he was looking down from.

"No. It's just a company with a conscience." That was the party line. The one that was scrawled all over their website and brochures. Gavin would be proud.

"It sounds like you've drank the Kool-Aid."

I could tell what he thought about that. I shrugged, tired of the interrogation, and him basically crapping on good people. It was time to turn the spotlight on him. "So what have you been doing?"

"I'm developing a new game for Microsoft. I'm on the lead design team."

"You're the lead designer?" I asked as innocently as possible. There was a huge difference between being on the team and being in charge. Fresh out of college? I knew where his place was in the pack. I'd play dumb if it knocked Luka down a few pegs.

"No." He shifted in his seat, angling his body a little further from me like I'd struck him. Score! "But I could be, you know. Everyone has to start somewhere. The salary is huge though. I have my own place, a new car, I get a couple weeks vacation."

I couldn't tell if he was selling me on Microsoft or him. I wasn't interested in buying stock in either.

"That's cool," I said noncommittally, tapping the tines of my fork with my fingernail. The disgruntled waiter appeared with the bottle of champagne, looking annoyed at my fidgeting as though it marred the atmosphere of the joint. He held it out for Luka to inspect, but he waved it off like it was fine. He really was determined to show off. Two glasses were poured and I watched the bubbles dancing in the pale liquid.

Luka raised his glass. "To new beginnings."

I hoped he didn't mean new beginnings with me. I clinked my flute against his and took a sip, amazed at how much it bubbled in my mouth. I'd never had champagne this expensive before. Now I understood the price tag, but I wasn't about to tell him that.

The alcohol had the effect of boosting my courage. I took a heady swig and dived right in. "So, I've been thinking since I ran into you about how our relationship ended."

"I have, too," he admitted to my surprise.

I hadn't expected him to be so open to a discussion about the past, but, hey, if I had the opportunity, I was going to take it. Carpe diem that bitch.

"I guess I just never understood why you cheated on me." I abandoned the champagne and waited for a response.

Luka took an extraordinarily long time taking his next drink. If he'd been thinking about us, he hadn't been considering that. Finally, he answered, "We all make mistakes, Cassie. I think it's best to leave the past in the past."

"Does that include leaving you in the past?" I couldn't help myself. My patience was beginning to crumble, especially if Luka was going to act like it wasn't a big deal. I decided to stand my ground. "No, really. You hurt me. I mean, we weren't in love or anything, but I did kind of think it was crappy of you."

"It was bad of me," he admitted "but I was a kid. I was surrounded by a campus of beautiful women. I've changed a lot since then."

I suspected that someone whose defense was to recall the sheer number of gorgeous girls on campus hadn't changed as much as he wanted me to believe. Before I could point that out, he moved closer to me. I felt his hand on my knee, and I jumped a little. Luka looked deep into my eyes, locking our gazes, and for a split second, I remembered how charming he could be. Yes, he was cocky, far too self-assured, but he had the moves to back it up—and the looks. As his baby blue eyes stared soulfully into my own, I felt like nineteen-year-old Cassie again and for just a second I was lost. "Cassie, I'm not going to lie to you. I have grown. I think that what we had was something really special. Sex that hot doesn't come along every day. I'm busy with work. You're busy with this internship. I think that maybe we could really blow off some steam together."

"Excuse me?" I smacked his hand from my leg like it was a mosquito. I'd prefer it had been a mosquito. I'd rather be dealing with a bloodsucking parasite.

"Don't take it the wrong way. I mean, maybe it will lead to something. Someday. And I'm not to going step out on you anymore. I understand the value of sticking to one chick."

"Chick?" I repeated. "I'm not a chick. I'm a woman." And the closest he was getting to me was paying the check. The waiter had the bad timing to show up with the foie gras at that moment. I stood up, ready to blow, and nearly knocked him over as I grabbed for my purse. "The problem is you never saw that. That girl—the one who was stupid enough to think your crazy driving was cool, the one who didn't notice when you were sleeping around—she's left the building. Now this woman is about to do the same thing." I took a step toward the door, paused, and spun around. Picking up the plate of foie gras I gave him a haughty glare. "And I'm taking this with me."

The waiter who had stood to the side did nothing to stop me as I stole the dish. I kinda hoped they charged Luka for it.

I was out the door, foie gras in hand, before I remembered that he had driven me here. Now I was in the middle of downtown Seattle with a plate of French duck liver and a pair of shoes that were not made for walking. I decided that despite that fact I needed to get moving. If Luka had the balls to follow me out, I didn't want him to find me standing there trying to figure out what to do next. I walked in the opposite direction of his car. It seemed like a safe bet that he would head the way we had come. He was the one wanting to take a tumble down memory lane after all. The trouble was I didn't really know where I was. It took some maneuvering to handle the dish I'd stolen and get into my purse to dig out my phone. Before I could open the Uber app, a car pulled up to the street in front of me with the window rolled down. I glanced down quickly at my little black dress wondering if I'd accidentally dressed like a street hooker. It didn't seem like I was advertising. Maybe it was someone looking to score some haute cuisine on the side.

"Cassie?" A familiar voice called.

I leaned down, which was tricky given the balancing act I was already doing, and saw the driver. Gavin's friendly, and very welcome face, stared back at me.

Eight

"OH MY GOD, I THOUGHT YOU WERE GOING TO solicit me."

Why did I have to say everything I was thinking around him? It seemed like I had absolutely no filter in the presence of Gavin North. I couldn't imagine what he thought about me. Actually, I could and none of it was good.

But he only laughed. "You looked a little lost."

That was probably the nicest thing he could say, given that I was wandering around downtown Seattle holding a plate of foie gras. Since I was probably going to say whatever popped into my head, I might as well be honest with him. "I just walked out on a really bad date." I held up the plate. "And I stole the appetizer."

"Is that foie gras?" Gavin asked, craning his head to see.

"It is. Or it was—if I don't get it out of this summer heat then it won't be much of anything soon." I glanced down at the delicate dish, hoping it wasn't ruined from standing outside. I wanted to eat it along with all of my feelings about tonight. Possibly with a spoon. Definitely with a bottle of wine.

"Tell you what, I'll give you a ride home, if you give me a little of that." Gavin waved me toward the car: a shiny, new Tesla.

As far as being propositioned on a street corner, it seems like a reasonable deal and I didn't have a better option. It would probably take 15 or 20 minutes to get an Uber down here this late on a Friday night. I got in and smiled sheepishly at him, clutching the foie gras like a French life raft. He was still dressed for work in his suit. I wondered if he had just gotten done with his meeting, but I didn't have the guts to ask. The last thing I needed was a reminder that he had chosen Trevor to go to that meeting.

"I'm all the way out in Bellevue if that's okay," I told him, trying to buckle my seat belt while holding the dish.

Gavin leaned over the center console, so close that I could smell the almond scent of his shampoo, and did it for me. His hand slid up the strap, smoothing and tightening it over my shoulder, before brushing swiftly over the bare skin of my collarbone.

Fireworks. It stole my breath for a moment.

"I was headed that way anyway." The words were thick as he turned his attention to the steering wheel and gripped it so tightly that his knuckles turned white.

"Okay," I said in a small voice as I struggled to regain control over my renegade faculties, all of which seemed alarmingly tuned to Gavin's frequency.

I wanted to ask him what he was headed to — or rather who. I kept my mouth set. Gavin checked both of his mirrors, put on his signal, and pulled back into traffic. Not only was he a perfect gentleman, he was a perfect driver. I was beginning to suspect the entire Gavin North package was almost perfect, except that girlfriend business. Still, as he began to drive me home, I wondered if I was getting more than I bargained for like a whole heap of wanting what I couldn't have.

"You saved my life." I shook mist from my hair as I flipped on the hall light. It had begun to finally drizzle as soon as we reached the condo, turning the summer night into an indoors-only affair. Typical, fickle Seattle move.

"I saved your shoes," he corrected me with a laugh. He paused at the door as though waiting for an invitation. He filled the door frame, small rain droplets dusting the broad shoulders of his suit jacket.

I beckoned him inside as I peeled my heels from my swollen feet. Asking him in was the least I could do after he'd driven me home through downtown traffic on a Friday night. There was no sign of Lillian, a small mercy since I'd sworn on my celibacy to get access to her guest room for the summer. I'd promised her no sex. No one-nightstands. I hadn't *exactly* promised her no men altogether. There had to be some rational exceptions for delivery guys and maintenance workers. Men who didn't count as men. Like Gavin, who wasn't a man. He was my boss.

Maybe I needed to wear a rubber band around my wrist to remind me of that very important fact.

Sure, he wasn't the boss I had been expecting. He had all

his hair for one thing. And yes, he had surprised me more than once. Taking things in stride, cracking jokes, delivering his intern and her shoes halfway across the city. Because Gavin was a good guy who despite some rough edges took time for other people. He genuinely cared.

About his job, I reminded myself as I eyed the wine rack in the corner. That was why he was here now. Because he saw his intern home in the rain. It was why if I offered him a glass of the Montepulciano I grabbed from Trader Joe's, he would say no. That, and the fact that he probably preferred to drink wine that cost more than ten bucks. Because if he accepted a glass of wine, that might signal that he wanted to spend time together socially. But was offering the wine the equivalent overture? In the end, the Texan in me—the part of me cursed with carefully cultivated social graces—won out.

"Can I get you a glass of wine?" I picked up the bottle so he could see the label in an effort at full disclosure. Cheap wine. Company intern. Gentlemanly boss. I knew what his answer would be before he opened his mouth.

"Sure."

My mouth fell open like a broken mailbox, and before I could clamp it shut again, he shrugged off his suit jacket and began unfastening his cufflinks. My jaw remained unhinged even as I backed into the kitchen to look for the corkscrew. It took mental coaching, the likes I imagined Olympic athletes employed, to talk myself into turning away from him to look in the drawer. I had no idea what to expect when I turned around. What if he took his shirt off? What if he'd stripped to his birthday suit?

It took two tries to get the cork out of the bottle and when it popped free, I felt a wave of relief. Grabbing two wine glasses, I quickly poured a safe amount of wine for each of us. There were no mental gymnastics needed to convince me to turn back around. Gavin was lounging on the sofa with his arms crossed behind his head. He'd rolled up his sleeves and loosened his tie but was otherwise clothed. My heart flipped with unreasonable, if fleeting, disappointment. Later, there would be a lecture in front of the mirror. One where I reminded myself that I'd chosen the path of being single, followed by a stern tongue-lashing regarding inappropriate fantasies about my boss.

"Sorry, it's cheap." I wished I could swallow it back as soon as I said it, my cheeks turning the same shade as the wine I handed him.

"No worries." He shrugged as if that didn't bother him. "I remember the college days and Two-Buck Chuck." He didn't bother swirling it, instead he took a long drink. "Definitely better than that."

"This one cost ten dollars," I said with mock smugness. I couldn't decide where to sit. Next to him seemed wrong—like a clear signal that we were on a spontaneous date. Across the room might seem like too much space as though I was afraid he would think we were on a date. I opted for the opposite end of the couch, leaving three-quarters of a cushion between us.

"I'm clearly paying you too much." He grinned and angled his body toward mine, a dark strand falling across his forehead. Even his hair seemed to be off the clock.

"You aren't paying me anything," I reminded him.

His eyebrow arched into a question mark, and he glanced around the condo. "Heiress?"

That made me laugh. I shook my head, incapable of imagining that as my reality. "If only. Daughter of a Texan rancher—and no. This is my best friend's sister's condo."

"Not a bad deal. She works late?"

I swallowed back the giddiness threatening to escape at his question. "She's a lawyer, so she works all the time."

"Then you're alone most nights." He took another sip, his mouth lingering longer on the rim. I wasn't certain if he was savoring the wine or the information.

Maybe I was reading into the questions, but it felt like more than friendly, small talk. Either he was casing the joint or I wasn't the only one entertaining crossing some boss-employee boundaries. It wasn't like it was that weird. There wasn't much of an age difference, and he wasn't actually paying me. Of course, I wasn't sure if that made it better or worse.

" That's usually when I get to actually talk to my best friends. They're both out of the country." It wasn't as if he was interested in what I did at night when I was alone, but I didn't want him to think I sat around solo in someone else's apartment.

"Together?" He asked as he abandoned his now-empty wineglass on the side table. I couldn't decide whether or not to offer him a refill. Too much alcohol and Cassie usually resulted in bad decisions. But I was sipping and in control.

"No," I told him as I retrieved the bottle from the kitchen and poured him another glass. It was the hospitable thing to do. "Jillian is in Scotland with her boyfriend, and Jessica is on her honeymoon."

"Honeymoon?" He didn't bother to hide his surprise, setting off my own internal alarms. I'd learned to steer clear of the M-word on dates, but this wasn't a date and it was a fact. Jessica was married. Never mind that I couldn't wrap my head around it either.

"Yeah, she got married a few weeks ago." So, so weird to say that.

"Is she...older?"

There it was, the wild-eyed look of a man trapped by a conversation about commitment with a girl he barely knew. Since this wasn't a date, and I was determined to keep it from heading down that path, I smirked. "We're the same age. She married an instructor."

"Her instructor?" He shifted on the couch, uncrossing his legs and looking distinctly *less* comfortable.

"Not currently." I did my best to look innocent, but I could barely contain my laughter.

"Wow." He paused and adjusted his loosened tie.

"He's about your age, so it's not like he's ancient."

"Doesn't the university frown on that?"

"The university doesn't really get a say in who we date. Jess wasn't his student and he was still a PhD candidate."

"You left that part out," he said accusatorially, but his eyes twinkled with his own suppressed laughter.

Okay, so maybe I was enjoying making him squirm a little. "I enjoy pressing a person's buttons."

Oh hell, I'd just said that aloud. What I'd meant and what I'd implied were on opposite ends of the spectrum.

Gavin cleared his throat, pulling at the loosened tie around his neck again. My thoughts went to what he could do with that tie—what I would let him do with that tie.

"I imagine it's different in the corporate world," I began, ignoring the alarm bells sounding in my head. I should stop. I shouldn't finish the thought. I did anyway. "Dating people at work, I mean. There must be rules."

"Probably at some places." He let that tidbit hang in the air without giving me any more information.

I couldn't help but bite. "And at Northwest Investments?"

"Half of our staff is married to one another. I don't care if people are hooking up if they're doing their jobs. I mean, we do have a sexual harassment policy," he added quickly. "So I wouldn't recommend you walking around and catcalling people."

Now he really was squirming. I had brought the subject up, pushed the topic of inter-office dating, but he was still the boss. However loose the rules were, they had to be different when it came to his relationships with his employees. "Good to know."

"Are you thinking about dating someone from work?" If he felt the least amount of shame asking such a forward question, he didn't show it.

Now I was the one with ruffled feathers. I stammered, trying to come up with a response that didn't make it obvious exactly who I was interested in. "Not really."

"It's hard for a lot of us," he said. "We don't get out a lot. It's just natural to date someone from the office."

"Is that how you met your girlfriend? At work?" Now I

had really done it. I had promised myself I would stay far, far away from this topic. Instead, I practically had him filling out a dating questionnaire.

"My girlfriend?" His confusion was obvious, which had the simultaneous effect of making me excited and sick to my stomach. I couldn't pretend that I hadn't been watching him now. Or that I wasn't interested in him.

"The girl who came to the office the other day. Pretty. Dark hair. Looks like a model." I knew her name. I'd asked about her. I wasn't about to admit that.

"Imogen?"

"Is that her name? You two looked cozy." There. I had put it on the table. It was stupid to keep beating around the bush. Especially since part of me wanted him to be beating around my bush.

Gavin leaned forward, placed his glass of wine on the coffee table, and then threw his head back and laughed. I wasn't certain what to make of that.

"I'm sorry. Are you gay?" It was the thing that made the most sense. If he wasn't dating the supermodel-gorgeous woman who'd been in his office, kissing him on his cheek, then maybe I had gotten the wrong impression altogether. He did dress well.

My question only made him laugh louder.

"No, I'm not gay." It took him a second to stop howling before he added, "Imogen is my sister."

His sister.

Sister.

Sister! Sister! Sister!

I did my best to look like this was merely interesting

while inside I was doing a hula dance. There *had* been another explanation. I just hadn't seen it. Maybe I'd gotten too used to expecting less of men.

"Wait, if she's your sister then...?"

Imogen Sound was the heiress to Sound Coffee. I didn't know that much about the chain except that I could close my eyes, point a finger, and there would be one waiting to make me a latte—*anywhere in the world*. The whole brand had been built from the ground up by Richard Sound, arguably one of the most famous Seattleite's living. He was universally beloved for his focus on his employees and his passion for his product. If Imogen was his daughter, and Gavin was her brother. "Your dad is..."

"Richard Sound," he confirmed with a sigh.

"That's incredible. I've read a bunch of his books."

Gavin's mouth tightened into a thin smile. "He's inspiring."

"You don't get along," I guessed.

"No, we do actually. We have a fantastic relationship."

It wasn't the answer I was expecting. I cocked my head as if a new angle might help me make sense of the conflicting information. There was definitely something that didn't quite add up. A puzzle piece that didn't fit. "But your last name."

"I use my mother's maiden name," he explained, slumping against the back of the couch.

"Why?" I blurted out. I could only imagine the doors that the Sound name could open. Big ones. Revolving ones. Locked ones. It would take less time to imagine the doors it couldn't.

"Let me guess. You're thinking that the Sound name would secure any business deal. It would mean guaranteed venture capital." He rubbed his index finger on his temple. I'd hit a sore spot. "But my dad built Sound Coffee with a vision and hard work. It's *his*."

"And you want to leave your own mark behind," I finished for him.

He cracked open an eyelid and studied me. "Exactly."

"I can't be the first person to figure out why you made that choice."

"You're the first person who didn't act like I was stupid because of it," he admitted.

"What's stupid about that? I can see the pros and the cons. Yeah, it would be easier, but as someone who hopes to achieve something in her life, I get why you want to do it yourself."

He stared at me like he was seeing me for the first time. His gaze burned through me, settled in my chest, and ignited a simmering ache.

"Oh, well, your sister is very pretty," I managed to force out, trying to head toward safer waters and hoping I didn't spontaneously combust from the heat he was throwing my way.

"And obviously she's not my girlfriend," he said with meaning.

"Do you have a girlfriend?" My voice piqued on the last word, betraying exactly why I was asking the question.

"I've been a little busy with Northwest Investments for the last couple of years. I dated a few women off and on.

Nothing serious. I guess I haven't been lucky enough to meet someone in the office like half my staff."

The hula dancing stopped. He hadn't been lucky enough to meet someone? Was he talking in the past tense? Did he mean currently? What did that make me? Invisible? Or simply undesirable? "I understand. I've been really focused on finishing my degree."

"So you are dating anyone then?"

Okay, I wasn't imagining the way he leaned closer as if he wanted to put less distance between us.

"No, I pretty much swore off men after the last one." Oh my God. Why did I have to say whatever came into my mouth around him? He was like a walking, six- foot- tall vial of truth serum. Sexy, sexy truth serum.

"Someone burned you," he guessed. He hesitated as if he wanted to say more. I could see he was holding something back. Probably he wanted to ask if it was Trevor. It was pretty obvious there was something going on there. If I was going spill my guts to him I might as well be honest up front.

"I was dating Trevor—the other intern. He cheated on me." It stung as I ripped that Band-Aid off and the air of truth hit the freshly closed wound, but not as much as I thought it would. Trevor might be around, but he was definitely wasn't in my life anymore.

"And then you both went after the same internship?"

I could see him trying to process this information. I needed to be sure he understood exactly how that had gone down, because it might be pretty easy to jump to the conclusion that I'd followed him to the company. "I had applied for the internship while we were together. He decided to as well apparently. I had no idea that he'd also gotten one. You might remember the first time we met in the office." I gulped down half my glass of wine and reached for the bottle. This truth stuff felt new. Usually, at this point, I was trying to flirt or sound smarter than I felt. With Gavin it was somehow easy to just open up to him, but scary at the same time.

"I remember that," he said with a smirk. Gavin ran a hand through his hair and I wondered what it would be like to run my own hands through it — to feel his body against mine — to kiss him. "Cassie?"

I blinked, he had said something and I was busy in la la land fantasizing about kissing him. "I'm sorry?"

"Is working with him going to be a problem?" Gavin's eyes squinted in concern and I refrained from hiding under a throw pillow.

"No! I mean, I'm a professional. Of course, I will put Trevor in line if need be." It was probably best that he know that now. I'd be totally professional until Trevor stepped out of line.

"I bet you will." Gavin didn't seem bothered by this idea, instead he seemed rather amused. "So you've sworn off men?"

This was my chance to take that back. Or to make my move. Instead, I nodded. Because it was the truth and I found lying to Gavin impossible. I had sworn off men. "I need to focus on me for a while. I have things I want to do with my life."

"I get it," he said. "I kinda said the same thing. I just have the list in my head of all the things I want to accomplish before I turn thirty."

"You still have a while then…" I was fishing for information. It was obvious and I should have been ashamed of myself. I wasn't. Finding out info from the source was less pathetic than Google stalking him later.

"Four more years," he said matter-of-factly. "The thing is I've checked off most of my list. It's kind of strange. I guess I have to figure out what I want to do next."

God, I hope I was on his next to-do list.

"I understand. I've decided I need to get out of school, graduate with honors, get amazing internships, and plan to land a kick-ass job. But now that I'm completely on the path to doing all of those things, I've started to think about what happens after all of that."

"Have any answers?"

I shook my head. "You?"

"No, but I'm excited about the possibilities." His eyes were blazing and I wondered if maybe he was thinking what I was thinking. What would it mean to be part of Gavin's life? From the way his gaze seared through me, he was wondering the same thing. Before either of us could find out, he stood and grabbed his jacket. "I should get home. My kid sister is staying in my apartment for the weekend."

"I'd love to meet her sometime," I said, my cheeks turning red. I'd gone from keeping him at arm's length to asking to meet his family. What a difference a non-date made.

Gavin didn't seem to mind my request, however forward it might be. "She'll be in the office. She's spearheading that preservation committee."

"The one that's trying to stop us?" I asked, taken aback. "Talk about a case of sibling rivalry."

"It's one of her great joys in life: to try to make things hard for me. Actually, we're pretty close, despite her need to be a pain in the ass." They had to be if she was staying with him while actively working against him.

He moved towards the door and I followed after. We lingered a moment, a few feet apart, before he reached for the handle. "Don't work too hard this weekend."

"Am I that obvious?"

"I think we have a lot in common."

"Then maybe we can figure out our next steps together." Did I just say that? Out loud? To him? I was going to have to glue my teeth together when he was around.

Gavin didn't say anything, but he was smiling as he left.

Nine

I WILL NOT FACEBOOK STALK GAVIN NORTH. OR Wikipedia stalk. Or Google stalk. I will be an adult.

No matter how often I repeated the words, my willpower didn't get any stronger. That was pretty much the opposite of how a mantra was supposed to work. Already today I had opened a web browser and started to type his name three times. I'd immediately closed it before I could hit enter, but that was the closest thing to restraint I'd shown. Searching his name would be reading too much into Friday night. So we'd shared a couple glasses of wine and talked. Nothing had happened. Only, nothing had happened and that fact was driving me crazy.

Besides, I'd learned a lot about him from our conversation over the weekend, including fun facts like he was only four years older than me.

Translation: there was a reasonable age gap.

Imogen Sound was his kid sister.

Translation: I didn't need to be jealous of her and, more importantly, Gavin was single!

None of what I'd learned made him any less my boss. Sure, Northwest Investments was cool with inter-office dating, but it didn't take a genius to figure out that the boss dating an intern was going to be frowned upon. It might also wreck my chances of landing a permanent position with the company when I graduated. Maybe we could date in secret like in the movies, because that always worked out. And what about the inevitable break-up? I didn't have the best track record with my ex-boyfriends. Despite the plethora of new information I'd learned from Gavin, my options were looking bleaker. It was easier to tell myself I shouldn't date him when another woman stood in the way. I was never going to be a cheater like my exes. But if the boundary line was purely propriety, I was completely screwed.

He hadn't come in for the day yet, so I was left to split my time making notes about the project and overanalyzing every moment we'd spent together. It was impossible not to think about him in the office, but I stubbornly redirected myself until my focus was mostly on the project. I'd finally begun to have an actual idea about how to approach the preservation committee. For some reason knowing that Imogen was the one behind it made things easier. I'd allowed myself to Google her. That was research—necessary research —not crazy-girl research. Still, I jumped every time someone walked by my cubicle. It didn't garner much info. Imogen was an It-Girl, which meant that I'd have better luck piecing together info about her life from Instagram posts.

I'd spent my weekend binging The Bachelor while thinking of any ideas I could about the Majestic Theater project. To avoid access to Google and the temptation to use it, I'd written 100 tiny notes on Post-its instead of opening my computer. Considering the first thing I'd done when I got access to a web browser was do a search on Gavin's sister that had been a wise move. This morning I needed to sort through all those notes. By the time I'd finished plastering them across my desktop and the walls of my cubicle, my entire workspace looked like a crime scene investigation. It was actually amazing what a weekend without access to computers or cell phones did for my creativity. Now, I didn't have one good idea, I had at least twenty good ones and probably about eighty insane ones.

By the time, I'd filtered through them, I was feeling pretty good. Good enough to pop down to Sound Coffee to pick up a latte and a drink for George. Danny was working the bar and he lit up when he saw me, prompting my usual waves of guilt. Thank God, caffeine usually assuaged it.

"Hi Cassie, how was your weekend?" he asked with a bright smile as he began to pull my shot.

I didn't know how to answer that. My weekend started with the bad date that had ended with... I wasn't sure what had happened between Gavin and I. Just thinking about it left me feeling warm and tingly inside, probably an inappropriate thing to share. I opted for the cop-out answer. "I mostly vegged and watched TV. You?"

"I was working. We get pretty busy on the weekends." He put a lid on my cup and passed it to me and then began working on the drink I'd ordered for George. "I put an extra shot in there for you."

The trouble with Danny was that he was so nice that he was boring. I hadn't given him exactly scandalous events to work with, but that was what our relationship boiled down to: small talk about work. He finished up George's Americano and handed it to me. I grabbed two sleeves from the tray next to the espresso machine. I couldn't help but stare at the Sound Coffee logo as I slipped them on.

Gavin, like it or not, was the heir to a giant coffee fortune, and yet, he'd chosen to work his way up from the bottom. It was really something special.

He was really something special.

The person behind me in line bumped my arm and I startled back to reality—the place where I had a job and shit to do. I waved goodbye to Danny and headed back to the office, eager to get to work on one of the one hundred ideas I'd thought up over the last few days. Pausing at the reception desk, I held the Americano just out of George's reach as was becoming our custom.

"You didn't tell me that Imogen Sound was Gavin's sister?" I accused him.

He wiggled his eyebrows and pursed his lips like I had been giving him sass. "Honey, you didn't ask. Why does it matter if she's his girlfriend or his sister?"

"It doesn't." I shrugged in a not-at-all convincing way.

"Umm-hmm." He took a sip of his drink with one raised eyebrow. He wasn't buying it, but he didn't push.

"Enjoy your coffee!" I called before he decided to ask more questions.

It had been a dangerous move bringing up Gavin at all. If I wasn't careful I would find myself distracted at my desk. I sat down at my computer, determined to get to work, and dug in. When Trevor popped his head into my cubicle, I looked up surprised to see an hour had already passed. So far I had outlined three separate proposals. They were skeletons —ideas really—but any one of them would work. I just had to choose the one that would impress NorthWest Investments most. I did my best to shield my screen from Trevor's prying eyes, but he craned his neck trying to see anyway.

"Are you working on the Majestic Theatre proposal?" he asked

I snorted. Even if he couldn't decipher the dozens of random thoughts scrawled on notes all over the makeshift walls, some things should be obvious. "No, I'm solving world peace."

"Come on, Cassie. I was thinking about it all weekend and it doesn't make sense for us to work separately." He leaned against my makeshift doorway and shoved his hands into his trouser pockets casually as he began to whistle his new tune.

If I knew Trevor, he hadn't spent his weekend working at all. Undoubtedly, he'd been out to the bars or taking some new girl out. He had a firm commitment to a work-life balance that usually tipped the scales firmly toward life.

"I'm actually pretty far along in my proposal already." I hit the sleep button so that he would stop trying to peek.

"Maybe you could show me what you have, and I can give you some tips."

"Do you really think I'm falling for that?" I asked. Clearly, he wasn't as prepared to tackle this project as he'd tried to let on before.

"I'll show you mine if you show me yours." He winked in a way that I used to find charming, but now it made me want to gag.

"No thanks. I've seen enough of yours already." I refrained from detailing how little interest I had in revisiting anything he had to show me.

Trevor's forehead crinkled and his mouth drooped down as he shook his head in a sad, slow way. "You know, we were in love once."

I didn't know what to say to this. I couldn't believe he was bringing it up *here*. *Now*. We hadn't been in love. I had been in love. "If that was true," I hissed under my breath, "then you wouldn't have cheated on me."

"We all make mistakes. You don't have to keep punishing me."

"Let me make this clear to you." I sat up in my seat and crossed my arms over my chest. "I nothing you. I'm not punishing you. I'm not helping you. I nothing you."

Trevor opened his mouth, the concerned look vanishing and morphing into white-hot rage, but before he could speak, we were joined by Gavin. He looked from Trevor to me and raised an eyebrow. Now that he knew about our past, it probably wasn't hard to figure out what was going on, especially with me in protection mode and Trevor on stage two of a nuclear-level meltdown.

"Everything cool here?" he asked nonchalantly. If I didn't know better, I'd think he was just checking in on his interns. Except, I knew better, which made the checking in feel personal, like he was worried about me. I liked it.

"Yeah, we were just working together on the Majestic

Theater project." Trevor shot me a cocky grin while Gavin's eyes stayed trained on me. I could sense Gavin searching for the truth in what he was being told. I hoped he found it.

"Yes, we were just talking about our *separate* proposals," I said with emphasis. Better to spell it out than let him get the wrong idea. I'd told Gavin I could work with Trevor, but I didn't want him to think I was choosing to do so. Somehow, that felt like it was sending the wrong message.

"There's definitely a time and place for teamwork," Gavin said, spreading his hands, "but I can see why you two would want to work on this project individually. If you have any concerns or want to bounce any ideas, come see me in my office." His eyes never left mine when he made this offer. A low fire lit in my belly and I hoped its heat didn't make its way to my cheeks. Technically, the offer extended to both of us, but I got the impression that it was meant for me. There was no stopping the flames from coloring my face now.

"Thanks," Trevor interjected, "I'll do that."

Gavin gave him a terse nod and then disappeared toward the corner office.

Trevor watched him walk away before he straightened up and adjusted his suit jacket. "Well, I guess I understand why you don't need my help now."

I was too busy fantasizing about bouncing ideas off Gavin in his office for that to process immediately, but when it did, I startled and looked up at him. "What does that mean?"

"That it looks like you clinched this competition."

"There is no competition. We're doing our best to help the company."

"I guess we weren't sitting in the same meeting," Trevor said. "There's a job at the end of this rainbow, and it's supposed to be mine."

"Remind me how you got this internship again?" I asked, not able to stop from fuming. Did he honestly believe that he deserved that job? He hadn't even done the legwork to find this internship. Now he wanted to steal the prize.

"You'd love to be the martyr on this one, wouldn't you? But I didn't think you'd sink this low." He shook his head. This time his disappointed face looked a little too practiced.

"Exactly what are you accusing me of?" I knew. I could hear it hiding under his words, but I wanted him to say it.

He had the decency to lean down and lower his voice when he did. "I'm saying that if you think screwing the boss will get you this job, then I'm disappointed in you. I guess I really can't help you out with your proposal."

I didn't have to tell him to get out, he walked away following his accusation. I sat at my desk, staring at my blank computer screen. How dare he claim he had a right to be disappointed in me? Gavin wouldn't be the only one making the decision about how to pitch the preservation committee. And it wasn't like anything had happened between Gavin and me. In fact, I'd been trying like hell to make sure nothing did happen. Was I guilty just because I'd had a few daydream fantasies and shared a glass of wine with him? So much for innocent until proven guilty. I wanted this job. I'd worked for this internship. I wasn't about to let my reputation be skewered by an ex's revenge- driven tactics. There was only one thing I could do. It took nearly a half an hour to screw up the courage, but I got up and walked toward Gavin's office. I paused before knocking on the door, but I didn't wait for an invitation before I strode in. Gavin looked up, obviously surprised, because he had a guest.

"Cassie," he said my name with a familiarity that wrapped itself around me like a warm blanket. "Is there something I can do for you?"

"I'm s-s-sorry," I stammered, losing some of my nerve. "I can come back later."

Or never. If I didn't do this now, I would never get up the guts again. I would just have to go into hiding. Maybe permanently. Maybe it was time to get a shopping cart and find a spot under a bridge and hide out forever. That suddenly felt like a much better life plan.

"It's fine. I did tell you my office was always open," he said. There was a double meaning in that. I could feel it.

Imogen, who up close was a more delicate version of Gavin with the same blue eyes and dark hair, bit her lip as if holding back a smile. Maybe I wasn't the only one aware of the simmering attraction between him and I. Nope. The list of people who'd picked up on it was growing. Trevor. Imogen. George. If I wasn't careful, by the end of the day, everyone in the office would know.

When I didn't say anything, Gavin rescued me. "Actually, I wanted to introduce you to my sister. Imogen this is Cassie. Cassie this is Imogen."

"It's nice to meet you," I blurted out before rushing on. I had to get this out. "I was thinking about what you said—about the presentation—I won't be needing any help. I really need to do this alone."

"It's really no trouble," he began.

I held up a hand. "No. I need to do this *alone*."

Gavin sat back in his chair, his shoulders slumping, and frowned. "I understand."

I didn't wait for him to ask me what was wrong. There was no need to confide in each other about this. We had almost taken things too far, and I just put a stop to that. He knew I wasn't on the market. I'd told him. We'd both needed a little reminder of that.

"It's nice to meet you too," Imogen added softly. I gave her a small smile before backing out of the office.

I wondered briefly if he had talked about me to her and what she must think of me after that bold intrusion, but it didn't matter. Because I wouldn't be getting to know Imogen outside this office. Because I'd made my choice. Because Gavin North and Cassie Hart were colleagues and nothing more.

Ten

I BURIED MYSELF IN WORK. I'D GONE WELL PAST workaholic and straight into *I live, I breathe, I work*. When I wasn't in my cubicle, ignoring every living soul around me and researching the ins and outs of the proposal I finally decided upon, I was at Sound Coffee. Having an in with one of the managers meant that I could set up shop and stay there for hours without anyone asking me to leave. It had become my unofficial office but with ready access to copious amounts of caffeine.

All the time I was putting into my proposal, two weeks' worth of effort, was finally starting to pan out. I was less than a month away from the presentation that could decide my fate. Waiting on permits had scored me more time to get things together. Gavin had been so busy with the planning and building commissions that the most I'd heard from him were short emails updating me on the status of the project. Impersonal ones at that, given that they were addressed to the entire office. He kept his distance and I had kept mine.

Hopefully, in a few weeks, the sacrifice would prove worth it.

I had no idea what Trevor was working on, but if he was staying up late at night working, he wasn't doing it in the office or at the coffee shop. I never saw him after hours when I was burning the midnight oil. All the better, because Sound Coffee had begun to feel like my second home. I felt content in the café surrounded on all sides by, but still protected from, the bustling street life of Seattle. Even its industrial chic decor had begun to grow on me.

"You know it's Friday night, right?" Danny sat down at the seat across from me and peered at the piles of notes on the table. By the end of this, he should get a job at Northwest Investments. I felt like his steady supply of caffeination had gotten me through this project and would be necessary for years to come.

I offered him a rueful smile and kept typing. "Ain't no rest for the wicked."

"Don't I know that," he said, leaning back in the chair and spreading his legs, "but even I'm taking off in a few."

I glanced at my watch in alarm and saw that it was only 7 o'clock. "You aren't closing?"

"Don't worry. They know to take care of you." He nodded toward the baristas still behind the bar. I knew each of them by name now, but that wasn't the reason I was alarmed. Danny had become a comforting presence in my life. There was no pressure. No expectation. But there was coffee. In a way, it was the healthiest relationship I'd had in a long time. No taking just giving. Unless, of course, you looked at it from his perspective. I was usually taking. Taking up space. Taking coffee. Taking free refills. He never complained though. "How's it going?"

I kept him apprised of my various ideas, and he'd offered suggestions along the way. Most of them hadn't been very helpful, but it was pretty sweet.

"I think I've nailed down the exhibit aspect," I told him, "and if I can just figure out the screenings, then I'll be gold."

"If anyone can do it, you can." He gave me a beatific grin, the one that had become such an important part of my daily routine.

I didn't feel any differently about Danny exactly. He was still Mr. Nice Guy. Still the dependable one. No, I didn't find my engines revving at the sight of him. But there was something reassuring about his presence. Maybe I'd discounted him. Maybe I should've given it a chance to see if it could have become something more. To his credit, he never acted like my late-night work sessions were anything more than a friend sitting in his café. Maybe I owed him more than that. The trouble was that even when I actively tried to consider Danny as an option, all I could think about was Gavin. Despite weeks of keeping my distance, even the slightest thought of him sent me into a tailspin. I'd never be able to give Danny a fair shot.

I'd begun to wonder if nailing this presentation was the best idea after all. How would I feel about Gavin in a few months? Would my initial interest have cooled off? Or would I still be battling this wild interest?

"So are you hoping to get a job there?" Danny asked, tipping his head in the direction of my office building.

I shrugged my shoulders, wondering how he'd managed

to hit on exactly what was preoccupying me. But Danny was just perceptive like that, another Mr. Nice Guy trait. "I don't know. I want to do a good job though. It could be a great reference."

There. That's how I needed to think of this. Maybe a future with Northwest Investments wasn't my wisest choice, but having them to give me a good recommendation could make all the difference. It was just the fuel I needed to keep the weekend fires burning. I was so close to figuring out the last part of this PR puzzle.

"Hey, I have a question for you." Danny leaned across the table, lowering his voice.

My stomach did a nervous little flip. If he asked me out, would I say yes? I considered it. I tried to talk myself into it. But with a sinking feeling I realized that no matter how much I wanted to want Danny, it would never happen. "Okay."

He reached below the table and I froze. Then he pulled out the last thing I expected. A ring box.

I didn't know what to say. I was pretty certain that I hadn't been leading him on to this level.

"I'm going to ask my girlfriend to marry me," he began, and I breathed a heavy sigh of relief. He paused, looking momentarily confused, but I waved him on. "I can't decide between the top of the Space Needle or on the big Ferris wheel."

"How sure are you that she's going to say yes?" I said without thinking. I could score points for my spontaneous idiocy. The last thing Danny needed to worry about was whether she would say yes or not.

Danny only chuckled. "Pretty sure."

"Good," I said with a relieved smile. "I wouldn't want to be stuck on a Ferris wheel with someone who'd said no."

"I hadn't thought of that," he admitted. "I just saw that Prince did it in London and I thought it was a pretty good idea."

"Yeah, but it should be more meaningful to you. Which one of those places has more meaning?" I asked him.

Danny thought about it for a moment before shaking his head. "Neither really. We haven't gone to either place. I just wanted a big, romantic gesture."

"Let me tell you a secret," I whispered, so it might have more impact. "Most girls don't want a big gesture. Most girls want to see that you remembered the small things."

"Small things, huh?"

"Like where did you meet? Or is there a special place to you? When did you first realize you fell in love with her?" I asked him, hoping I inspired some smaller, more intimate romantic gesture.

"Cassie, you're a genius!" He didn't share any answers because at that moment he stood up, almost knocking over his chair as he waved excitedly at the door. It was boyish and charming and part of me melted a little.

I glanced over my shoulder and saw a petite blonde looking around the café. Judging by the way she grinned when she saw him, he was right about the answer he was going to get. She practically skipped over and gave him a big kiss.

"You ready?"

"Tracy meet Cassie." He didn't bother to explain that I

was his ex, which I was glad for. It didn't really seem necessary.

I stuck out my hand and smiled back at her.

"Let me go lose this apron and then I'll be with you."

Danny abandoned us, and to my surprise, Tracy plopped down into the seat he just left behind.

"How do you know Danny?" she asked, blinking at me innocently. Did I lie? Or did I come clean? My hesitation must've been enough, because she giggled. "Oh wait! *Cassie*. You two used to date." She said this like it was a matter of fact and not all something that bothered her. I nodded.

"Like 1 million years ago," I said.

"He told me about you. He said you were just better at being friends," she repeated as if she had memorized it.

"Yeah. I guess that's true," I said. We were really, now that I thought about it. I'd been so obsessed with whether he was still interested, I'd missed that we'd clearly exited to Friend Avenue. At least, it was one less thing to worry about and my java fix wasn't in jeopardy.

"Danny is my best friend," she said dreamily as if she wasn't in the same room as me anymore.

"I thought you two were dating," I said, momentarily confused.

Tracy perked up. "We are. I mean that's love. Being with your best friend. I can be myself around him."

"That sounds... amazing," I finished. It really did. None of my romantic relationships had ever achieved best friend status. I thought to my two best friends and how little they came to me with their problems now. They were still around when I needed them, but they both had new best friends now I realized.

"It is," she sighed. "And he's super hot."

I laughed at this. Tracy didn't strike me as the jealous type, so I added, "He is pretty cute."

Danny reappeared, and Tracy popped up to meet him. They were holding hands before I could blink my eyes. The love between the two radiated off them. I had never seen something so obvious in my life. No matter where he decided to ask her—even if he dropped to his knee right here and now in front of his ex-girlfriend, I knew what her answer would be. Somehow it even made me believe that true love was a possibility.

"Have a good night!" I called after them. My eyes lingered on the door long after they had left.

Danny hadn't been the guy for me. I had always known that, but I never really stopped to consider what Tracy had said about love and friendship. Maybe that was the one ingredient I'd always been missing. I dated guys but I had never really been friends with one of my boyfriends before. It was dates and sex and work, but we didn't hang out. Watching the two of them together, hearing how they talked about each other, that was what I wanted.

I'd be an idiot to settle for anything less.

Eleven

AFTER THE WORLD'S MOST ADORABLE COUPLE LEFT the coffee shop, I couldn't focus. Maybe it was the happiness lingering in the air. It was like being really hungry and smelling something delicious that I couldn't have. I needed a change of scenery to clear my head.

The conference room at Northwest Investments was naturally empty on a Friday night, so I seized the opportunity and spread out all of my notes, plugged in my laptop, and got to work. The meeting space had the added benefit of a large white board I could use. I just had to remember to erase it when I was done or run the risk of ruining my surprise presentation. Grabbing a couple of different colored dry-erase markers, I began to make notes on the first element of my soon-to-be winning proposal. I wanted to showcase the history of the Majestic Theatre first, then I needed strong community programming in order to help the residents feel like a part of the process. It would take some careful planning with the development and building departments to make sure everything went off without a hitch timing-wise. Given that this project would probably drag into the fall semester, I was a bit nervous that I might not be around to see it through. Still, when I stood back and surveyed my ideas as part of the big picture, I was pleased. Seeing them like this made all the difference. Usually, I had dozens of scattered notes and computer spreadsheets, but I'd never looked at it as a whole.

"This is going to work," I whispered to myself as a tremble of excitement raced through me.

"It just might," Gavin said from behind me.

I startled, whirling around to face the intruder. Gavin was no longer in his business attire—the navy blue suit that he'd worn to the office today. Not that I had been paying attention. Now he was dressed down in a pair of dark washed jeans that hung on his hips and a black V-neck that clung to his torso. No wonder he always wore suits to the office. Dressed down he didn't look like the CEO of a major real estate investment group, he looked like the kind of guy you saw at a bar and made eye contact with—the kind of guy you hoped bought a drink for you. The kind of guy you might buy a drink for yourself. I realized I was gawking, my hand pressed to my chest, my heart still racing, but no longer because of surprise. Possibly because I'd stopped breathing.

He'd seen my notes. The thought filtered through my oxygen-deprived brain, and I angled my body to try to shield the whiteboard, suddenly self-conscious of the fact that he was looking at all my plans. "You aren't supposed to see this yet."

"What does a guy have to do to get a little peek?" he

asked. I got the distinct impression he wasn't talking about my plans for the Majestic Theater.

It was Friday night and I was alone in the office with Gavin North. Gavin North, who didn't look like my boss, who wasn't acting like my boss, who I didn't want to be my boss. I wanted to show him a lot more than my project proposal, but I planted my feet and my resolve. "Once the permits are in and I can officially present, then you'll get to see—along with everyone else."

He moved a few steps closer, but he didn't try to look over my shoulder at the board. "Maybe I can give you a few helpful suggestions."

I wouldn't mind if you gave me a few, helpful orgasms, I thought to myself. It took a fair bit of moxie to keep that suggestion in my head and off my tongue. I wasn't usually the girl that shrunk back and waited for a guy to make the move. Usually, I went after what I wanted. There was no denying that I wanted him. Now, I not only wasn't going after him, I was actively avoiding him. Or I had been. Avoiding him was a little harder to do with him standing alone with me in a room, especially while he made suggestive comments.

"I'm sure you have something better to do on a Friday night," I said, hoping he would take the hint. *Or someone better to do.*

I hoped that he wasn't on his way to a date. But why else would he still be in his office? Why would he be so dressed down? Why couldn't I stop wondering about him? My heart plunged like an anchor into my stomach where the sinking feeling continued to grow.

"I do have plans. The better question is: why don't you?" he asked.

"I do," I lied unconvincingly. "I have a hot date with a sailor."

I had absolutely no idea why I had said that. Maybe it was because I was working on the Majestic Theater and my only good photo of it in its heyday was while *South Pacific* was showing. Maybe it was the proximity of the Puget Sound. Maybe I had officially lost my damn mind.

Now, I didn't just look pathetic for being at work so late, I also looked crazy.

"A sailor?" Gavin bit down on his lower lip without further comment. The gesture was enough.

"Why is that so strange? We live near the ocean. There are lots of sailors here." Apparently, I wasn't only going to toss a lie out there, I was going to go all in on it as well.

"I'm sure there are," Gavin said, his eyes twinkling with mischief. "What's his name?"

"His name? His name is...um," I searched for any answer I could come up with. Any name. My mind was a total blank. I had forgotten every name in the blessed world except two. I didn't dare say Gavin, so I said the other, "The Majestic Theater."

It was a relief to let go of the ridiculous story. Even if it left me feeling a little silly.

"That's what I thought. Come on. Grab your bag." Gavin walked past me and picked up the eraser perched on the board's ledge.

"What are you doing?" I shrieked.

"I assume you don't want everyone to see your proposal." He began erasing it without waiting for an answer.

"Including you!" I snatched at the eraser, but he held it out of reach.

"Calm down. I had it memorized the moment I saw the board." He tapped his forehead with his free hand. "Photographic memory."

That was hardly playing fair. I let him continue, but I didn't gather my things. When he finished, he turned around and waited.

"Do you need help packing that up?" he asked.

"What, you aren't going to do it for me?" I asked dryly.

He shook his head. "No way. My mama taught me to never to go into a woman's purse."

"I've still got a lot to do," I hedged. I'd begun to eye my belongings. It would only take a few minutes to pack up, but I shouldn't.

"Not on a Friday night."

"Gavin, I just don't think it's a good idea—"

He cut me off, "I'm heading out to dinner with my sister. You can grill her on what the preservation committee's beef is with our plans for the theater."

That changed things. I started stacking my notes into a pile and shoving them into my overworked Kate Spade bag. Then, I paused. "Isn't that kind of cheating?"

"Your best friend Trevor has been tagging along to any meeting that isn't closed doors. Without an invite. I think it's okay for you to get a leg up, too."

I narrowed my eyes, but then returned to the task at hand. I was packed up in a matter of twenty seconds. I shrugged my bag onto my shoulder and turned to him, "Where are we going?"

He didn't answer, he only grinned.

THIS WASN'T what I expected. When Gavin told me he was having dinner with his sister, I'd expected a fancy, formal dining room or a trendy, new restaurant. Instead, we were jammed into the back booth of a Cheesy Pete's. The restaurant, which catered to adults who wanted to act like children for a few hours, was a West Coast staple. Growing up I had gone to the family-friendly versions aimed at actual kids, but I had never been to one of these.

We were currently engaged in a hot debate over what pizza toppings to order.

"I don't eat meat, Gavin," Imogen said with a weary sigh, the kind usually reserved for conversations between a sister and a brother.

Gavin rolled his eyes. "So that this week's diet?"

"Behave," I muttered and elbowed him in the side. Engaging in physical combat was one of the perks of sitting next to him. It wasn't the only one though. Even in the crowded restaurants, I caught the spicy notes of his cologne, which smelled like smoky leather combined with heaven. It was taking considerable effort not to bury my nose against his neck and take a deeper breath. "Be supportive."

Imogen pointed a manicured finger at me. "I like this one. Keep her."

"We're just—"

"It's not like—"

"Sure." Imogen shut her menu and shot me an impish smile. "My brother is a pain in the ass, but he's a pretty hot, eligible bachelor. Even *Seattle Magazine* says so."

Gavin's head fell backwards as he groaned to the heavens. "I don't need you to get a date for me."

"Obviously, you do."

"My sister," Gavin gestured toward her, "making my life hell since 1997."

"I can't help it if you're relationship-challenged. I mean, some of the girls he brings to these functions our parents make us go to, I wouldn't be surprised if I found out he was paying them to be there."

I mashed my lips together, holding down a giggle. I was glad I'd come out after all.

"I have never paid for a date. I just don't have the greatest taste in women," he said to me as if he needed to do some damage control.

"You actually have to put some effort into it," Imogen advised "or, even better, just date *her*. She's perfect and she's your type."

"I don't date," I asserted myself into the conversation, but I'd caught the last bit. I was his type, huh?

In-ter-est-ing.

"Neither does Gavin," Imogen said with meaning. "I have an idea! You guys could not date each other, not get married, and not have beautiful babies!"

"I begged my parents for a brother," Gavin grumbled next to me.

We were delivered from the sibling bickering by the arrival of the waiter. Ten minutes later, and two pizzas ordered, I realized that these two could fight anywhere. It wasn't obnoxious though. I'd watched my best friend fight with her mother and that had been awkward to be around. Instead, this reminded me of my relationship with my own siblings. The love between Gavin and Imogen was tangible. I could feel it. I could see it. They just chose to show it through good-natured ribbing and doing their best to embarrass the hell out of each other.

"As I was saying, Gavin doesn't date." Imogen leaned across the table and covered her mouth with one hand as if sharing a secret. "He's looking for *the one*."

"I'm not looking for anything, except for the reason why I invited you to come out tonight," he broke in, tugging at his collar. It was warm in here, but I suspected his sister's need to dish his secrets was what really had him bothered.

"You called me," she accused. "I had other things to do tonight, but then you're on the phone telling me I have to get dressed and be ready—"

"You guys want to play Skee-Ball?" Gavin interrupted her.

My eyebrows shot up at this development. "She was in the middle of a sentence!"

But he grabbed my hand and dragged me toward the arcade section before she could finish it. I guessed the conversation was on pause. He whipped out his credit card and purchased two gameplay passes so fast my head spun.

"Aren't you going to get one for her?" I asked, tipping my head toward his sister.

"Imogen can take care of herself."

"So can I," I said defiantly. I wished I hadn't left my

purse at the table, so that I can take out my credit card and buy my own pass on the spot. Before I could head back for it, Gavin pressed a card into my hand.

"Yes, you can," he said genuinely. "But you shouldn't always have to. Let me do it. Just for tonight."

If I wasn't careful—if I let him keep saying things like that—they were going to be mopping me off the floor of Cheesy Pete's.

"Okay. But I have to warn you that I'm going to kick your ass at Skee-Ball." I marched over toward the machines, not waiting for him and swiped my card. The familiar sound of nine plastic balls rolling down a chute greeted me instantly. Gavin took the spot beside me and started his own game.

"I don't think you know how good I am at Skee-Ball," he warned me as his own balls racked up.

"Care to make a wager on that?"

He straightened, a blue, plastic ball in hand and asked, "What do you have in mind?"

I looked over to the prizes section where a variety of ridiculous, nostalgic toys and items were on display. They ranged from before my childhood up until the new millennium. Everything from Pound Puppies to Britney Spears posters was on display, all meant to elicit a sentimental reaction from someone who was far too old to go out and buy these things now. I spotted exactly what I wanted on a top shelf.

"I bet you I can get you something off the top shelf." These were fighting words. Anyone who had spent any time in arcade as a kid knew exactly how many tickets were needed to claim said top shelf prize. He studied the bounty of choices on display, grinned, and nodded.

"You're on." He didn't wait for me to start instead he assumed a crouched position and let the first ball role. Right out of the gate, he hit a fifty pointer.

Damn, he was good. Too bad for him that I was better. Bending down, I angled my body until I had the perfect position. Then, I let my ball go. It took just the right amount of finesse to hit one of the coveted corner rings. Most people believed it wasn't even possible and that even if one could get a ball near them, the holes were too small and would send the ball shooting back out to be collected by the ball hop at the end. I knew differently. My ball sailed up and dropped into the coveted ring.

Gavin paused mid-roll, his mouth dropping open. If he had any further thoughts on the matter, he didn't share them. Instead, he reached for his next ball.

I waited to see what he would do. A rookie would try to do the same. A seasoned Skee-Ball player, who wasn't good at 100 point ringers, would stick to his strengths. Gavin nailed another fifty-point score.

So, he did know what he was doing. That was kinda hot. I managed to hit another 100-point mark, putting me firmly at double his score.

"Your luck isn't going to hold out forever," he warned me as he rocketed off another ball.

"It's not luck." I shot back. But my smack talk proved to be too big a distraction. My next ball skimmed over the plastic ring and then fell down into the ball hop without giving me any points. I couldn't remember the last time I'd whiffed so hard.

Gavin didn't say anything, but I caught a smug grin on his face. Oh, it was on.

I didn't bother to keep track of individual games. We were playing too fast for that. Instead, every few minutes I would dare a glance at the stream of tickets his Skee-Ball machine was awarding him. I thought I still had him beat, but it was close. Without stopping to actually count, and because I wasn't keeping track in my head, I couldn't be sure. Gavin had loaded our play cards with more digital tokens than we could get through before our food would arrive. When he finally tapped me on the shoulder and nodded toward the table, I've been so in the zone that I hadn't looked over to check his score for at least ten minutes.

"Food's there."

"Giving up?" I asked him as I snapped my tickets off the machine and began to fold them into a large pile.

"Never." He grinned. "But kicking your ass is making me hungry. Intermission?"

"Okay," I agreed reluctantly. We headed back toward the table where Imogen was already serving herself a giant slice of veggie pizza.

"You two abandoned me." She pretended to pout, but I had no doubt that someone her age had spent most of the last half hour on her phone.

"I've never been here before," I told them as I helped myself to a slice of veggie and a slice of pepperoni. Gavin's eyes widened at the pile of food I was making myself on my plate, but he didn't say anything.

"Lucky you. Gavin makes me come every week and he never lets me win." Imogen stuck her tongue out at her brother.

"We come once a month," Gavin corrected her. But I saw the look he shot her. It was full of warning.

"So, you come every week?" I said with a laugh, folding my pizza in two so I could take a bite without losing half the toppings.

"I do, and when she's in town, she's forced to come," Gavin admitted. "She's not a Skee-Ball addict like me."

"Skee-Ball addict?" I raised my eyebrows, pretending to be impressed before I shook my head sadly. "And you still can't hit a 100."

"You're going to have to show me how you do that," he said as he shook Parmesan on to his slice.

"Not until I win," I told him.

Across the table, Imogen smirked, pizza paused midair. "You two are perfect for each other."

THE SKEE-BALL BATTLE continued after we finished our pizza. This time Imogen joined us. She might act too cool to be in an arcade, but she had some serious moves. She might not come with him every week, but she came often. I watched as Gavin pretended to steal her tickets and felt a twinge of homesickness grip my heart. My entire family was too far away for me to get to spend much quality time with them. Most of my interactions with my younger siblings were over the phone. Gavin and Imogen were lucky to get to see each other as often as they did.

It took me far too long to figure out the Gavin hadn't loaded up our cards with an insane amount of gameplay, he had actually purchased the unlimited pass. Every time I expected the card to come back and tell me I had run out ,it only sent the balls funneling down the chute one more time. It was why I didn't notice that Imogen was the one playing next to me instead of Gavin. I straightened up, arching my back to stretch it out. We'd been playing so long that I was starting to get sore. I had the tickets to show for it though.

"Where did your brother go?" I called over the noisy restaurant.

She shrugged, abandoning the waiting balls and following me in my stretches. "Bathroom probably."

"So how often does he really drag you here?" I asked.

She returned my grin. "It's usually once a week. Unless one of us is traveling."

"And you hate it?" I didn't believe that she did but getting her to admit otherwise in front of him would never happen. That was sibling rule number one.

"No. I just enjoy giving him a hard time."

"That I understand. What got you into historical preservation?"

"I've seen a lot of strip malls." She pretended to gag. "It's a hazard of your dad having a coffee shop in every city in America."

Or five in every city, but who was counting?

"Not a fan?" I asked.

"Have you ever been to London on Paris? If they tore down buildings for strip malls, imagine what they would look like." Her voice was rising slightly, filled with passion. I'd found what made her tick.

"America isn't nearly as old as those cities. Those buildings are hundreds, sometimes over a thousand, years old," I pointed out.

"Well, five hundred years from now, I don't want America to be full of preserved strip malls."

"That's a long-term plan." Apparently, Gavin's younger sister wasn't going to be content to sit around and spend the family money either. She might not be building her own empire, but she seemed to be putting the family name to good use.

"What's up with you two?" she asked, shifting the subject from the relatively benign topic of architecture. "Are you dating?"

I shook my head. Trust the very young to not see why us dating would be problematic. "He only got me to come out tonight, because he said you would be here."

"Ouch. You *wanted* a kid sister buffer? He really does need to start dating. He's losing his mojo."

That made me laugh. I couldn't imagine any woman who would want to go out with Gavin and his kid sister when she could get Gavin to herself. "I wanted to talk to you. I'm working on a presentation for the Majestic Theater."

"Double ouch. You used him to get to me! I'm going to have to rub that in later," she teased.

"Getting to play Skee-Ball was just a bonus," I added.

She edged closer, ball in hand, and glanced over her shoulder as if looking for him. "Really? You're not interested in him at all?"

"Gavin is my boss," I explained. Why did I get the feeling he had put her up to this? I felt like I was being passed a note in study hall. "He's just taking pity on me, because he found me in the office late on Friday night. Nothing is happening between us."

"He's so not taking pity on you. He's got it bad for you. But don't tell him I told you that," she added conspiratorially.

So, she wasn't put up to this, and she wasn't just playing matchmaker—if it was true. And if it was true, did it change anything? No. Did it still make my insides feel like they were melting into a pile of gooey cheese? Yes.

"And you've got it bad for him," she guessed.

"Who's got it bad for what?" Gavin asked, coming up to us with his hands behind his back.

"Me!" Imogen chirped. "I've got it bad for historical preservation. I was just telling your brilliant intern that. She was asking about the theater."

I liked Imogen. I couldn't help it. I suspected she would make our lives a living hell as we tried to move forward on this project, but it was nice to know that she was all bark and no bite. Plus, whatever sibling rivalry—however good-natured it was—that caused her to want to embarrass him at every turn didn't include me. She could have told him the truth: that I was totally into him. I knew she had she seen right through my flimsy excuse. Still, she hadn't. I could see myself becoming friends with her. Maybe if I wound up with a job in Seattle next year, we could hang out.

"I'm going to grab a beer," Imogen announced far-too-dramatically before disappearing into the crowd.

Maybe in a year I wouldn't be humiliated by her blatant attempts at matchmaking.

"Where did you go anyway?" I eyed him suspiciously and tried to grab for the hands he still kept behind his back.

"I told you I would win," he said smugly. From behind his back he produced a top shelf prize, and not just any prize, the very one eight- year-old me would have picked out: a My Little Pony with rainbow hair and a variety of accessories.

To my everlasting horror I squealed.

"I chose correctly then?" he asked.

I grabbed it out of his hands. "How did you know?"

"You told me you were from Texas. That you grew up on a ranch. I assumed a pony was a safe bet."

He had assumed correctly. Although it was really less of an assumption and more that he'd paid attention. That made the prize that much sweeter. "I haven't had one of these since I was a kid."

"I can probably win you another at the rate you're keeping up with me." He rubbed his hands together like he was warming up for the next round.

"Oh please." I scooped up my pile of tickets, plucking the last one from the machine, and beelined toward the prize counter. He might have been the first to win, but neither of us were walking away empty-handed. As they counted the tickets for me, I tried to ignore the staccato beat of my heart. He had been paying attention. He'd picked the thing off the top shelf of prizes that I would have chosen as a little girl. He'd been paying attention. I couldn't get over that fact. I scanned the other prizes looking for the perfect one to win for him. What did I really know about him? Except that he was humble when he didn't have to be. That he loved his family and obviously treated them like a priority, even when his kid sister was being annoying. That he worked hard and he chose to build his own success. All of that told me that he was a good man, but it didn't tell me about who he was as a kid. I wanted to find that giddy, optimistic, inner child, he'd learned to keep hidden in the office. Just like he had found mine.

I bypassed a selection of superhero toys and transformers before my eyes landed on the perfect thing.

"That one." I pointed up to the highest possible shelf, the one that stocked the best prizes. The guy behind the counter had to use a step-stool to get it down.

"You still have five left," he told me.

I opted for a Tootsie Roll.

When I found Gavin at our table, I pranced up holding my own prize behind my back. Imogen was nowhere to be seen. "Where did your sister go?"

"She begged out early. Apparently, there are bars and clubs that she needed to get to," he said wryly.

"Doesn't she know this is the hottest place in town?" I teased.

He spread his hands on the table. "I tried to tell her."

"Well, all is not lost. I got you a prize." I pulled it out from behind my back and presented him with the box of Legos. When complete, the set would create a replica of the Seattle Space Needle.

"This is," he hesitated, before adding, "perfect." The words were thick and spoken with emotion. Gavin looked up, his eyes smoky with some barely suppressed desire, but before he could express what he was feeling, I placed the Tootsie Roll on top of the box.

"Does this count as bonus points?"

It affectively broke the heady tension building between us. Gavin tore his eyes away from me and grinned. "You win."

Somehow tonight it felt like we had both won.

Twelve

By the time we left, we'd earned enough for a pile of candy. We ate it shamelessly on the drive home, scattering wrappers all over the floor of his Tesla. It was the strangest, and somehow most fun, date I'd ever been on. Except it wasn't a date. It was two friends— no, colleagues— hanging out together. With the colleague's kid sister. The trouble was that the term colleagues didn't cover how I felt about him. I wasn't certain what did. I wanted to have sex with him. That was the one thing I was certain. It was also why when we pulled up in front of the condo, I didn't ask him to come inside. I was hopped on Skee-Ball victories and sugar, I couldn't be trusted to make decisions.

Before I could get out, Gavin jumped out of the car ran around to my door. That was a date move. It was in the dating handbook on page one. Maybe I should ask him in for a drink. Except that even if this was a stealth date, asking him in was a couple chapters later. Instead, we lingered on the steps, making idle chit chat.

"I had a lot of fun tonight." I meant it. I'd never had that much fun outside time with friends. So why couldn't Gavin and I just be friends? Probably because I was dying to see him naked.

"Yeah? I wasn't sure what you would think," he admitted, running his hand through his dark hair as he leaned against the door frame. He looked like a poster of James Dean, not the CEO of a real estate development firm. No wonder my head and my heart were at war.

"I loved it. I haven't done anything like that for years."

"Oh man. You haven't been practicing? Then I'm in trouble. I play every week. It's how I blow off steam. I'm not sure that my ego can take being beat by someone who rarely plays." He clutched his chest as if wounded.

"Give me a few more weeks and there won't even be a competition," I warned him.

"I don't think there was much of a competition now," he admitted

I hesitated, a question poised on the tip of my tongue. I wasn't sure if I wanted to know the answer. If I asked, it might change things. If I didn't ask, things might not change. I wasn't certain which possibility frightened me more. "Why did you ask me to come out?"

"Truthfully?"

I nodded. I had the audacity to ask and now I wanted to know the answer.

"You've been working so hard. You don't think I notice, but I do. You eat lunch at your desk and then you pack up when everyone leaves and go work at the coffee shop. I thought you needed a break," he told me.

The answer crushed me. It was sweet. Thoughtful. Just like him. But it wasn't what I wanted to hear. He'd merely been delivering his workaholic intern from herself. Nothing more.

"Thank you," I managed to force out. What did I want him to say? That he spent all week trying to get me alone. That I was all he'd thought about for weeks, too? Of course not. I was being silly. I fumbled with my keys, trying to get them in the lock. It was time to wrap things up before I started to cry. "Dammit, I can never remember which one it is."

Make it look like the keys have driven you to the point of tears. That will fool him.

Gavin reached out and placed his hand over mine. He took the keys from me and inserted one into the lock with one swift, sure motion. It was the perfect fit.

"Thanks." I turned the knob, but before I could step inside and wish him one final, definitive goodbye, his hands found my waist.

There was one brief pause as he drew my body to his—a moment where his eyes searched mine as if to say 'is this okay?' I didn't know what he saw there, but he found his answer. His palm stayed on the small of my back as the other found my chin and tipped my face to his. He lowered his mouth to mine slowly, hesitating once more at the last possible second. The world stopped, everything slowed down, and I waited for Gavin North to kiss me.

Our lips met in a soft crush that was urgent, but not insistent. He lingered as if savoring the taste of my mouth on his before the kiss deepened into something more, something that could never be mistaken for anything other than what it was: want.

I wanted him, too. Now that whatever invisible boundary we'd erected had been breached, I could admit that to myself. I could relish it.

I wanted him. I wanted his body against mine. I wanted his lips on my own, on my skin, on every inch of me. I wanted to taste him and feel him move against me. I wanted to take him inside, and I wanted him to take me to bed.

Gavin pulled away, his mouth hovering inches from mine before he whispered, "Sweet dreams, Cassie."

He left me on the stairs, still wanting, and when I went in, I noticed, with a thrill, that he waited in the car until I turned out the porch light.

MY DREAMS WERE INTERRUPTED by the incessant chime of the incoming video chat, which was too bad considering my dreams were mostly of Gavin and what might come after that kiss. I checked the time and realized it was only midnight. Either I was getting old or the frenzy that followed Gavin's kiss had worked me into an early bedtime. Somehow my best friends seemed to have sensed something was up, because they were conference calling. I answered, immediately hating them for making me face them in this groggy state.

"Who's dying?" I asked in a gruff, sleep-heavy voice.

"You if you don't spill the details," Jillian informed me. She was alone for once. Liam, her perpetual shadow, was nowhere to be seen. That meant serious business.

"I don't know what you're talking about" I said coyly. But really, how did they know?

"Oh! Spill already!" Jessica yelled into the screen. Unlike Jillian, she wasn't alone. Roman looked up in the background, wincing at the sudden exclamation.

I waved to him. "How is Mexico?"

If they thought I couldn't think of ways to draw this out they were wrong.

"You texted us an hour ago. What did it say?" She looked to Jess.

"A very cryptic 'Skee-Ball! Kiss! Love?' What are we supposed to do with that?"

"And then you don't respond to any of our texts," Jillian jumped in.

"I was asleep!"

"Are you kissing Skee-Ball machines? Because if so we need to have a serious conversation. I know you swore off men, but..." Jillian trailed off.

Both of them were perched cross-legged on their respective beds like we were gathering around the campfire for stories.

"I kissed Gavin." My announcement was met with silence.

"Your boss?" Jess finally asked.

"I thought you were keeping your distance," Jillian added.

This wasn't the response I had expected nor the one I had hoped for. "Don't tell me you have a moral objection."

"That's not it," Jess said, taking on the diplomatic tone I knew and loathed.

"Good, because you married a professor," I reminded her. Where was the support? The squeals?

"We're just surprised," Jillian said. "What was the Skee-Ball thing about?"

I filled them in on the details of the night. By the end of my story, their attitude had softened toward Gavin, but I still felt like crap. I didn't need them to be excited. Okay, that was a lie. I did need them to be excited. Instead, they'd gotten in my head and screwed everything up.

"Are you going to see him again this weekend?" Jess asked. The hits kept on coming.

"I don't know," I admitted. "Tonight wasn't really planned."

"Maybe he'll call," Jillian said in a soothing voice.

"And if he doesn't it's just because he's busy with his sister," Jess added.

But it was too little too late. It took a little effort to get them off the call. They seemed to sense that they'd screwed with my head. When I finally did, it took hours to fall back asleep where only nightmares waited.

Thirteen

I wore my nerves to work on Monday, doing my best to cover them up with a cute, black wrap dress. The encouraging phone call I received from my best friends on Friday night had been so discouraging that I thought about it all weekend long. What was I doing? I was risking everything and for what? I did not have a good track record with relationships, so why should I risk one now. As soon as I walked into the lobby of Northwest Investments, I wished I could turn around and leave, especially since Trevor was coming off the elevators, his hands shoved into his trouser pockets and a smug grin on his face. He spotted me before I could run.

"Did you hear?" he called over.

I had no idea why he was so early on a Monday morning. Technically, I was early, but even he had beaten me here. A note of panic crept up the back of my spine. Trevor wouldn't be here if he didn't have a good reason. He'd probably been hanging around the lobby, waiting for me to come in, so he could rub that reason in my face.

"I'm just getting in. What's up?" I asked, trying to sound as nonchalant as possible.

"The permits came through. We're going to be doing our presentations next Monday." He looked a little too happy about that—like he was prepared to face the hiring squad. If only I felt the same way.

I shrugged my bag higher on my shoulder and shifted uncomfortably in my heels. "Next Monday?"

In truth, I was ready. I knew that. There was really only so much more I could do to perfect my plan for dealing with the preservation committee and getting the neighborhood on board for the restoration. But despite all of that, it felt like a teacher had just announced a pop quiz. I hadn't even begun to think about the actual presentation. The part where I had to stand up and wow a bunch of people who didn't even know my name was Cassie and not Kathy. I was so screwed.

"You okay?" Trevor asked, looking not the least bit concerned.

"Don't get all touchy-feely on me," I scoffed. "People might mistake you for human."

"You sure now how to start a fella's week off right. I'm going to miss you when you aren't here in a few months and I have the job." He hit me with that parting shot as he strode off. At least, he was finally showing his true face.

"There wouldn't be enough room for me and your ego to work in the same office anyway," I called after him. I limped over to the receptionist desk, my pride wounded, and dropped my bag in a heap with a heavy sigh.

"I thought you were supposed to relax over the weekend," George said as he eyed me with concern.

I couldn't tell him that I had relaxed. Friday night had been perfect. I'd blown off steam just the way Gavin usually did. Then I'd spent two days over-analyzing every second of it. Trust a girl to negate whatever R&R she managed to get. "It's no big deal. How was your weekend?"

"I binge-watched Netflix and ate an entire pizza in my pajamas. So it was pretty much like every weekend," George said.

"Maybe I need to hang out with you on the weekends." It seemed like a much safer choice for everything but my thighs.

"Any time, girl. Consider that an invitation."

I left him at the desk with promises of a coffee run later and decided it was time to get to work. I might be ready in theory for this presentation, but I needed to hustle if I wanted everything to go off smoothly by next Monday. But no matter how hard I tried, my eyes kept wandering toward the corner office area, hoping to see Gavin coming in or out of it. His blinds were closed, but the door was cracked open. Was he in there? I kept expecting to see his head poke out and look in my direction. Wasn't he the least bit interested if I had come in for the day?

Cut it out, Cassie, I scolded myself. If I had spent half as much effort tweaking my presentation, I would be done with it already. Hell, I probably would've won a Nobel Prize by now.

Meanwhile, Jillian and Jess had decided that they needed to be more involved in my off-limits, office romance. The texts had started arriving at ten and hadn't stopped, despite my trying to ignore them.

Jillian: Have you seen him yet?

Jess: I bet he's waiting for you to go in there.

Jillian: She can't make the first move.

Jess: She didn't. He did when he kissed her. The ball's in her court.

It seemed like I didn't have to actually be a part of this conversation that they were having about me. I wanted to tune it out, but I was thinking all the same things that they were discussing. Maybe Jess was right, and he was waiting for me to make my move. That kiss. *That kiss*. It had been one hell of a first move, so it would only be fair for him to wait for me to respond. The trouble was that after 48 hours of analysis I still didn't know what I should do. We'd crossed the line. That much was clear. If he hadn't been such a gentleman, we probably would've crossed more lines. Maybe even dotted a few i's and checked my list twice. But things hadn't gone too far.

Yet.

Or maybe he would pretend like nothing happened. If so, I would follow suit. Perhaps he had spent the weekend realizing what a huge mistake he made. What if he was in his office right now hiding from me?

I stood up, my chair rolling backwards so hard it hit the cubicle wall. Well, I wasn't going to just sit here while he pretended I didn't exist. Before I'd really processed what I was doing, I was marching toward his office. My courage faltered as soon as I got there. I peeked inside and nearly collapsed with relief. Gavin was nowhere in sight. Agnes, the redhead from the meeting, came up behind me.

"Oh, he's not in here," she said. I stepped to the side to

allow her access, and she bustled in, picked up a pen, and began scribbling a note. When she was done, she straightened up and smiled warmly at me. "You're the new intern, right? If you need something from him, you can leave a note. He'll get back to you sometime today."

"Thanks, I'll do that." Now I was on the spot. I took the pen and paper she held out to me and waited awkwardly for her to go.

She stayed.

"How are you settling in? That seems like kind of a silly question since it's only a temporary gig, right? But I know you're working on the Majestic Theatre project. Let me know if you need any help with that."

I remembered how vocal she had been at the initial meeting and made a mental note to take her up on that. "I think it's going okay, but I won't really know until we present."

"Don't let any of them scare you," she lowered her voice. "Half of us don't know what we're doing half the time. That's the real truth about being an adult. Were all just feeling our way through it."

"So this sick to the stomach feeling that I'm getting it all wrong isn't going away anytime soon?" I asked her.

"No," she said, shaking her head with a laugh. "But there are perks."

I was all ears. So far the only *perks* I'd experienced were taxes, bills, and an ever-growing list of responsibilities. "Like what?"

"No one can tell you when to go to bed," she teased.

"I guess I'll settle for that," I said as we both laughed. She headed back out and I turned toward Gavin's desk, alone with the notepad at last. I had no idea what to write. The things I wanted from Gavin probably shouldn't be in writing. Not in a building with an HR department. Also, there was the fact that I really needed to deny what I wanted from Gavin. In the end, I settled for 'I need to talk to you. Cassie.' I hesitated, almost signing an XOXO and then decided against it. The hesitation cost me because before I could leave, Gavin reappeared.

"Cassie." He sounded happy to see me. I guessed he hadn't been avoiding me after all. "I just stopped by your desk and you weren't there."

He'd been looking for me. I twisted at the pen's cap nervously, the movement mirroring how my insides felt. "I've been in here waiting for you."

Now that sounded pathetic. I should have said that I ran into Agnes or made up an excuse for where I had been for the last ten minutes. Instead, I held up the pad of paper. "I was leaving you a note. Agnes left you one, too."

He took it as he circled to the back of his desk and read it over, his nose crinkling with concentration as he did. I took a small step backwards. If I went slowly and quietly, maybe he would forget I was here until I was out of the room entirely. Gavin tossed the notepad down.

"You wanted to talk to me," he said. It was amazing how one simple sentence could make me feel backed again the wall. My eyes shot toward the open door. It wasn't really a conversation to have if half the office could hear it. He noticed my glance and walked over to close it. I wasn't entirely sure that was any less obvious—the boss closing the

door with the intern inside felt like the beginning of a porno
—but it was going to be the first step in having this conversation that I still wasn't sure I wanted to have. Before I could
screw up the courage to open my mouth, he turned around
and hit me with, "About Friday night."

His words hung heavily in the air between us as ominous
as the gray clouds blocking the sun outside.

I had my answer. I really didn't want to have this conversation, and now he was blocking my only escape route. If he
noticed my deer in the headlights terror, that didn't stop him.
"That kiss might not have been the best idea."

I'd been thinking the same thing for 48 hours, but
hearing it from Gavin's own lips—the lips that had kissed me
—crushed me. I squared my shoulders and forced a smile.
"That's exactly what I was thinking."

"I think you're misunderstanding me." Gavin ran his
hands through his hair in frustration. He done the same
thing on Friday. I realized it was a nervous tick. There was
some solace in knowing that I had gotten under his skin, too.
"I shouldn't have kissed you."

"I think I'm understanding you perfectly," I said. I really
didn't need him repeating himself if it was just going to be a
series of direct blows to my heart.

"You told me you weren't interested in dating. I keep
pursuing. I'm sorry," he said, spreading his hands. "If that's
what you really want, then I'm going to respect it. I got a vibe
on Friday, but it wasn't—"

I didn't let him finish the sentence before I was kissing
him. He wanted me and that was all that mattered. All the
questioning, all the analysis, I really, truly had my answer as

to what I wanted. I didn't want Gavin to stay away. I wanted him closer, consequences be damned.

Gavin broke away, breathless, his mouth hovering dangerously close to mine. "I just need to know this is what you want."

"Well, I didn't want you to stop kissing me," I grumbled. He took the hint. His arms snaked around me and I reacted instinctively as he lifted my body and pressed me against the wall. My legs wrapped around his lean torso, urging him closer. I had no doubt where this was leading. Not right here. Not right now. But soon. This was a sneak preview. A coming attraction. A restricted trailer for an R-rated evening. When we got to the feature presentation, I wanted him all to myself.

Gavin trailed away from my lips, brushing kisses along my jaw until he reached my ear. "I haven't been able to stop thinking about you this weekend."

"Me either," I whimpered.

"I'm not sure how I'm going to get anything done today," he admitted.

"Sick day?" He laughed and I joined him. It would definitely look suspicious if suddenly we both became ill. "Dinner, tonight? At my place, or... dammit."

"We can go wherever." I just wanted to be with him.

"I want you alone. But Imogen is staying with me still."

I conveniently overlooked Lillian's no boys rules. She would be at work late anyway, and someone needed to get laid in that house. "My place will be empty. We can order takeout."

He shook his head. "I'll cook."

"You cook?"

"Don't sound so surprised." He grinned at my disbelief. It was little lopsided and I swear I almost fell in love with him on the spot.

I took a deep, steadying breath as he lowered me back to my feet. "Okay. My place. Seven?"

"I'll be watching the clock." He lifted my hand and kissed the inside of my palm softly.

I'd be watching the clock, too.

Fourteen

I DIDN'T TELL ANYONE THAT GAVIN WAS COMING over for dinner. My best friends' method of cheerleading usually just left me freaking out and there was really no one else to tell. As far as I knew we weren't advertising this around the office. I might have told George if so. My perpetually absent roommate didn't need to know, especially since I'd promised her no boys in the apartment. Since he was cooking, that left me to obsess over all the little details. I picked up the place, which only took me five minutes given how little time Lillian actually spent here and how terrified I was of making a mess in the spartan living space. My bedroom was another story. I decided, though, that if I straightened it, I'd be asking for trouble. It was better to take it slowly—a concept I hadn't really tried before. Instead, I scrubbed down the already clean appliances. We never cooked. Then I set the table in the dining room. I stood back, Olive the cat circling around my ankles, and thought better of that.

"Does it seem like too much?" I asked the cat. That was what my life had come to: seeking romantic advice from my roommate's cat. She meowed as if she had opinions on the matter. "You're probably right."

I took everything back off the table, which was in no way an insane move or anything. Then I decided to do something I was actually good at: figure out what to wear.

The entire contents of my closet had been emptied out onto my bed as I searched for the perfect outfit. I'd changed out of my office dress the second I got home, opting for pajama bottoms and a tank top. The dress had seemed too formal as if I wanted to keep him at arm's length and in a tiny box of professionalism. Still, I couldn't wear the pajamas either. But what exactly was a girl supposed to wear when a guy came over to make her dinner? I could go for casual and look like this happened to me all the time. Dressing up seemed like a no go. I didn't need to look like I was heading out to a gala. I tried on a dozen different outfits, nearly breaking down to call the girls to see if one of my friends had a suggestion.

"What do I wear?" I asked no one in particular.

Olive had been weaving in and out of the piles of clothes. She meowed loudly and settled onto a simple, floral sundress.

"Perfect!" I told her.

She looked distinctly ruffled as I picked her up and took away her chosen ensemble. "Sorry, I'm going to need that."

I really did have to get a life if I was going to continue to have conversations with the cat. Olive jumped from the end of the bed all the way to the dresser, which was pretty impressive given that it was at least 6 feet away. She batted at the top drawer. I hadn't caught her with my special friend in a while, but clearly she still knew where I kept Mr. Dependable.

"With any luck, I will not be needing that thing anymore," I promised her. I wondered how Lillian would take it if I gifted her cat a vibrator.

The dress was cool and Seattle was hot. The clouds had lifted after my morning meeting with Gavin, like a good omen. But an afternoon of sun had left the condo stuffy. Since no one up here had air conditioning, a fact which the Texan in me could not fathom, the strappy cotton sundress was a welcome relief from the heat. I opened all of the windows and set out a box fan to try to clear out some of the air. I had no idea what he planned to cook, but since the kitchen didn't get much use, I wasn't sure how much hotter it could get.

Since Gavin was involved I was guessing a whole lot hotter. I swept my hair into a topknot that sat loosely at the crown of my head and inspected my makeup. It was still done for work, maybe a little much with my more casual outfit choice, so instead of reapplying my lipstick, I wiped it off and settled on some gloss. I'd purposely taken off my watch when I'd gotten back, so I wouldn't drive myself crazy checking it. As such, I lost track of time, so I was surprised when I heard him knock on the door.

He was even more dressed down than on Friday night. This time he'd opted for a thin white cotton T-shirt and another pair of jeans. As much as I liked seeing him in a suit, seeing him like this was even better. Maybe because it felt clandestine. I'd gotten the boss out of his clothes. I couldn't help but wonder who else got to see him this way. He grinned and held up the bag of groceries. "Show me the kitchen."

I stepped to the side to let him enter and then quickly led him to the kitchen as he requested. He glanced around at the shiny appliances. "Does anyone ever cook here?"

"I cleaned it," I explained.

"These appliances look brand-new."

"Sometimes we use the microwave." To heat up the food, we ordered from restaurants. "Two working women don't have a lot of time to cook."

Gavin opened the refrigerator and let out a low chuckle. "You two really don't cook much do you?"

I looked over his shoulder and realized that there was half a gallon of milk with an expiration date from three months ago, a carton of eggs of dubious age, and something that might have once been a vegetable. Or cheese. It was hard to say.

"I guess it's time to confess that I don't know how to cook." I buried my face in my hands. If my mother could hear me, she would be ashamed. She'd tried so hard to teach me how to cook and I had thwarted her at every turn.

"You can't cook anything?"

"Macaroni and cheese and sometimes eggs, but those don't always turn out."

"So, I guess I'll be doing the cooking in this relationship." He moved past me and began to un-bag the groceries.

In this relationship. Had he really just said that? Had we gone from possibly this is a date to a relationship that quickly? My head was still spinning as he turned and handed me a bundle of vegetables in a netted plastic bag.

"What are these?" I asked suspiciously.

"Don't tell me you don't eat Brussels sprouts," he said.

I held them up and studied them for a moment. Yes, I recognized this vegetable. I tried not to show my dismay. "My mother made them when we were kids. I don't remember them looking like this."

"They were probably frozen. Do me a favor. Give my Brussels sprouts a fighting chance."

I set them on the counter with a nod. When it came to Gavin, I was determined to finally keep an open mind. I spent too much of the last few weeks fighting against my attraction for him. The least I could do was try his vegetables. That left me thinking about his cucumber.

"Can you wash those?" he asked me.

"Um, sure." It took an embarrassing amount of time for me to find a pair of scissors to cut the bag open with. Then, I began to take one out and wash it.

"Not like that. It'll take forever." He moved behind me, his arms circling my waist, and picked up the entire bag to hold under the water. I was pretty certain he could be doing this without me as a buffer, but I wasn't complaining. Instead, I leaned against his firm chest, more than willing to let him show me how it was done. When he finally stepped away, I missed him immediately.

"Now what?" I asked. If I had to be in the kitchen to be near him, I might as well be helping, and with any luck he'd have to show me what I was doing again.

"Washing the vegetables was the easy part," he warned me.

"I'm a modern woman," I told him, "I don't just let my man cook for me. Teach me."

He laughed at this and gestured to the package of steaks left on the counter. "Can you find me a pan for those?"

I screwed up my face. "Is a pan the one you put cereal in?"

Gavin looked stricken, and I burst into laughter.

"I'm not exactly that helpless in the kitchen."

"Okay, sassy. Find me a pan."

"We're eating steak." I might have been a little too happy about that. Seattle had spectacular access to seafood, and while I love me some lobster, sometimes all I wanted was red meat. You could take the girl out of Texas, but you couldn't always take Texas out the girl.

"Yes. We're going to reverse sear it."

I waited for him to explain what this meant. Finally, he looked over and sighed. It sounded strangely contented like he was actually enjoying walking me through the cooking process.

"We're going to cook it in the oven and then finish it on the stovetop."

"Really?" I wasn't sure I was buying this method. Maybe it was a weird Pacific Northwest thing.

"Who's the one who knows how to cook here?"

He had a point. "Will this work?"

I pulled a skillet off of an upper shelf surprised to see it wasn't covered in dust and cobwebs. I'd half-expected bats to fly out when I'd opened the cabinet door.

"That's perfect." He took it from me and began to show me how to prepare the meat. He rubbed down one of the steaks with a little bit of oil and then cracked some pepper on top of it before stepping to the side. "Now you try."

"Me?"

"I'm beginning to wonder if the whole Texas rancher's daughter story is a lie," he teased me.

I grabbed the oil and poured a bunch into my hands, mimicking what he had just done. So, it wasn't exactly cooking. It was more like combining a few things and then heating. Still, when Gavin put them into the preheated oven, I felt a strange sense of accomplishment.

"What's for dessert?" I asked him mischievously.

Gavin jumped a little and dashed over to the bag. He pulled out a pint of mint chocolate chip ice cream. "This is going to have to go in the freezer for a while. I totally forgot to put it in there."

"That's okay. We probably have a few minutes until the steak is done, right?"

"We have about 45 minutes," he told me.

I heard my stomach rumble in protest. I hoped he didn't catch it. "Oh. What else do we need to make?"

"I'll wait until the steaks are close to being done before I start the vegetables," he said.

"So, what are we going to do until then?" I eyed the bottle of wine peeking out from his grocery bag, and he nodded. I'd just reached in to pull it out, discovering it was the same Montepulciano that I had served him a few weeks ago, when Gavin hooked an index finger under the strap of my dress and tugged me toward him.

"I had a few thoughts about an appetizer."

"Can't wait?" I asked, already wondering what else he had in the bag.

"You could say that." I started to turn my head to gesture toward the bottle of wine at the same moment he tried to kiss me. The result was a catastrophic bumping of the heads. We both took a step back, me rubbing my cheek and him rubbing his nose.

"Let's try that again," he suggested.

This time I was ready for him. *So, so ready.* His mouth found mine, but this time it wasn't the hesitant first kiss or the desperate second kiss we'd shared, this was a full range of motion. Our limbs tangled together, our bodies fighting to be closer. Gavin pulled back and said, "About that appetizer."

His eyes were the color of the ocean on a stormy day, fogged over with his own desire, as he picked me up and set me on the counter. We kissed like we were each other's oxygen. I was lost to anything but him. I'd been waiting for this—dreaming about this—and it was finally happening. My breath hitched when I felt his hands sliding up my thighs, under my dress, and coming to rest on my bare hips. There was another pause, another chance for me to stop this in its tracks. Instead, my hand fisted in his T-shirt. I nearly had to refrain from shoving him even further down.

"I've been thinking about what I wanted for dinner all day," he told me, as his thumbs wiggled under the band of my panties. I lifted my hips instinctively, allowing him to slip them down until they fell to the floor. "There was only one thing that I really wanted."

"Steak?" I asked in a small voice.

"Something much, much sweeter." A slow, wolfish grin spread over his face before he disappeared from view, then I felt his soft, warm lips pressing to my inner thigh.

"Oh that," I moaned as he continued his progress toward the promised land. Before he reached it, his hands sunk into my hips and yanked me forward until I was teetering on the edge of the counter.

"There you go," he coaxed me as my legs spread in invitation. I felt the heat of his breath first, caressing a long my bare skin.

My head fell backwards at the sensation and I yelped with frustration. "Oh God!"

"Is everything okay, Miss Hart?" he asked, his voice somewhat muffled by his mouth's location.

"Don't spoil your dinner though" I scolded him.

He laughed, which tickled a little. My legs, sensing an intrusion, tried to clamp shut, but Gavin nudged them apart, his five- o-clock shadow scratching the soft skin promisingly. I was about to grab onto his hair and get this ride going when his lips made contact. The soft, gentle kisses slowly became deeper until I felt his tongue split me open. I nearly lost control of my entire body. I had to prop my toes on the top of his shoulders to keep from falling over, but he helped steady me. A low groan of appreciation rumbled through his body as his mouth settled into place and began to flick and suck and tease. He wasn't in a hurry. He was savoring every moment, judging from the primal, masculine sounds he was making.

I'd never gotten off this way before. I had always been a

little self-conscious about a guy going downtown, but Gavin was making it pretty clear that this was exactly where he wanted to be. Without thinking—because that was pretty impossible at the moment—my hands found his hair and gripped it tightly, urging him on faster and harder. For a split second, I wondered if he could breathe. That thought flew out of my mind as my body began to crack and shatter on his tongue. He didn't let up, even as my legs collapsed on his shoulders and my body went slack. It was only when I slumped, completely spent, onto the counter that he pressed one soft kiss to my trembling thigh and stood up. A second later, I felt my underwear being drawn back up my legs.

"You don't want to keep them as a trophy, Mr. North?" I asked him. "I feel like you deserve some type of award for that."

"The sounds you made," he said, helping me back up into a seated position, "are all the reward I need. I'm going to be recalling those pretty much every moment until I get you to make them again."

"That sounds dangerous." I tried to hide against his shoulder, but he tipped my chin so that I could see his face.

"What's wrong? Did you not want..." he trailed away.

"No! It was great! Really, really great." I shook my head, almost dizzy from it still. "I've never really.... that way...you know."

"You must have dated some real idiots. I'm pretty certain I just found my happy place," he told me

I tried to turn away, my cheeks flaming, but he stopped me. "Seriously, Cassie, you are so beautiful. Do you know that? I can hardly think of anything else when I'm around you."

"I sound like a distraction," I said softly.

"The best kind. Do you want to know what makes it even hotter?"

I managed to nod. How could he think I even held a candle to him?

"Your brain is just as sexy," he murmured. "You're the whole package."

"Hmmmm....package." My fingers slid down to the button of his jeans and I began to free him.

"You don't have to," he said, gently gripping my wrist. "That's not what this is about between us."

But I wanted to. For the first time in my life, I wanted to drop to my knees for a man. Then I want to do a whole bunch of other dirty stuff with him. Fate had other plans. Before I could finish releasing the Kraken, the front door swung open and a harried- looking Lillian bustled into the apartment. She dropped her bags on the dining room table along with her keys without noticing us.

I jumped off the counter quickly and did my best to look innocent. "Um, hello."

She looked up, startled. It was clear she still hadn't gotten used to me living there. "Cassie." She caught sight of Gavin and did a double take. "I'm sorry. I didn't know you had company."

"I should've told you," I said apologetically. "I just figured you'd still be in the office." It sounded like the lamest excuse ever, especially since I was breaking her no boys rule. In fact, I'd pretty much broken every rule on the counter just now. Guilt washed over me and before I could kick Gavin out, he stepped forward.

"We're cooking dinner. There's more than enough. Have you eaten?"

"Steak," I added.

"That sounds amazing. I'm famished."

Had we actually gotten away with it? Did it really look like we were innocently cooking in the kitchen? Lillian excused herself to go change in her room and I collapsed against the counter as soon she was down the hall.

"You look so guilty right now " Gavin told me.

"I did pretty much break the only rule she gave me. Next weekend I could hold a kegger, then I could disregard everything she asked of me when she let me live here for free."

Gavin brushed his index finger down my belly, sending a tremble of anticipation running through me. "Next time we'll do it at my house. I'll kick Imogen out if she's not run off to a beach somewhere. We can even put a sock on the door if that makes you feel more comfortable."

"Put a what on the door?" Lillian asked as she reentered in a pair of lounge pants. The evening had become increasingly casual, it seemed. Nothing killed a date like your roommate coming to dinner in her pajamas with your pseudo-boyfriend.

"Nothing!" I chirped. The kitchen timer went off saving us all from this embarrassing turn in the conversation. Gavin showed me how to sear both sides of the steak now that it was cooked internally. Then we made the Brussels sprouts. Okay, he made the Brussels sprouts and I watched. I did, however, contribute by pouring everyone a glass of wine.

After nearly getting caught in the act by Lillian, my nerves were rattled, but Gavin was a natural at easy conversation and the discussion flowed as we sat around and ate. The evening began to draw to a close and I was left to wonder if I dared to ask him to stay for dessert. Lillian seeming to sense my dilemma, stood up and grabbed all of our plates. "I'm exhausted, I think I'll head to bed."

I shot her questioning look. If she was going to protest his being here, I'd rather know about it now. She only gave me an encouraging smile. She stacked the dishes in the sink and turned to head to her room when Olive appeared with my large, purple vibrator clutched in her jaws.

How had that damn cat figured out to turn it on?

She dropped it on the floor in the middle of the room and began batting it around. All three of us shared a look before Lillian dashed over, scooped Olive into her arms and began to scold her under her breath, "Not yours. Although I think Cassie might not be needing that any longer."

She winked at me as she whisked the cat away to her room.

"So that's what having an older sister is like," I said out loud.

Gavin was obviously trying to look everywhere but at the vibrating elephant in the room. Why Lillian had to take the cat was beyond me. It seemed simple enough to me. Leave the cat and take the vibrator.

I got up, mustering as much dignity as possible, went over and turned it off. It whirred to a stop with a sad mechanical sigh. Turning to Gavin, the vibrator still in my hand, I said, "Best date ever?"

He got up and crossed to me, stopping for a moment to study his competition. He didn't look intimidated. "Absolutely."

"Is there any point in asking you to pretend you never saw this?" I asked him, my voice taking on a desperate edge.

"Hold on. Trying to judge if I measure up."

"You're terrible." I smacked him on the shoulder with it.

"Did you just hit me with your vibrator?"

I gasped, realizing what I'd done, but Gavin only chuckled. "I mean, I don't want to get between you two."

"Why can't a giant piano fall on me right now?" I asked. Gavin caught me around the waist and planted one soft, promising kiss on my lips.

"I'm not the jealous type. Although I think your roommate might be right about how much you're not going to be needing that."

Knees buckled? Check. Niagara Falls down below? Check.

Why didn't I have my own apartment?

He stepped back and surveyed the mess we left in the kitchen. "We should clean that up and then I should get going."

This evening wasn't turning out how either of us had planned. And I understood why he wanted to get out. Lillian, her cat, and my vibrator weren't exactly the welcome committee most guys expected. "I've got this. I'll see you in the office tomorrow."

We would take our time. There was nothing wrong with that. I did my best to avoid the nagging voice in the back of my head that worried I had scared him off. That bitch never shut up anyway.

This time, I shoved Mr. Dependable in a box at the top of my closet. Lillian was right, I wouldn't be needing him anymore. Not since I had found Mr. Right.

Fifteen

The next morning, in a shocking turn of events, I was running late. I skidded into the kitchen, my lipstick in hand, praying that Lillian had put coffee on. Even terrible, automatic machine coffee would be better than nothing at this point. I didn't expect to actually find Lillian there.

She was leaning against the kitchen counter, a mug clutched in her hands. She looked over to the clock on the microwave. "Running a little late?"

That was an understatement. I nodded. "Tell me there's more of that."

"Put your lipstick on." She turned and pulled a mug out of the cupboard and began to pour me a cup of liquid happiness. "Long night?"

"I have a lot on my mind. Big presentation." I was lying, but not about the long night. I'd been awake fantasizing about what had happened between Gavin and I—and what might have happened if he'd stayed over. I'd been too giddy to overthink things. All I had done was bask in the orgasmic glow of our first serious alone time.

"You were probably thinking about your boyfriend, too," she tacked that bit on like the lawyer she was—a quick rebuttal to my claim but a loaded one.

Was this the part where she told me off for breaking the rules? I paused and sized her up, for the first time realizing that she wasn't even dressed to go into the office. What was she doing here at eight in the morning? As far as I could tell, she worked sun-up to sundown plus overtime. I was in real trouble if Lillian had called in sick just to tell me off.

She held out the cup of coffee like an olive branch, so I took it tentatively, wondering if it was a trick. Was this the Trojan horse of roommate offerings? Would I take it and find myself under siege? I didn't know what I would do if she kicked me out. It was only midsummer still. There was no way I'd be able to find somewhere else to crash. I didn't know anyone else in the city well enough. How long could I get away with sleeping in the office before anyone noticed?

"Where did you meet him?" she asked conversationally.

"At work," I said slowly. She seemed to be trying to put me at ease. Maybe she was hoping I would spill my guts and tell her exactly what had happened—on the kitchen counter she was now leaning against. My eyes flashed to the spot, wondering if she could sense the promiscuous activity like some people claimed to experience paranormal activity. "He's actually my boss."

"Your boss?" she repeated archly. "The one you thought hated you?"

"That's the one."

"Well that explains that." She spoke matter-of -factly as though I could translate what she meant. I suspected I should understand her. The trouble was that I didn't.

"Explains what?" I'd managed to lift the coffee mug near my lips, but I hadn't been brave enough to take a sip yet. I realized looking down at it that my hands were shaking. I couldn't imagine facing her in a courtroom.

"It explains why you thought he hated you. Everyone always thinks that boys grow out of being mean to the girl they like, but they don't really."

"He's pretty nice. I think I had the wrong impression of him."

"When did you to start seeing each other?" Apparently, the interrogation was going to continue.

I stayed on my guard, abandoning my coffee on the counter. If I was going to face this, I didn't want to risk third-degree burns by dumping it down my shirt due to trembling palms. I took a deep breath and came clean. "I know I broke the rules," I began, "and I should have warned you he was here. We'll hang out at his place from now on. I hope you can forgive me."

I felt so grown up that I half-expected her to hand me a gold star sticker.

"I'm not upset," Lillian said quickly. "I know I said no boys. It's just that Jessica told me once about your boy-catching thing."

I cringed at the memory of our freshman pact. None of us had ever been very good at it—except maybe Jillian. Come to think of it, boy catching had been Jillian's idea. It was the kind of thing that sounded cool and worldly to eighteen-year-olds. Now? It was a bit silly. Basically, we'd agreed to stay away from serious relationship and be total players. I had lasted one week before I met Luka. Jessica had gone a little bit longer before she met her ex. Jillian had clung to the concept the longest, but even she had fallen victim to the lure of true love after a one night stand gone right and was now off the market. Boy catching was something to laugh about now. "I really don't do that anymore. I don't even date—until last night. I didn't even want to date him."

"If he's acting inappropriately..." Lillian began, instantly shifting from cross examination to attorney-client privilege.

Oh crap. Now I had given her the wrong idea. I quickly reversed my tune. "No. It's not like that. He's made it perfectly clear that I have every right to kick him to the curb."

"Do you want to? He's kinda hot." Just like that she was back to older sister mode.

"I thought it would be smarter if I stayed away from him. I didn't want to cause problems at the office. I know it's kind of a gray area to date someone you work with, especially your boss."

"He's not Donald Trump," she scoffed. "He can't be much older than you. If you showed interest and he respected your boundaries, it doesn't seem all that questionable to me."

"He's 26," I told her.

"That seems reasonable to me. I'm guessing he's a worka-holic. The twenty-six- year-old boss of a real estate investment firm probably doesn't take much time for dating." She paused, her coffee cup hovering near her lips. "He must think you're something special."

He was a workaholic, and his role in the success of NorthWest Investments proved that. I didn't tell her who his father was or why he'd spent more time at the office than picking girls up in bars. I wanted to respect Gavin's desire for people to know him before they knew who his family was. "We'll still hang out at his place."

"Just put a sock on the door if you don't." She winked as she started toward the living room. "Your coffee is getting cold."

It was mercifully cool enough to chug and warm enough not to suck. It turned out, Lillian was taking the day off. That was something I thought I would never see. I left her home on the couch, cuddled up with Olive. I was a little jealous. Part of me wanted to stay in my pajamas. A bigger part of me wanted to get to work though.

I wished it had to do with my job—which I loved—and not what was waiting for me at the office. But I couldn't lie to myself. I wanted to get to work, so I could see Gavin. The second I got to my desk, he appeared. "Cassie! You're here. There was something I needed to discuss with you about the Majestic Theater project." He spoke so casually that no one would have guessed what was really going on between us. I, however, caught the simmering desire heating his words.

"Let me get my stuff put away and then I'll head into your office." It was better to pretend like I didn't need to run after him. Not only because walking together to the office might be a little too obvious, but also because I didn't want him to think I was too eager. I kinda enjoyed the fact that he was chasing me. I took as long as I could before my patience gave out and headed in. I paused in the doorway and tilted my head. Was this official business talk or something more private?

"Can you shut the door? I think it's best if we speak alone," he said loudly enough that anyone passing by might hear. The door had barely shut before he was on me. His hand snaked behind me and I heard a lock click.

This was definitely something more private.

He'd shaved and part of me missed how his stubble had felt on my skin. But work Gavin was equally sexy. Maybe it was the suit. Or the tie. Or just him. My hands slid up his black jacket and found his broad shoulders. How were we going to get anything else done for the day? Thank God, I'd worn the no smudge lipstick.

"What did you want to talk about?" I asked breathlessly between kisses.

"This dress to start with." He kissed along my neck and down to the hollow to my collarbone.

"What is wrong with this dress?" I demanded. I thought the black sheath looked pretty sexy, in a work-appropriate way.

"Absolutely nothing. I just wanted a closer look." His hands roamed over my hips as though a look wasn't all he wanted. Before he could take it any further though, I placed one hand on his chest and pushed him away. Gavin backed up without argument.

He really was such a gentleman. I couldn't wait to see what he was like when that careful, responsible part of his personality gave way to his more primal instincts. I had a pretty good idea how to get a preview. I kept my palm planted there, marveling at the firmness of his pectorals as I urged him backward toward his desk.

"If we're going to have an affair in the office," I told him, "then I want the whole cliché."

"Cliché?" he asked.

"Haven't you ever read a romance novel?"

"I can't say that I have." His loss.

"Let me show you what I mean." I kissed him firmly on the lips, my tongue slipping past his teeth and licking across the roof of his mouth. Now that I had him where I wanted him, I gripped his tie tightly, then I used it as leverage to lower myself to my knees.

Gavin looked down at me, his eyes hooding over with want. "I think I would like romance novels."

I practically purred with delight as I unbuckled his belt and yanked it free. I unbuttoned his pants slowly, allowing him to keep them on, as my hand stroked past his fly and found his rock-hard dick waiting for me. He was wearing black boxer briefs that probably hadn't been so tight a few minutes ago. Now they were struggling with their increased capacity. I pressed a few kisses to their elastic waistband before I pushed them down, allowing him to spring free.

Holy crap. I sat back on my heels just so that I could get the full view. I'd been too close to see *all* of it. I needed to zoom out. Magnificent didn't begin to cover it. He made Mr.

Dependable look like a joke. As I knelt there almost drooling, I couldn't wait to get my lips on him. I wanted to hear him lose control. I needed to.

I took my time though. Running my fingers down the silken length of him, I marveled at the spectacle. Gavin groaned, a low guttural noise that emanated from his chest. The sound made me wet. When I finally lowered my mouth to him, I ran my tongue from his tip downward, relishing the power I held over him. His hands clutched the desk behind him as though he needed to brace himself.

"Jesus, Cassie. You're going to kill me."

"I haven't even gotten started jet." I murmured as I ran my tongue back up and swirled it over his crown.

"You are so unbelievably hot," he murmured in a low voice, "with your red lipstick and your little black dress and my cock in your mouth."

I felt an uptick of interest between my legs at his words. I didn't think I could be any more turned on. God, I wanted to make this man feel as good as he made me feel every moment we were together. My lips closed over him, sinking lower until I'd taken him into the back of my throat. Gavin growled in response. He actually growled. I wondered how much louder he would get, if he would lose control entirely. I should be more worried that someone would hear, but part of me got off on the idea of it. We were doing something dirty and sexy with only a door and a couple walls shielding us from dozens of people.

I stroked along his shaft as I continued plunging my mouth over him. Gavin's hand shot out and caught my pony-tail, guiding me to go farther and deeper. It wasn't forceful, but rather encouraging, and to be honest, I loved it. I loved how he looked down at me with such naked need. I loved how I felt under that gaze. When he suddenly tensed, I prepared myself, pulling back with his crown still between my lips

"I'm going to come," he warned me.

Such a gentleman. He was about to find out I was no lady.

I kept him in my mouth as he finished, allowing one single drop to drip down over my lips. I waited until his body had stilled before I sat back again and licked my lower lip. Gavin watched without comment but his jaw tightened.

It was how I'd felt last night, when he kept going after I'd climaxed. I'd wanted to return that feeling of being wanted, so there would be no doubt that he could have me any time and anywhere.

"Come away with me this weekend," he said. I hadn't expected that. It wasn't a question, but it wasn't demand either.

"Where?" There were one million reasons why now wasn't the time to go away. Gavin seemed to sense my hesitation. Somehow, it didn't wreck the mood though.

"You can't possibly be more ready to present on the project," he told me, offering me a hand and pulling me to my feet. He tucked his dick back in his pants and buttoned them, ignoring his belt which still sat on the desk. When he was decent, he pulled me to him, his hands on my hips. "You'll just spend all weekend worrying. Spend it with me instead."

"You think you can distract me from worrying?" That was a challenge.

"I'm already thinking of a dozen ways to distract you." He pressed a kiss to my ear, which made my whole body shudder. "Come away with me."

I was powerless to resist.

Sixteen

THE WEEK PASSED AT AN EXCRUCIATINGLY SLOW rate. I had two run-ins with Trevor, who seemed intent on catching me in the act with Gavin. Gavin, on the other hand, continually reassured me that no one in the office would have a problem with our relationship. Still, I wanted to keep it private for now. We hadn't even slept together yet. It hardly seemed like the business of the rest of, well, the business. When Thursday night finally rolled around it was like Christmas Eve. I couldn't sleep. Instead, I managed to get both Jess and Jillian on video chat to help me decide what to pack. Since I'd finally told them about my dinner with him the other night, they'd adjusted their attitudes about him. It felt good to have my outfit-prepping, over-analyzing, twenty-four hour cheer squad back together.

"Will I need a swimsuit?" I asked them, studying the meager choices I had to work with. I kept most of my suits back in Texas where I usually spent the summer. There wasn't a lot of call for swimwear in the rainy Pacific Northwest.

"Yes," Jillian said definitively as though she was an expert on my itinerary. "It's better to have it then to have to go au natural."

"I don't know." Jess jumped in with her opinion. She was back in the hammock, even though it was dark outside. "Gavin might find au natural pretty inspiring."

"Look at her," Jillian exclaimed. "She could wear a burlap bag and he would be inspired."

"I'm packing this one," I announced. Gavin had been a little less forthcoming with the details than I would like. I didn't know if we were staying in a hotel, a bed and break-fast, or a tent. I really, really hoped we weren't staying in a tent. This was one weekend where I wanted a bed at my disposal.

"How are you getting there?" Jess asked. The wind blew a strand of blonde hair over her freckled nose and she pushed it away with a puff. She was like a talking advertisement for a Mexican vacation.

"Driving? Where is Friday Harbor?" I didn't really have any clue where that was located. Since I'd found out our destination only a few hours ago, I'd jumped straight into packing.

"It's on an island in the San Juans," Jillian said dryly.

"There are plenty of bridges that connect the islands," I pointed out. Gavin had left that detail out, but he'd probably assumed I'd know after three years of college here.

"It's like a four-hour ferry ride," Jess informed me. She had lived in the Pacific Northwest the longest of any of us.

Naturally, she knew exactly where Friday Harbor was. I wished, though, that she thought to mention this fact before.

"Four hours?" I was aghast. "Will we be stuck in a car for four hours? Or on a boat for four hours? How does he expect me to wait that long to..."

"You can do it on a boat," Jess said.

"You can do it on in a car," Jillian said at the same time.

"Are we writing a Dr. Seuss novel or helping me out?" I was frustrated. Sexually. And otherwise. But mostly sexually. "I don't want our first time to be in a car or on a boat."

"You haven't done it yet?" Jillian said with a look of horror that mirrored Jess's. I'd been a little light on the details of our first date. Mostly, because I didn't want them to psych me out about the sex stuff.

I shrugged as if this was no big deal. "We messed around. We've just been waiting."

"Who are you and what have you done with our best friend?" Jess asked.

I stopped trying to shove another pair of shorts into my overstuffed weekender bag and looked at the phone screen. "I always jump into bed with a guy too soon. You both know that."

"We know that. We didn't know that you knew that." Jillian looked mildly impressed as though I told her that I'd taken a vow of silence or that I had swum the English Channel. Given that she had slept with Liam before she knew his name, I could see why this was the case.

"Gavin is... different." I didn't even want to say it. Those words felt like a jinx. I'd thrown around the term 'the one.' I talked about long-term possibilities with Trevor. There was even the terrible choice of a certain tattoo. Thank God, it wasn't his actual name. I had been that girl who wanted the real thing so much that she was willing to settle for the knock-off. Now, I couldn't believe that I'd landed the genuine article.

"Uh-oh." Jess sat up in the hammock, nearly falling out of it, her legs tangling as she tried to get up while still holding the phone. "Is this more than a fling?"

"No way!" I held up one finger. Yes, I had been hinting that Gavin was Mr. Right, but they weren't going to get me to say it. Doing that would really screw my chances to make it work with him.

"Oh my God!" Jillian squealed, then clapped a hand over her mouth and looked over shoulder. I assumed Liam was asleep at this hour. "She's falling for him!"

"I don't see why you two are happy about this. I usually have terrible taste in men."

Both of them averted their eyes from the camera on their phones at the same time. That was more than a little suspicious.

"Spill it," I demanded. They had been up to something. Something behind my back. They were being a little too cool about Gavin, especially given how concerned they'd been after I told them we kissed.

"I called my sister," Jess said in a rush. She sighed heavily, as though she felt relief for keeping such a serious secret for so long.

"She had dinner with him. That doesn't make her an expert," I said. Lillian's own workaholic tendencies and commitment to her job didn't exactly make her a matchmaker.

"She's a lawyer," Jillian explained.

"She knows how to read people," Jess said. "I believe her exact words were: Cassie has finally caught herself a real man."

Now I was definitely jinxed. Not only was I having a hard time not thinking of Gavin as Mr. Right, my friends had already decided he was the one. It was going to be hard enough for our fledgling relationship to live up to my expectations. I couldn't imagine how hard it would be to live up to theirs.

"And we Googled him," Jillian confessed. My friends had stalked him more than I had.

"Did you run a background? Get his FBI file?" I sat down on my bed, crushing a pile of clothes underneath me, ensuring they'd be a wrinkled mess, but I didn't care. My friends had given me a headache.

"We like him even more now," Jess said.

"You two really are determined to jinx this."

Jillian shook her head furiously. "Don't worry. Trust me on this. Sometimes life surprises you."

"What is that supposed to mean?" I pinched the bridge of my nose as my temples began to throb.

"Good guys still exist," she told me. This time she smiled as she looked over her shoulder at her own Mr. Right. "You're going to have to trust us on this."

"Jillian is right," Jess added, "and believe us when we tell you that when the right one comes along, there's nothing you can do about it."

"I mean, even my mother didn't scare Liam off." To Jillian there was no greater proof that she'd found a keeper.

They were making a lot of sense. They'd found true love. They'd fought for it. After my last relationship disaster, their stories had given me hope. It was just that I had finally accepted that the right guy might never come along. Now I had to face the possibility that he had. "How will I know?"

"You just will," Jess promised.

Seventeen

I WAS GOING TO DIE.

And not an unexpected death. No, I pretty much expected it. I hadn't asked questions when Gavin picked me up in his Tesla. After my conversation last night with Jess and Jillian, I'd looked up the ferry information for the one that went out to the San Juans. I'd felt prepared, so when Gavin began to drive, I didn't think anything of it. To be honest, I didn't know this side of the Puget Sound all that well. If I had, I might have noticed that he wasn't heading in the direction of the ferry at all. That, and the fact that he'd given the entire office a day off, stating that we all had to rest up before the big Majestic Theater presentation, had led me to believe that we would be spending the whole day traveling.

I stared at the small, four-person aircraft he expected me to get on. Gavin hadn't noticed my reluctance yet. He'd been putting our baggage into the cargo hold and speaking with someone who worked at the private airfield.

I hadn't moved. I was still sitting in the passenger seat.

The car was off and it was beginning to get hot, but despite the dangers of the greenhouse effect, I felt a whole lot safer in here.

I wasn't an enthusiastic flyer on a good day. I usually had to remind myself that statistically I was more likely to die in a car accident then I was in an airplane crash. I didn't know how much that changed on a Cessna, but I was going to guess those figures skewed a little when the plane was the size of a golf cart. I was considering whether I should call my parents and tell them I loved them when Gavin opened the passenger door and leaned down.

"Are you going to join me?" he asked.

"I was just deciding that," I admitted. My hands were still on my seat belt buckle. I really hadn't gotten far in the decision-making process.

"Will it help you to know that I've been flying for 12 years?"

I did the mental math on those numbers. "You can fly at 14? Your parents let you do this? Do your parents even love you?"

"I learned with my dad. When he bought his first plane," he added.

"So this plane is yours?"

"My family's."

I stared at it. Gavin owned a freaking plane. The longer that information stewed in my brain, the more silly I felt. Of course, his family owned a plane. They were gagillionaires, which meant they probably could have afforded something a bit larger. Or at least big enough to have a nice flight attendant serving vodka.

"Oh, I guess I would have expected..." I shut my mouth before I said something truly stupid.

"That we would have private jet? We do. I just don't like to use it. Dad insists that we have a pilot fly that. I prefer to be in the cockpit."

I really wished he didn't have that preference. Right now I wanted a pilot and a plane that looked a little less like child's play toy than this one.

Gavin extended his hand in offering. "Do you trust me?"

That was a loaded question. An hour ago I would have said yes unequivocally. Now, I had something to quibble about. He helped me out of the car slowly, letting me take my time, or maybe giving me time to change my mind. Once I was out, his fingers knitted through mine and the simple gesture—the first time we'd ever held hands—calmed me. He led me toward the Cessna, chattering about various near misses and how he'd handled each one.

"Please don't tell me about the times you almost crashed," I said, gripping his hand a little tighter.

"The weather is perfect today," he said in a soothing voice. "It's going to be a perfect flight and it will take less than an hour."

One hour. I repeated it over and over again like a mantra. I could handle anything for an hour—except dying. Gavin helped me climb into the co-pilot's seat, which proved to be a little tricky in my sundress. When the wind caught my skirt and tried to blow it over my head, he grabbed it and kept me covered up.

"That's for my eyes only."

Normally, I might have languished in those words,

savoring the possessive suggestion of them. Now? I was glad I would die with my dignity.

Once I was inside, he handed me a bulky set of headphones with a mic attached. "You'll need these when we're in the air. It will be too loud for us to hear each other otherwise."

"Since I'm probably going spend the entire flight screaming, you might regret giving me these." I took them as my stomach began to churn.

"There's a floatation device here." He motioned to a pouch on my belt as he helped me buckle up. "But you aren't going to need it."

"I never understood why they do that," I began, nervously rattling out everything in my brain. "Before you take off—when they tell you what to do with your mask or flotation device or how to get to an exit. We're all just going to be praying and crying if the plane goes down."

Gavin stood back, his mouth gaping open, and I realized what I'd done. I thought I'd gotten control of my sailor mouth.

"Sorry," I said sheepishly. "I did the cursing thing again, didn't I? What did I say?"

"I don't think I could repeat it without blushing," he said with a chuckle. He tucked a strand of loose hair behind my ear and kissed my forehead. "You're going to be fine. Trust me."

For a second that appeased me. Then I remembered that my issue wasn't Gavin's 12 years of flight experience. It was with the Cessna. The plane didn't care about me. The plane could not be trusted. I kept these thoughts to myself lest I unleash another stream of foul-mouthed, verbal diarrhea.

I closed my eyes and concentrated on everything Gavin had said about how safe we were. Nothing helped. I tried to picture being in my happy place – a white, sandy beach. All I saw was fiery wreckage on the sand. When the engine turned on, I nearly jumped out of my seat, which would've been hard given how tightly I was strapped in. The propellers whirred to life and Gavin's voice filled my ears. "Sound One requesting the runway."

Sound One? Later, when I wasn't about to vomit, I'd have to ask if there was a Sound Two. Although, I didn't want him to think I was interested in flying in it. I never wanted to be on this thing again. Wherever the San Juan Islands were, I hoped they were nice, because I was going to be living there forever. He'd talked me into this once. It would take drugging me to get me on it again.

"Sound One you are cleared for takeoff."

We taxied forward, gradually gaining speed. I felt it in the pit of my stomach, but I kept my eyes clamped shut. So far it was a lot like every other flight I had taken, except that I could feel air rushing in at me. There wasn't much separating me from the outside and as the wheels left the ground I realized that I must be suicidal.

"How are you doing?" Gavin's voice filled the headphones.

"What happens if I barf all over the cockpit?" It probably should have occurred to me this question before take-off.

"There should be air sickness bags on the floorboard."

I didn't risk trying to bend over to search for them. My

belt would have made it harder and I didn't want to risk pressure to my already queasy stomach. Instead, I began to count. One number after the other. Gavin, wisely, stayed mostly silent. I had no idea how much time we'd been in the air until he spoke again. "If you look out, you can see the islands.

I cracked open one eye, followed by the other and dared to look out the window. There was nothing but blue water hatched with lines. Waves, I realized. In the distance, I could make out land. I imagined that if I turned around I might still be able to see the rest of Washington. But while it was beautiful, my stomach did a nose dive when I looked at the open water. One of the perks of mostly flying between Washington and Texas was that there was usually land below. Not that I wanted to crash into that either.

Gavin cautioned me as we began to circle the Friday Harbor Airport. "This is going to be a little rough. It always is."

Thank God, he wasn't a nurse or doctor. He had terrible bedside manner. Still, I appreciated the warning. That said, I was pretty excited to see solid ground.

The plane descended rapidly, much faster than I was used to. As the landing gear came out, I closed my eyes again and braced myself. We hit the tarmac fairly hard and then braked with a whoosh. When we finally stopped, I couldn't even bring myself to open my eyes. Finally, my door opened and Gavin began to unlatch me. I practically fell into his arms. Pushing him aside, I stumbled a few steps away and proceeded to hurl all over the pavement. I tried to wave him away, but Gavin was at my side instantly, making sure my hair was out of my face. He rubbed circles over my back as I dry heaved a few more times.

"I'm so sorry," he said. "I just thought you were nervous. I promise we'll find another way home."

I straightened and forced a small smile. I was grateful when he found a napkin for me to wipe my mouth with.

"We can either take my motorcycle up to the house," he said, quickly reversing when I blanched at the suggestion, "or we can walk into town. Is there anything that might make you feel better?"

"Besides a new stomach?" I was only half joking. "Maybe a milkshake and no more motorized vehicles on land or sea."

"A milkshake?" he repeated as though he expected me to spout some WebMD bullshit about how it settled the stomach.

"I figure there's still a 50% chance I'm going to throw up, I might as well have my favorite thing in the world," I explained.

He settled for that logic. "Done."

Gavin wouldn't let me carry anything other than my purse. I was glad that I had packed light for the weekend, since I'd been hoping to spend it mostly nude. He looked a little like a pack rat with his bag and my bag slung over his shoulders, but he didn't complain. Downtown Friday Harbor was only a mile away. We took it slowly, allowing my stomach to make peace with finally being back on two feet.

"I didn't expect you to take flying so badly," he said, obviously feeling guilty.

"I probably just need some Dramamine or something." I didn't bother to tell him that I doubted I would ever take flying well. I hated that something he loved made me lose my breakfast.

"There are other ways to get here. That was just the fastest."

"Fast isn't always better," I said, allowing a hint of suggestiveness to creep into my voice. Now that I didn't want to toss my cookies all over him, I was starting to think about what I had planned for the weekend. He was the only item on my to-do list.

Friday Harbor was a charming collection of local restaurants and shops, all owned by community members. As far as I can see, there were no corporate stores or big chains. There wasn't even a Sound Coffee. The various establishments were brightly painted, standing out against the blue background of the marina. It was a refreshing change of pace from downtown Seattle.

I had wanted to ask if he'd come here before, but I'd been too nauseous during the flight. Walking through downtown, I realized everyone here knew him.

Every corner we turned on and every street we walked down, someone waved hello or stopped to catch up. They knew his name. They felt comfortable around him. It was clear he came here often. By the third time I was introduced to a total stranger, it began to dawn on me that he hadn't simply asked me on a weekend away, he had invited me into a deeply personal part of his life. I tucked that realization away for later contemplation.

His familiarity worked in my favor because he knew exactly where the ice cream shop was. Friday Harbor Ice Cream Co was a local establishment, like everything else here, and given that it was the height of summer, there was a line. That was fine because there were 72 flavors to choose from. In the end, I opted for a classic: chocolate and strawberry mixed together. Gavin watched me nervously as I took my first sip, probably worried that it would come back up immediately. Instead, I moaned with pleasure. It had been a crazy summer and I hadn't taken enough time for milkshakes.

"You're going to make me jealous," he told me.

I held it out to him. "You can try some if you want."

"I'm not jealous that you have a milkshake. I'm jealous that it makes you moan."

"Some girls know what they like." I bit down on the tip of the straw trying to stop myself from jumping him on the spot.

Gavin swallowed hard as though he was doing the same. His eyes lingered on my mouth and he cleared his throat. "Do you want to see the family house?"

"Lead the way." I hadn't been sure exactly where we would be staying. After seeing him walk around downtown, I wasn't surprised to hear that he had a family home here.

We barely made it half a block before the door to a restaurant flew open and a man came running out with his apron still on. "Gavin!"

"Thomas, it's good to see you." The men shook hands before Thomas pulled him into a hug. The other man had to be at least 20 years older than Gavin. I'd noticed a slight limp in his step as he'd come out to us. Gavin stepped away and smiled broadly at me. "Allow me to introduce my girlfriend, Cassie."

I was temporarily struck dumb. I fumbled, taking

Thomas's outstretched hand, and tried to come up with words. I got as far as "Hi."

The two of them didn't seem to notice that I couldn't speak and began to chat.

So I was on holiday with Gavin. We'd messed around a few times. My entire weekend plans focused on having sex with him as many times as possible. But I hadn't been sure until this moment that I was his girlfriend. I liked the way the title sounded.

"He's a good man," Thomas informed me, taking my hand in his as if to impress this upon me. "You two must come to dinner tonight. On me. It's the least that I can do."

We reassured him that we would. I was only mildly disappointed that there would have to be a break in tonight's sexual Olympics to go out to eat. Then, I remembered how much I loved food. I surveyed the restaurant's handprinted sign which read The Weekend Café with interest. With any luck, I'd be really hungry this evening.

"He really likes you," I told Gavin as we started up the hill and away from downtown. It had been charming, but I finally had him to myself.

"I've known him my whole life. We've been going to his restaurant since my parents bought the house here."

"Why does he owe you?" I couldn't help asking, curiosity getting the better of me. It had been clear that the two were old friends, despite their age difference, but there must have been more to it. Thomas had seemed grateful to Gavin and I wanted to know why.

"A bad storm hit here last year. The restaurant was damaged and I helped him out." Gavin spoke as if this was no big deal. That made me suspect there was more to the story, but I didn't press him on it. He had said he wanted to make his mark and it was becoming pretty clear that he would leave the world a better place.

Friday Harbor was hillier than I'd expected and I'd almost begun to regret not taking the motorcycle when Gavin finally paused and said, "Home sweet home."

The house was nothing like I had expected. The Sound family was full of surprises. Just like when we had taken the Cessna instead of a private jet. This looked like a family home, not the vacation house of one of the world's most successful business men. True, it sat on the side of a hill overlooking the glorious waters of Friday Harbor. I could only imagine what it was valued at. As we got closer, I began to notice that it wasn't a simple house either.

"Is this one house?" I asked trying to figure it out as I followed him up the cobblestone path.

"It was one house," he explained, stopping to take a key from under a rock. This really was a whole, other world if they just left their house keys under a rock. Although, if the rest of Gavin's family was as loved as he was by the town's residents, the house was probably in safekeeping while they were absent. "My parents bought this part of it 20 years ago when Sound Coffee first really took off. Over the years they've added on. I think one wing came about when we were preteens and the other came about when we were teenagers. At first, they just needed to get away from us. Then, they needed to keep us apart. Imogen and I were always fighting."

"You don't say," I said dryly. I had been witness to their

good-natured sibling disagreements myself. I found it endearing, but I could imagine why his parents wanted a break from it when they were on vacation.

He unlocked the door with a grin and it swung open, creaking on its hinges. This was no lavish vacation home. It was the heart and soul of a family who worked hard, but had found a quiet spot to escape. We entered into a large living room that joined with a huge, country style kitchen. An island surrounded by barstools was the centerpiece. I could see Gavin and Imogen sitting here while his mom cooked. The floor was a warm oak that matched the wood trim and beams overhead, and the walls were painted a deep green. There was no fancy artwork on the walls. Instead, dozens of family photos had been hung.

A lump formed in my throat. He'd brought me here. He'd chosen to share this with me.

"This place is perfect," I breathed.

Gavin looked pleased, but he didn't move from the doorway. He was still carrying both our bags and now he looked torn.

"I usually stay over there." He nodded toward one of the adjoining buildings. "But I can show you over to Imogen's place. Or the guest room in here."

"Show me your room," I said, putting an end to the gentlemanly charade. It was adorable that he wanted to pretend we'd come here for any other reason than to bone.

We exited through a series of French doors onto a bridge that connected Gavin's part of the property to the main house. It was lined on either side by lush Douglas firs. It was a bit like walking into the forest. It must have been tricky to add on to the property, given its hillside location, but the effect had an almost magical feeling. It was like finding a Woodland Castle or a fantastic treehouse.

Gavin showed me to his quarters, setting our bags inside the door. He stood and shoved his hands into his pockets. "This is it. Is there anything I can get you?"

Your penis? I thought to myself. I bit that back and stuck with "I'm good."

I looked around the room, taking it all in. There was a little balcony that looked out over the water. Not the marina side, but rather a calm, unbroken expanse. The view was breathtaking. The room itself was spartan save for a couple of book piles and a few more filled bookshelves. There was no television, which was just fine since I had other plans for entertainment.

And in the dead center of the room was my favorite part: the biggest bed I'd ever seen.

"The bathroom is in there if you'd like to freshen up," he suggested.

That was probably a good idea. I supposed that after throwing up all over the runway, I needed to do that. I grabbed my bag and ducked inside with a shy grin. Digging into it, I found my toothbrush and brushed my teeth three times to be safe. While I did, I wandered around the bathroom. It was probably as big as his bedroom. It seemed like he'd decided to sprawl here. In the city, space was at a premium. Here, he had the freedom to indulge. Behind the duel sinks was a large walk-in shower with four rainwater heads. It looked like it belonged in a show home. But what really caught my eye was the large, jetted bathtub in the corner. It was surrounded by oversized windows that looked out over the trees. The condo didn't have a bathtub. Neither had my dorm room. Maybe I had one more thing to add to this weekend's to-do list.

Once I'd finished my final brushing, I stepped back and surveyed myself in the mirror. My dark hair swung over my shoulders, still fresh thanks to Gavin's intervention at the airfield. Since I'd opted for the natural look, I didn't need to touch up my make-up. Despite my breakfast's encore appearance I didn't look half bad. I considered digging into my weekender for the one slip of a nightgown that I had brought along. I hadn't been sure if we were at the full-blown lingerie stage, so I had decided to keep it simple. Would it be presumptuous to go back in there in something like that?

Of course, I was well past the point of presumptuous. We were here, in very close proximity to a very empty bed, and I was ready to seal the deal. I found the nightgown and changed into it. After a quick check in the mirror, I decided it wouldn't do. It looked like I was ready to go to bed. And not in the way I was hoping for. Nope, I needed something that screamed 'take me now.' Or I would actually be screaming take me now. I whipped it off and dropped it back on my bag. Catching sight of myself in the mirror, I realized that I didn't need anything at all if I wanted to send a clear message.

Even with a summer of questionable fitness practices, I didn't look half bad. There would also be no mistaking what I was after if I wore absolutely nothing out that door.

I loved how careful Gavin was about making sure we

were on the same page, but I was ready to let him take control of me—my body and my heart.

"Now or never, Cassie," I said in a firm voice. Squaring my shoulders I marched toward the door and stepped out, with a flourish, to an empty room.

It was more than a bit of a letdown. Gavin was nowhere to be seen. No doubt he was off checking on some other part of the house. Or he'd gone to grab something. It wasn't a blow to the ego exactly, it was more like the split second I needed to feel embarrassed by *my complete and total nudity*.

I was naked and alone and really regretting my choices in life. I started to back toward the bathroom and the safety of my clothing when Gavin walked into the bedroom holding two bottles of water. He froze as soon as he spotted me.

"Where's a fig leaf when you need one?" I said under my breath. Instinctively, I tried to wrap an arm around my torso, but couldn't decide what parts of me were most important to cover. My double Ds put up a fight, spilling over my arm and refusing to play along and I could nearly hide my cootchie if I crossed my legs right. "I'm so sorry."

It was all I could think to say. It was probably the first time a woman had ever apologized to a man for being naked.

"Don't be sorry and don't leave," he tacked on hurriedly as I kept backing into the bathroom.

"I should put something on."

"Whatever you do don't do that." He tossed the water bottles onto the nightstand and strode quickly toward me. I'd given up on trying to cover my body and instead hid my face with my hands as though if I couldn't see him he couldn't see me. Gavin gripped my wrists and drew them from my face. "God, you're beautiful. You shouldn't be ashamed."

"I'm feeling a little exposed," I whispered. All the confidence I had when I walked out here had completely deflated, leaving half a Cassie in its wake.

He dropped my hands and stepped away. With one fluid motion he pulled his shirt over his head. "Then allow me to even the playing field."

I'd already seen some very impressive parts of Gavin, but with his washboard abs on display, I almost forgot I was naked.

"Better?"

"Much." I couldn't tear my eyes away. Would my tongue vibrate if I licked that six-pack?

He reached down and slowly began unbuttoning his jeans. "What about these?"

All I could manage was a nod. Apparently, that was good enough, because they hit the floor. I'd seen what he was packing under his boxer briefs, but with his legs on display I realized that he must have spent a lot of time at the gym. I should have known they'd be as powerful as the rest of him after he had held me against that wall. He clucked his tongue, catching my attention. "Your eyes seem to be wandering."

"Hey, you can't blame a girl for looking." I was about to scream 'show me your peen' when his boxers hit the floor revealing the full Gavin package.

He really was Mr. Right.

"I kinda like this nudist lifestyle." He strode around the room strutting and showcasing his lean, muscular body. "Are we going to do this all weekend? I'm not sure how they'll take it at the restaurant. I wish I'd known you were into this."

I began to laugh, somehow he'd made the whole thing feel ridiculous. But not in a 'I want to run and hide way'—in the way a friend would.

Of course, he was a friend I wanted to fuck.

He lit up at the sound of my laughter and before I knew it, he caught me in his arms and swept me off my feet.

Gavin carried me to the bad and laid me across it. Dropping down beside me, he ran a finger lazily from my collarbone to my bellybutton. His touch practically sizzled on my skin.

"I can't decide where I want to start with you. Long and slow? Fast and hard?" His hand circled back and wandered to my breast where his thumb began to stroke my nipple. It pebbled under his touch and I bit my lip as new sensations crowded my body.

"Part of me can't wait a second longer to be inside of you," he continued. "The rest of me wants to see how many new ways I can make you come first."

I practically came on his words alone.

"Option D," I panted. He pulled back, his eyebrows arching into a question mark. "All of the above."

A slow, self-satisfied smirk spread over his handsome face before he lowered his mouth to take over for his thumb. I felt the wet heat of his tongue as it flicked across the furl of my nipple, then circled around it, before he took it into his mouth and began to suck. My head fell back into the pillows and I reached up to grab one, needing some type of leverage. Gavin took this as an invitation to continue. His mouth moved to my other breast, repeating the same action until both breasts were swollen and tender. He trailed downward, leaving a wake of kisses until he reached my bellybutton.

I decided I didn't need to eat after all. I could live on this alone—feast on the way he touched me.

A hand pressed between my legs, urging them to part and I felt his finger stroke along my sex. I pulled the pillow over my head, afraid that I would scream as he plunged inside me and began to work. But Gavin had a free hand and he reached up and took the pillow away.

"We're all alone here. I want to hear you," he said in a husky voice that left little room to doubt the sincerity of his words. He continued his gentle assault until I was breathing heavily and nearly there. He seemed to sense that I was close, so he lowered his lips to my ear and whispered, "There's a condom in the drawer."

"Bring a lot of girls here?" I asked through gritted teeth, circling my hips against his hand. A wave of jealousy broke over me, which only made me want him more.

He loosed a gruff laugh that made my stomach clench. "We'll be lucky if they aren't expired."

I reached for the drawer and fumbled around inside, barely in control of my own body. Gavin wasn't helping as he continued to cajole me toward my breaking point. When my fingers closed over a foil packet, I grabbed it and checked the date. I found an unexpired condom at the same moment his thumb found my clit. I bolted up at the contact, coming with a throaty cry that tore through me.

Gavin caught me around the waist with his other hand and kept me up right. It took me a second to stop shaking and then I reached for the condom I'd dropped. That had been more than enough foreplay. I tore it open. Then with a pretty smile I popped it between my lips, careful not to catch it on my teeth and dropped my head to his lap.

So it was a college trick, but it was still a showstopper.

"Holy shit," he hissed between his gritted teeth. He flipped me onto my back and hovered over me before pausing. He seemed to think better of it before he sat up and propped himself against the headboard. "Come here, baby."

I didn't need him to ask twice. Crawling onto his lap, I lowered myself carefully. Having seen the full size of him, I knew I would need a second to adjust. He stayed sitting up, his arms wrapping around my waist as my legs wrapped around him, and guided me onto his dick. Our gazes locked as we shared the moment. It was incredibly hot and undeniably intimate. When I finally was sheathed to the root, I groaned with the pent-up desire that I'd been holding back since the moment we met.

He began to move, at first with no urgency. We found our rhythm together—a slow, steady rocking. My head fell back, eyes closed, as I savored the fullness of him. Soon, though, nature took its course and I began to feel anticipation building inside my body. It clawed at my skin, which felt too tight to contain everything I was feeling. I bucked against him, wanting more contact, wanting more of him, and he responded matching me thrust for thrust. As I felt the first ripples of my climax, his hand tipped my chin down and he murmured gruffly, "Open your eyes, baby. I want to see."

I pried my eyes open, feeling vulnerable and secure at the same time, and met his smoldering gaze. It was the final push and I fell over the edge, safely in his arms the whole time. I rode out my orgasm as his body went rigid. He groaned and brought his mouth to mine and we shattered together.

There were no words as we collapsed onto one another, sweaty and boneless. Gavin rolled me to the side and tucked me against his body, holding me closely as we lingered in the afterglow.

I counted his breaths with the beats of my heart.

Eighteen

I DIDN'T REMEMBER FALLING ASLEEP. I WOKE TO the sound of Gavin softly snoring behind me. It was twilight outside, far too early to fall asleep for the night. But I couldn't bring myself to wake him. Instead, I lingered in his embrace for a moment before realizing that I really needed to go to the bathroom. I wiggled out from his arms, which were quite heavy when he was unconscious.

The girl in the mirror was glowing and rosy-cheeked. My dark hair had a wild, tousled style that I could never replicate with every product in the world. This was a look that only getting laid could achieve.

"Fancy meeting you here." I said to myself. It had been a long time since that face had greeted me. Too long and somehow just long enough. No other man could have put that smile on my face.

I tiptoed out of the bathroom and found Gavin's T-shirt on the floor. It was just long enough to cover my booty, and since I didn't really know how close any neighboring houses might be, I decided it was best to cover up before I explored. I needed a glass of water and a moment to commit every detail of what had just happened to memory. I grabbed one of the water bottles from the nightstand and snuck out of the bedroom. In the kitchen I found a glass and filled it with ice before dumping the now tepid water in, then I began to wander.

Outside the living space, there was a large patio and another cobblestone path leading off in the direction of Gavin's room. I wandered down it aimlessly, struck by the rosy hues of twilight over San Juan Island, one of the most beautiful places I'd ever seen the sun set. The path led to a small garden that sat directly under the balcony of Gavin's bedroom. Like most foliage in this area, it hadn't been tended to in a while and didn't really need to be. Wild flowers grew recklessly, unconcerned with whether they were wanted or not, but there was a small sitting area and two Adirondack chairs where I sat down and watched the sun began its descent over the water.

This was the most beautiful place in the world. Calm and lush and richly colored. My infatuation with this place might have had something to do with the company I was keeping. I really had it bad if I was getting poetic.

The real poetry existed in the memories we had just made though.

I recalled how his lips had felt on my body, how his hand moved between my legs, how we found our bliss together. The connection was undeniable, and I could see it in his eyes, too.

Why had I ever thought I'd been in love before? The

thought rocked through me. Because if I hadn't been in love before, could I be in love now? It didn't seem possible. It didn't seem rational. But admitting it to myself felt right. A deep peace settled over me and I knew.

I loved Gavin North. I loved him beyond reason or expectation. I should have felt scared—to lose him, to move too fast—but I didn't. I couldn't.

It was just right.

Overhead I heard doors swing open and Gavin came out on the balcony. "There you are," he called down, "I thought you'd finally gotten what you wanted out of me and left."

"You think that's all I've come for?" If so, he had another thing coming. How many positions were in the Kama Sutra? We might have to give up sleep if we stood a chance at satisfying me.

"Are you hungry?"

I remembered with a start that we had promised to go to his friend Thomas's restaurant. It was a good thing that I was famished. I nodded and popped onto my feet. "I'll be right up to get dressed."

"Those are the saddest words ever spoken," he said, shaking his head as he made his way back into the bedroom.

It turned out getting dressed was a lot harder in Gavin's presence. Mostly, because neither of us wanted to be dressed when we were around each other. But, he gave in and finally let me throw my sundress over my head when my stomach growled so loudly that he heard it over my moaning.

The walk downhill was much easier, but I still stuck to a pair of flat, strappy sandals with extra cushioning. We walked hand-in-hand toward the twinkling lights of downtown. The sun hadn't faded entirely, but the dusky pink was gradually settling into violet as the moon began her appearance. Summer was my favorite season, because day and night seemed to dance with one another, and I had never experienced a more beautiful summer night than this one. It was amazing to think that a place like this existed on earth—quiet and magical.

Downtown was still full of life though, and the Weekend Café was packed. Clearly, Friday Harbor wasn't hurting for tourism. But we were ushered into a quiet corner of the restaurant as soon as we arrived. A few tourists shot us dirty looks, and I smiled sheepishly as we were led to our table. I did feel bad about it, but I needed sustenance after my afternoon shag. The restaurant was charmingly simple with rustic wood floors and a large stone fireplace on the far wall. Its most stunning feature, however, was its waterfront location. Gavin ordered a bottle of wine and the waiter disappeared to bring it.

"They didn't bring us menus," I said, looking around as if one might appear on the table.

"Thomas would never hear of that," Gavin explained. "He'll bring us something delicious. Probably too many delicious things."

"Then we'll have something to work off," I said coyly. I grabbed my napkin and placed it over my lap.

Gavin took my hand and brought it to his lips. "Earlier was amazing."

I bit my lip, unsure what to say. Amazing wasn't quite the right word for it.

Spectacular.

Life-changing.

Earth-shattering.

All of those it seems apply. I was saved from falling victim to hyperbole by the appearance of Thomas.

Thomas was thinner than I might have expected from someone who loved food, tall and reedy with graying hair and a perfectly-lined face. At the moment, he looked tired but happy, just what I would expect from a chef coming off the evening rush. Wiping his hands on his apron, he grabbed a chair, spun it around and sat down. "Any allergies I should know about?"

"You're getting broad-minded," Gavin said, studying his friend as if he hadn't seen him before.

"You've never brought a woman here," Thomas retorted, "I don't want to scare her away by nearly killing her if she has a shellfish allergy."

"You've never asked me if I have a shellfish allergy," Gavin said in a mock-accusatory tone.

"I would kill you if you did," Thomas said. "Put you out of your misery."

"That's very sweet. There's nothing to worry about," I reassured him. "I'm easy."

What I said took a second to register and when it did I closed my eyes in embarrassment.

Thomas only guffawed as the matter was settled and that was that. "That's the best news I've heard all night."

"Her lack of shellfish allergy is the best news?" Gavin said, as if seeking clarification.

"Sure," his friend said, his eyes twinkling a bit as he

clapped him on the shoulder. "It's probably the best news for you, too."

"I should tell you now that I have foot-in-mouth disease," I said to Gavin when Thomas was safely back in the kitchen. "I'm always saying the wrong thing without meaning to."

"I know. Why do you think I find you so fascinating?"

"I assumed it was my ass," I said dryly.

"Believe me, that caught my eye. What caught my attention though was when you unleashed more curses than I had ever heard come out of a human's mouth in the elevator that day—and I watched *The Wolf of Wall Street*."

"I've got to work on that." I'd gotten better or at least that's what my best friends had told me. Maybe they'd developed a filter, too.

Gavin shrugged and took a sip of his water. "Why? They are just words."

"That's what I've been saying!" It was clear he understood me.

"I do have to wonder: do you talk like that around your parents?" he asked with interest.

So, he had brought up my parents. No guy had ever brought up my parents. On one hand, it only seemed fair given that I met his sister and that we were staying in his family home. But I couldn't remember the last time a boyfriend had just casually inquired about my family. "The only time my filter works at 100% capacity is around my parents. I think my mom might have a heart attack if she heard me say crap."

"I can't wait to see you around them." Gavin brushed his thumb over the back of my hand before taking it in his again.

"Oh yeah?" I tried to sound nonchalant as though the idea that Gavin had just suggested he meet my parents wasn't a big deal. Inside, half of me was twerking with joy and the other half of me was shaken. No boyfriend since high school had met my parents. That guy—the one who had taken me to prom—was met at the door by my father, shotgun in hand. I couldn't picture what it would be like to bring a serious, adult boyfriend home. This time the gun might be loaded.

"Yeah," he confirmed. "Actually, that's something I need to talk to you about."

That sounded serious, so it was a good thing that the waiter showed up with our bottle of wine. I took it from him, skipping the unnecessary tasting ritual and poured myself a large glass. Once booze was safely in my hands, I addressed the previous topic. "Talk about what?"

"Imogen told my parents I was seeing you. I know." He held up a hand before I could protest that we had not technically been together at that point. "We weren't really seeing each other at the time, but she's a bit of a psychic when it comes to these things. Anyway, they have been shamelessly calling, emailing, and texting—something I didn't know my mother even knew how to do—and asking when they can meet you." He ran his hand through his hair, that adorable, nervous tic he had. "Suffice it to say, I haven't gotten involved with anyone in a long time. They're chomping at the bit."

Gavin was worried about *me* meeting *his* parents, but it

197

seemed like he wanted me to. It was awfully early for something like that. Yet, it also seemed perfectly natural. The war between my head and my heart rearing its ugly head. Rationally, I realized we hadn't been dating that long. We'd spent some time together and we'd tried to ignore our attraction to one another. We'd known each other a couple of weeks. I might have expected to wait longer to meet most people's parents. Given that I had never met any of my boyfriends' parents either, I didn't really have a typical timetable for these things. My best friends' own experiences weren't helpful. Jillian's mother tended to show up like a hurricane, unannounced and intent on destruction. That's how she had met Liam. Jess's mother hadn't even met Roman until after they were married. I supposed that what Gavin was asking was something safely in the middle. But even as I overthought it, my heart settled on the idea.

"It's cool. If they're anything like you, I'm sure I'll love them." It slipped so easily from my mouth: the L-bomb. Foot in mouth activated. Had I said that out loud? Because the implication of it was pretty clear. *If they're anything like you, I'll love them?* So, I'd been feeling a lot like I was in love earlier. Saying it was a whole other thing. One I wasn't sure how he would handle. It was like I had a relationship destruct button.

But Gavin only smiled and leaned over to kiss me. "I know they're going to love you, too."

Well, that didn't help. It soothed my nerves a little regarding my faux pas, but I didn't know how to take what he said. Did he mean if I loved them, they would love me? Or did he mean that they would love me like he loved me? I took another long swig of wine, hoping I'd find the answer at the bottom of it.

Things were moving pretty fast. In my experience, I was usually the one behind the wheel, pressing the gas. I'd sworn not to be that way in any future relationship I might risk. But it didn't feel like I was the one in the driver's seat here. It wasn't just Gavin speeding along either though. Was it possible that we were both moving at the same rate?

"You look a little pensive," he noted. "I knew I shouldn't have brought up my parents. Forget it."

"No, I want to meet them," I said quickly.

"It feels like we're moving fast, doesn't it?" He'd read my mind. "I don't know what to say, Cassie. I can slow down. It just feels right to me. Normal."

"Honestly? Me, too," I whispered. So I'd moved fast in relationships before, but deep down, I'd always known I was making mistakes. I just wanted to believe that everything would work out in those instances. Mostly, because I'd been so eager to find the one. It was time to confess that to him. "It's just that I've moved fast in relationships before and that's not always turned out well. Usually, I'm more into it than he is. It's just that I've wanted to find the right person for so long. I watched my parents be in love my whole life. They met when they were sixteen, and they've shared everything together."

I stopped, realizing I was unloading a whole lot of emotional baggage on to him. But Gavin handled it as well as he had handled carrying our bags up that hill earlier today. "I know exactly what you mean, actually. My parents are the same way. I can't say that I went out actively looking for love.

I just kept waiting for the right person to come along. My dad told me something once and it stuck with me." He shook his head and took a sip of wine. "I won't scare you off with that one."

I leaned forward, my interest piqued. "If I haven't scared you away already, then you should feel pretty safe that I'm not going anywhere."

"You're amazing," he said, as if I'd just handed him a winning lottery ticket. "I told my dad that I didn't know when I would have time to find the one. It was a couple years ago when I was just getting NorthWest Investments up and running. I dated a few girls off and on in college, but nothing stuck. I'd confided in him that I didn't think I would ever have what he and my mom had. He said to me that life wasn't about finding the right one, it was about reaching her. I'll never forget that."

I sat back and digested his words. Not finding the one—reaching the one? Somehow it made perfect sense. I thought back to the first day of my internship running into Luka and then Danny and then Trevor—a string of boyfriends past to remind me where I had been—and then meeting Gavin.

I hadn't found Gavin. I had reached him.

"Are you sure I haven't scared you off?" he asked after a few moments of silence.

"No," I said softly, "I think you're stuck with me."

"*That's* the best news I've heard all day." He kissed my hand again as if sealing his words as a promise.

"So, you've never brought another woman here?" I tried to emphasis here as in this restaurant, which was not at all what I wanted to know. Thomas had made a big deal about my presence, which had left me with a few questions.

"No, I haven't. I've never felt like bringing anyone I dated to Friday Harbor," he admitted.

I preened a bit at this revelation. Reading between the lines that meant our relationship was different. It also meant...

"Why do you have a drawer full of condoms?" I blurted out, shutting my mouth quickly as our appetizer arrived: a pile of oysters on a bed of ice.

"You really do say whatever comes in your head, don't you?" Gavin mused as he picked one up and slurped it back. "I put them there when we arrived while you were in the bathroom. I didn't want to seem presumptuous, but I, uh, presumed."

"Oh." That made a whole heap of sense. It was the gentlemanly thing to do and as long as he was being responsible I should be, too. We were sleeping together after all. "I'm on the pill. Well, the shot. Less to remember."

"Good to know," he said, sounding genuinely relieved.

"No little Cassies or Gavins." *For now.* Had I actually just thought that? Had the thought of having this man's babies just *appealed* to me? Sure, I was picturing like twenty years from now, but still. What was he doing to me? I scrambled for any change in topic before I overshared those thoughts with him. "I don't get oysters."

Yes, Cassie. I internally rolled my eyes. *Insult his friend's food. That will win you points.*

"Don't eat a lot of oysters in Texas?" he guessed.

"To say the least. I never know what to do—and how are

they an aphrodisiac? They're just chewy," I confessed. "There are no oyster eating lessons on a ranch."

"Let me show you." He picked another up along with a tiny fork and gently moved it around in the shell. "So, you take it like this and you suck it in your mouth, but don't swallow. Just bite it once or twice. You don't have to chew it up. You just want to get all the flavors. Really savor it."

He demonstrated, a look of revelation coming over his face, as he tasted it. I blushed a little recognizing that was how he looked after he'd gone down on me. I gulped some wine and did my best not to get lost in thoughts of that.

"Here." He handed me one.

I took it with some trepidation. Yes, it looked easy. But I had a spectacular ability to make an ass out of myself. I did exactly as he did, except I closed my eyes to try to concentrate on the experience, hoping I could see why he loved them so much.

I sucked it onto my tongue then chewed once. Twice. A salty, sweetness flooded over my tongue. I let it linger for a moment before swallowing.

"It tastes like the whole ocean in your mouth," Gavin said softly. "It's mysterious and unexpected every time kinda like making love."

Oysters were not taking my mind off sex. The rest of the meal was less suggestive. Although still full of foods known for their more sensual qualities: salmon in a butter sauce with a hint of chili pepper, long spears of asparagus, and for dessert a tray of ripe, red strawberries, locally grown, with a pot of melted chocolate and freshly whipped cream. Thomas was one hell of a wingman.

I left pleasantly full but not overly stuffed. By the time we walked back to the house, I'd be ready for more dessert. Gavin offered me his arm and I took it, marveling at the subtle electricity I felt whenever I touched him.

"Look," he said, pointing to the sky, which was clear and full of stars, "a shooting star. Make a wish."

I hoped it would always be like this. Simple and magical. I wished it would be.

Nineteen

THE NEXT MORNING, I WAS ACTUALLY SORE. I LEFT Gavin in bed still sleeping and decided to take a quick shower. The jacuzzi tub looked tempting, but if I played my cards right, I could sneak down and make Gavin breakfast before he was awake. It would be eggs—the only food I knew how to cook—but it was something and he was going to need to rebuild strength after last night.

It took an embarrassingly long time to figure out how to turn on each of the four separate shower heads, since I'd only been blessed with normal showers until this point in my life. But it seemed rude not to enjoy the whole experience. I stepped under the water and allowed the heat to wash over my tired muscles. I felt like I'd done hours at the gym yesterday. It was a cardio plan I could get behind. Gavin was tireless, which probably accounted for why he was still sleeping now.

I'd just begun to wash my hair when a pair of strong hands caught my hips. Startling and getting soap in my eye in the process, I stepped backwards into his embrace. God, his body felt amazing.

"That's the second time I've woken alone," he said. "I don't like it."

My heart did a little flip. Not that this was something to get used to. Tomorrow we would return to Seattle and to our separate lives, which meant figuring out a lot about how this was going to work. For now, I was going to soak up all the romance I could get.

I turned around, splashing water in my eyes to stop the burning from the shampoo.

"You scared me," I accused him, rubbing at them until the irritation started to subside.

"It looks like you're having a hard time. Let me help you." Reaching up, he massaged the remaining shampoo through my hair, his fingers working magic on my scalp as he helped it rinse away. This man really did know all the ways to make me moan. He followed it with conditioner, his hand sliding down to knead my neck for a few seconds as though he sensed how sore I was.

"That feels good," I murmured, allowing myself to press closer to him, the only thing between us a stream of water.

"I want you to feel good, baby." Gavin grabbed a bar of soap and began to lather up his hands. Once they were covered, he began to massage me, rubbing across my shoulders, down to my breasts. He lingered there, rubbing and circling until they began to swell with interest.

"I'm not sure those are as dirty as you think they are," I said wryly.

"If I was concerned about you being dirty, I'd be washing out your mouth."

He might have a point. Gavin continued his attention downward, kneeling on the shower floor and sliding soaped up hands along my thighs down my calves, then back up toward the space between my legs, which he conveniently ignored. I had no doubt that was on purpose. He straightened back up and maneuvered me around so that my back was to him before he slipped his hand to my forbidden zone, which was off-limits to everyone but him.

"I've got to wash this"—he nipped my ear—"so I can get it dirty later."

He continued to stroke me until the soap had washed away, his thumb delving until it settled over my clit. My palms found the tiled wall and braced myself for leverage. I had no problem with his thoroughness. In fact, I rather enjoyed it. Still, it was feeling a trifle one-sided.

"I thought we were taking a shower," I said.

"This isn't how you shower?" he asked. "I'm disappointed. I like the idea of you wet and touching yourself."

"Is that so?" His teeth had found my ear again and he was beginning to nibble. It took all the self-control I had to squirm out of his arms. I stepped away, sliding my hand down the wet plane of my belly and found the spot he'd been so expertly manipulating a moment ago. Gavin watched as I put on a show for him, his eyes hooding with unrestrained desire. It wasn't hard to find something to inspire my exhibition. Not with him standing under the shower, water flowing over his lean form. Little drops had begun to collect in the chiseled lines of his abdomen. They ran down to his groin where they collected off his most impressive organ.

Gavin always wanted to make sure that I felt good. I needed him to know that was important to me as well. Very carefully, so I didn't bite it on the wet tile, I lowered down to one knee and then the other until I was on all fours. I crawled under the water until I was at his feet. Sitting back on my heels, I dipped my hand between my legs again before reaching up with my other one and grasping his shaft. I spluttered a little on the water as I began to suck him off. His hand fisted into my wet hair, urging me on faster. I began to build with him, my fingers massaging furiously until he released his grip on me, reached down and grabbed me under the arms. Gavin lifted my entire body up and slammed me into the tile wall, plunging into me with one powerful thrust.

I lost control. Filter off. "Oh God! Hell, yes!"

This was definitely new territory. Skin to skin. Nothing between us. We had the talk about me being on the pill and we hadn't come to any conclusions, but right now I didn't care. I wove my hands through his hair and crushed his mouth to mine. There was so much water I thought I might drown.

But not in it, in him. I was already lost, crashing against him, surging forward as his hips rolled against me. He had my thighs tightly clasped allowing him to control the amount of leverage he had over me and he used it to slam into me over and over until I was crying his name and a whole lot of other things that would make a porn star blush. I dissolved into him, melting as pleasure lit up every nerve ending in my body. My arms wrapped around his shoulders holding on to him as he continued towards his own release. When he finished, he kissed me as he lowered me carefully onto my feet.

"I think I might have to wash you again." He grinned crookedly as though he was proud of this fact.

I shooed him away, my legs still shaky and one hand firmly planted on the wall. "I'll never be done with the shower if you keep helping me."

"It's built for two," he argued.

"No way," I said. "You can have it in a minute."

I finished up my shower with record speed. Partially, because I expected him to come in and repeat what had just happened at any moment, but also because I wanted to get downstairs and make him breakfast before he finished. As soon as I was out, I sidled past him, having to dart away before he could get his hands on me. Throwing my hair up into a wet mess, I found a shirt hanging in his closet and threw it on. I buttoned it up to a point nearing modesty as I skipped down to the kitchen through the magical forest canopy. I was humming to myself, completely lost in my thoughts, my lips swollen, my face still flushed with post orgasmic glow when I walked into the kitchen and discovered his parents.

Richard Sound was flipping pancakes at the kitchen island while Gavin's mom, whose name I didn't even know yet, sipped coffee. They both looked up at me as I stumbled in and froze in place. At least, I assumed they were his parents. Either that or two people who looked freakishly like him had broken in and decided to cook breakfast.

I didn't know what to say. Was there something to say in a situation like this? I couldn't imagine what they were thinking. A strange girl in their house, wearing nothing but their son's shirt. I scrambled to fasten a few more buttons.

"You must be Cassie." Richard looked up and smiled warmly before returning his attention to the sizzling griddle.

"Are you hungry?" Gavin's mother asked me.

I had just entered an episode of *The Twilight Zone*. Gavin told me last night that they wanted to meet me. I tried to think back on when he possibly could have called them to invite them up here, but I'd kept him pretty busy. Had we all just conveniently wound up here?

"I was going to make some eggs," I said lamely. My fingers found a lock of hair and began to twirl it absently. Was the polite thing to do to excuse myself and go get dressed? Warn Gavin his parents were here before he showed up naked? Sit down, half naked myself, and make conversation? It didn't seem like there was a way to win the situation.

"I'm sorry for the intrusion." Richard lifted a pancake off the griddle onto a plate and then turned to face me. "We couldn't help ourselves. When I saw that Gavin filed a flight plan for the weekend... Well, we decided to surprise him."

"I told you that we should have called him first," his wife said archly. "The girl looks like a deer in the headlights. We scared her. That won't do. We promised Imogen that we wouldn't ruin this for Gavin."

It wasn't coincidence. His family had ambushed us. After having met Imogen, I couldn't say that I was surprised exactly. Except that I was—as was evidenced by the fact that I was standing half naked in their kitchen.

"I'm going to go tell Gavin you're here." That seemed like a safe way out of the situation. It would also provide an opportunity to put on underwear.

"Tell him I made chocolate chip pancakes," Richard called after me.

I heard Gavin's mother scold him as the door closed, "Oh Richard!"

They didn't seem shocked to meet their son's girlfriend in this way. Nor do they seem terribly put off. In fact, it felt as if they were falling all over themselves to impress me. I hustled back up the interconnecting walkway, muttering under my breath the whole time. The first time I had met a boy's family and I hadn't been wearing panties. What were the girls going to say about that one?

Gavin, unlike me, was dressed when I entered his bedroom. He was towel drying his hair, and he dropped it on the bed when he spotted me.

"Hey, I was just about to come..." He stopped the moment he caught sight of my face. "Is everything okay?"

I planted my hands on my hips, took a deep breath and said, "Everything's fine. Your dad wants you to know that he has chocolate chip pancakes downstairs."

I was pretty certain the stricken look on Gavin's face mirrored my own. He definitely hadn't known they were coming. "They didn't."

"Oh they did." I huffed as I started tugging his shirt off. I couldn't find my clothes fast enough. "I'm pretty sure breakfast is getting cold, so we better hurry."

Gavin didn't move. He just watched me as I dashed

around the room hoping to pull myself together enough to not look like a crazy person.

"I'm so sorry," he said

"Don't apologize," I said, glancing over my shoulder to find he was still standing still, "and don't just stand there. Help me find my bra."

Why didn't I pack another? The one from last night was missing in action. I would be damned if I was going downstairs without both a bra and panties this time.

"I can tell them to leave." He joined the search, lifting the covers on the bed and checking on the floor. "Or we can leave. You don't have to meet them like this."

"That would be rude." I stood up and whipped around to face him. "They're here. They came to see you. I'm your girlfriend. That's how this works."

A strange look came over Gavin's face and he strode across the room, grabbed me around the waist and kissed me. Breaking away, he looked past me. "I see a bra."

It had fallen—or been tossed—onto the bookshelf.

I hadn't packed anything that was meet the parents appropriate. Not that I knew exactly what would fall into that category. It wasn't like I'd brought a bunch of stripper clothes or anything. But I hadn't brought another dress or a blouse. Those seem like the appropriate attire for what I was about to do. Instead, I was stuck with a pair of cropped jeans and a nice but somewhat casual tank top. I thought this weekend was about going away. I hadn't expected that I would need to be dressed up. I considered the dress I'd wore to last night's dinner, but I'd left that on the floor as soon as we got in and it had turned into a wrinkled mess. Since Gavin was also in jeans and a T-shirt, I decided to follow suit. I couldn't remember what his parents had been wearing downstairs. I'd been too preoccupied by what I *hadn't* been wearing.

We made our way toward the main house with grim determination. Gavin still hadn't said much, but I got the feeling he was a little pissed.

"What your mom's name?" I whispered, clutching his hand like a life preserver.

"Rebecca," He told me. He breathed a heavy sigh and paused before we went in. "Thank you."

"For what?" I asked him.

"For being you. I'm still sorry to put you in this position. You have every right if you want to run."

"That would be a tad dramatic. Besides they already saw me without underwear on. It can't get much worse." It was worth the look on his face to say it, but I added quickly, "I had that shirt on, remember? I don't think they saw anything. It's just not how I would've chosen to meet your parents."

"Believe me, this isn't how I wanted it to be either."

I did my best to sound upbeat. "Maybe this way there's less pressure."

I would've been obsessing for days over what to wear or worrying about spilling wine all over myself. Now, I didn't need to worry about embarrassing myself, because I already had.

"You're really an optimist aren't you?" Gavin reached for the doorknob. "You ready?"

"As ready as I'll ever be."

It was distinctly more comfortable to enter fully clothed. In the mad dash I'd made to get dressed, they'd set the table and laid out a full breakfast. My stomach rumbled at the scent of vanilla and chocolate chips. I thought I even smelled bacon. At least if they were going to ambush us, they had brought food.

"Morning, honey. Would you like some coffee?" Rebecca Sound beamed at her son, French press in her hand. She looked so much like him: dark hair and blue eyes, although she was more petite than either of her children.

"Mom." Gavin went over and hugged her, kissing her on the cheek. "I wasn't expecting you."

There was no missing the edge to his words.

"I tried to tell your father," she said defensively.

"She did." Richard carried pancakes to the table. "But I didn't listen."

He was where his kids got their height. He looked older than his wife, but in that distinguished way. His hair had grayed but he wore his age with grace.

"You could have at least called," Gavin reprimanded them as Rebecca brushed some invisible lint from his shirt.

"You are too skinny. Are you eating enough?" She bypassed his comments altogether.

"I don't cook," I said apologetically, feeling like I needed to put a foot into this conversation and only realizing at the last moment that it was the wrong thing to say. Foot in mouth struck again.

"Well, that's no excuse. It's not your job to do it for him," Rebecca spoke as though this suggestion was ludicrous. "My son can cook. You look too skinny, too. Gavin, you need to be cooking this girl dinner. I taught you better."

No one had ever called my size fourteen butt too skinny before. I fell in love with his mom on the spot. If things didn't work out with Gavin, I was keeping her.

I watched as Richard Sound, the founder and CEO of one of the most successful businesses in the world, prepared the table and made everyone plates. She obviously believed in this philosophy. No wonder Imogen had such a mind of her own.

"What are your plans for today?" Richard asked as we all sat down and began to take in to our ready-made plates.

I decided to let Gavin field that question. He was the one that knew this island. Besides, he was probably going to have to come up with something. I doubted he had plans to get farther than the bedroom.

I'd just lifted the first bite of pancake to my lips when Rebecca shook her head. "Richard, they were probably going to spend the whole day in bed, having sex like normal twenty-somethings, and you decided this was going to be a family weekend."

The bite of pancake I had just taken lodged in my throat, and I tried to get it back up. Hopefully, my choking would explain the way my cheeks colored. Gavin knocked me on the back as though that would be helpful, but I finally got it back up. I swallowed hard and reached for my glass of orange juice, hoping that Gavin's mother didn't continue to be so forthright.

"Mom, can you try not to kill my girlfriend?" Gavin

requested. He hadn't started eating yet. Instead, he was pinching the bridge of his nose and looking rather ruffled.

"They can have sex later. He has his own wing of the house." Richard seemed oblivious to everything that had happened.

"Dad!"

"You're an adult. Which is why we never see you. Okay, I'm sorry," His dad gave in. "I just want to spend some time with you."

"What did you have in mind?" Gavin asked. "Piling into bed with me and my girlfriend?"

It still sent a thrill bursting through me when he said *girlfriend.*

"We'll call next time," Rebecca promised. She reached over and patted Gavin's hand in reassurance. Then, she turned her attention to me. "So you're an intern at North-West Investments."

I wasn't sure what to make of the tone of her voice. Would his parents not approve of him dating a lowly intern? I guessed there was nothing I could do about that. I nodded. "For the summer."

"With any luck, I'll be able to keep her longer," Gavin said, his voice taking on a suggestive undertone. I knew he meant at the company. I couldn't even consider us not being together.

It was a weird feeling—this certainty that had settled inside me, centering me like an anchor.

"I have to finish school first," I stammered, aware that I was gawking at him.

"But then you'll come back to work there full-time?" she asked.

"I don't know." I dared a glance at Gavin. I didn't want to assume anything. "Gavin might want a break from me during the day."

Oh my God. Had I just said that? To his mother? I bit my lip before anymore presumptive comments spilled out. Rebecca only beamed. She looked like I'd just told her the wedding invitations were in the mail. Gavin squeezed my knee under the table.

"I doubt it," he said.

I melted like the pat of butter on my stack of pancakes.

"What does everyone think of your relationship?" Richard asked, bringing us all crashing back to earth.

"We haven't told anyone yet," I jumped in.

Richard raised an eyebrow at his son.

He disapproved.

Crap.

"Better not keep it a secret. These things always come out. Remember transparency is the key to good leadership," he advised his son.

"As you've told me about 1 million times," Gavin said. "Everyone loves Cassie at the office."

"Of course, they do," Rebecca said as if she had already decided that I was worthy of such affection.

"She could always come work for me," Richard said.

"Are you trying to steal my girlfriend?" Gavin pretended to be offended as he stabbed another piece of bacon off the center plate.

"I'm more interested in the CEO."

Rebecca sighed heavily as if she'd heard this conversation before. "He's got his own company, Richard."

"Then when do I get to retire?"

"When you appoint a new CEO," Gavin pointed out.

This was the first time I was hearing about this. Gavin had said he wanted to build his own business, but he had never mentioned that his father wanted him at Sound Coffee.

"I know you want to make your own mark," Richard said, "but this family built this business and I'd like to keep it in the family. I need someone who will stay true to my vision."

"What about Imogen?" I suggested.

Everyone turned to look at me. Clearly, they had opinions on that idea.

"If we could get her to stay in one place long enough, that might be a possibility." Gavin chuckled at the thought

"Imogen is a free spirit," Richard explained to me. "Maybe in another five years she *might* be ready."

There was a lot of doubt in his words. I bristled a little. Imogen wasn't a kid and I liked her. We were about the same age. Then again, I definitely wouldn't be prepared to take over the reigns of a Fortune 500 company. They might be right.

"Then I guess you get to retire in five years," Gavin said, in a way that suggested this conversation was over.

"So what are you two doing today?" Rebecca said quickly, as though she sensed the topic needed to change.

I looked to Gavin. This was his town. His vacation house. I was just along for the ride. He shrugged. "We hadn't really planned anything out."

"Spend the day with us," his mother said. "I promise we'll be on our best behavior."

"And we won't keep you to out too late." Richard added. Rebecca shot him a scathing look, but he feigned innocence. "What? I heard these two need to get back to bed. It's amazing that they look so young, but they're so tired."

Twenty

THERE WERE EVEN MORE TOURISTS TODAY. THE handful of shops in the historic downtown district were all packed. I didn't see where they could all be coming from. We did our best to stick together as we walked. For the most part, conversation flowed easily, save for a few minutes of bickering here and there between Richard and Rebecca. Despite their arguments, they held hands and stayed close to one another. It was clear they were very much in love, just like Gavin had said. Apparently, good-natured arguments were a Sound family tradition.

Rebecca stopped in front of a storefront and peered inside. "Oh! The gallery has a new artist." She shooed us all inside.

I didn't know much about art, except the poor and starving part. As a college student, I could relate to that easily. Rebecca, on the other hand, was greeted the moment she walked in the door with a friendly hug from the gallery owner. "Let me show you Joshua's work. You'll love it."

Rebecca wandered off with the woman while Gavin, Richard, and I studied a few landscapes. Most looked local. Given how beautiful it was here, it wasn't hard to imagine painters finding inspiration.

"That looks familiar," I said to Gavin, pointing at a landscape that featured a rocky shoreline and gray skies. I looked down to see the name of the piece and realized it was Olympic Falls. "That makes sense. It's where I go to school."

"Do you like it?" Richard asked.

"The painting or the school?"

"Both."

"I can't complain," I told him. "They gave me a full-ride scholarship. I'm a first-generation college student, so that really helped my parents out."

"A full ride?" He sounded impressed. Elbowing his son in the ribs, he pointed at me. "This one's a smart one. Keep her."

"It would help if you didn't try to scare her off," Gavin said, in a wry tone.

Rebecca came back over, positively buzzing about the newest artist, whom she proclaimed a genius with watercolors. She lowered her voice conspiratorially and told me, "I know nothing about art. I just buy what I like."

"Which is everything," Richard added.

She shot him a look and then turned to her son. "Gavin, take your father, so us girls can be alone. These shops are too full for all of us to be together anyway."

"And she doesn't want me to see how much money she spends," Richard told me.

"Come on, Dad. Let's go find some coffee."

The guys left us and we continued to peruse the art. She showed me the new watercolor artist's work. I had to admit it was striking. She'd already bought three pieces.

"This is better," Rebecca said with a relieved smile, as we made our way to the next store. "I'm not one of those women who has to be with my husband all the time. Of course, we usually are anyway. You two are young, so it's natural to want to be with each other all the time.

I laughed at this. "We haven't been together that long. I guess he's not sick of me yet."

I didn't want her to get her hopes up about us, which she clearly already had.

"Well, just remember, stand your ground. He'll respect it. If he doesn't, call me, I'll knock some sense into him," she promised me. "I raised him right."

We spent the rest of the morning ducking in and out of shops. Rebecca was a prolific spender, and no matter how hard I tried to refuse, I kept winding up with more and more shopping bags full of things she had to buy me.

"Imogen doesn't let me buy her anything anymore. You have to indulge me. My children are too independent," she said, a streak of pride in her words. No doubt they had gotten that trait from their parents.

It had been a long time since I'd spent the day shopping with my own mom. I hadn't realized how much I'd missed it. Rebecca felt like a surrogate mother.

We passed the Weekend Café which, if the two days I'd seen it were any indication, was characteristically full. There must always be a wait there. After dinner last night, I understood why. "We ate there yesterday. It was amazing."

"Oh, Gavin's restaurant?" Rebecca said, looking over to the bustling café.

"I thought it was Thomas's restaurant," I said slowly.

"Thomas is the chef, but Gavin owns it." She spoke matter-of-factly, like this was common knowledge. One look at my face and she realized she had let the cat out of the bag. "He didn't tell you, did he?"

"Your son is full of surprises."

"He doesn't like to brag," she explained to me. "Could be worse, I suppose. Richard and I did our best to show him that having money wasn't everything. I think it's stuck."

I thought about how humble Gavin was, how hard he was working to invest in his community and city, how respectfully he treated everyone we encountered. "I think you did a pretty damn good job."

"Thank you," she said sincerely. "He bought the restaurant last year when there was a storm."

I nodded. Gavin had shared that much with me.

"Thomas was hurt when part of the building collapsed and crushed his leg," she continued.

I thought back to the slight limp I noticed when I had first met the man. He was still getting around, but if it was still bothering him after a year, the damage must have been significant.

"The restaurant almost went under while he was recovering. Gavin just bought the place. He insisted on making Thomas half owner, but he wouldn't hear of it. He wants to pay Gavin back. Stubborn men."

"Is there any other kind?" I said with a laugh, while my mind began to wander. So, Gavin didn't tell me everything. He seemed intent on keeping small secrets. Not dangerous or hurtful ones, but rather things that most men might boast about. I didn't have to ask myself why he would do that. Gavin didn't want people to see him that way. He wanted to be his own man. Not a man with money. But I appreciated these glimpses from other people, because they showed me that he was even more amazing behind the scenes when no one was watching. I'd known that already. I'm glad other people got to see it as well.

We ran into the guys a little while later. They were still holding coffee cups from wherever place they had finally found some caffeine.

"Can I have some?" I asked Gavin. He offered me his without objection.

"It's the best coffee on the island," Richard told me.

"I guess you would know," I teased him. It wasn't half bad. A little strong for my taste, but I guessed that the Sound family drank their coffee stronger than the rest of us. "Are you ever going to open a Sound Coffee up here?"

It would make sense to expand. This town had a huge tourism trade. A lot of people would be looking for the familiar brand.

But Richard shook his head firmly. "This coffee shop has been here for twenty-five years. It was here when we bought our vacation home, and it will be here after I die. It's too small of an island support too many competing businesses. There are plenty of Sound Coffees in other places in Washington."

I could see that after spending the day here. Most of the shops were full of unique items. The shopkeepers seemed to dance around one another, trying to offer a wide array of merchandise without stepping on one another's toes. It made spending time down here all the more enjoyable.

"There's the added bonus that I don't get reminded of work," he whispered to me.

Gavin and his mother had begun to walk ahead of us, chatting about something, the subject of which I couldn't catch from this distance.

"Gavin says you're in PR," Richard said to me.

"I'm studying PR," I clarified. "I graduate this year."

"Well, if my son doesn't hire you, we have a pretty robust PR department at Sound Coffee."

I had no doubt about that fact. Still, I didn't want to take advantage of his kindness. "That's so nice of you. I really don't know—"

"You sound like my son," Richard cut me off. "You two seem like two peas in a pod, so I don't expect this advice will make a dent. Gavin is stubborn like his old man. But do yourself a favor and be a little smarter than him. He thinks that no one will respect him if he uses his family connections. The truth is, though, that family is the only thing we have in this life. We have to lift each other up. You can call it nepotism, but at the end of the day your family is loyal before everyone else. That's one of the reasons I hope that someday he'll run my business."

"My family are Texas ranchers," I explained to him. "Not exactly a PR-heavy position. But definitely a family business.

I know what it's like to want to make your own mark. But I also believe family is important."

I did. It was how I was raised. It was why my parents had driven their old car up for me to get to an unpaid internship this summer. It was why I always went home for Thanksgiving.

"You've got two families now," he said in a firm voice.

"Oh, well…" I didn't know what to say to that.

"My son is falling in love with you. That makes you family in my book." Richard looked up at his son walking a few hundred yards ahead of us. "Gavin doesn't give his heart easily. I know he would only choose an extraordinary woman."

"He's had an extraordinary example," I said softly.

"What are you two whispering about?" Gavin yelled over to us.

"Nothing," his dad called back. "I'm telling her embarrassing stories from your childhood. Remember the time you were convinced that there were tiny people in the radio?"

THE SOUNDS PROMISED to show me their boat the next time we were all on the island, an occasion I dreaded a little. I'd spent even less time on boats than I had on planes. I suspected if I was going to get serious with Gavin, I needed to look into the best ways to cope with motion sickness.

As early evening rolled around, my stomach began to grumble, our large late breakfast finally wearing off.

"Shall we sit down somewhere?" Rebecca suggested. "Grab a bite?"

I was grateful for the suggestion, but I wondered if she'd actually heard my hunger pains.

"I could cook," Gavin offered.

"Not tonight. I want to enjoy you," she said to him.

"How about something quick?" Richard suggested.

Something quick in San Juan Island language apparently translated into going to *the* drive-in. It was less of a drive-in and more of a walk-up these days with the amount of tourist foot traffic. The small, blue fast-food joint seemed like it had always been there. The Sounds were greeted by name and I was introduced to the man behind the counter who owned the place.

Gavin didn't let me order. He just returned with a bulging sack of everything. His dad held one for them.

"We lucked out," he told us. "There's a movie in the park tonight: *Bringing Up Baby*."

"Oh!" Rebecca clapped her hands with delight.

I didn't want to admit that I had never seen this movie. My face must have given something away, because Gavin looked at me incredulously. "Don't tell me you've never seen *Bringing Up Baby*."

I shook my head sheepishly "Is it a new one? I don't get to the movies a lot at school"

Being a scholarship student didn't allot for much spending money. Plus, I tended to spend my weekends at Garrett's, the campus bar, with my friends.

"You haven't seen a lot of classics, have you?" Gavin asked.

"How old are we talking?" I asked suspiciously. I was familiar with the John Hughes oeuvre.

"I think we got a classic films virgin," Richard said.

"That is one character flaw that we're going to have to fix," Gavin told me. "Thank God, I was beginning to think you were too perfect. I was going to start checking to see if you were a robot while you slept."

The movie in the park was a popular event. Families and couples were setting up picnics and lounging in lawn chairs. I nearly tripped over a renegade toddler. Gavin caught her and returned her to her frazzled mom.

Rebecca and Richard hopped into Island Mercantile and got two blankets for us to spread out on. Thanks to Gavin's eyes being bigger than his stomach, we had a feast to share. Rebecca lectured both men on their eating habits while they unpacked half of the drive-in's menu.

"What do you think?" Gavin asked, as I took my first bite of my burger.

I rolled my eyes with pleasure.

"It's good," I told him with my mouth still full.

When the movie started, Gavin sprawled across our blanket, resting his head in my lap, and I ran my fingers through his hair. It felt good just to touch him, to be connected and relaxed. The film was the funniest thing I had ever seen. I kept catching Gavin looking up at me with a goofy grin on his face, as if my reactions were as entertaining as the movie. Rebecca and Richard sat on the blanket next to ours, holding each other closely. I couldn't help but glance over occasionally and see what I suspected we would look like thirty years from now. I haven't known what to expect from this weekend when Gavin asked me to go away, but I hadn't expected to feel this way.

I felt like I had come home.

That night there was no discussion after we said good-night and went to his room. We made love slowly, our eyes on each other and our bodies joined, as though we could fuse our hearts into one.

Twenty-One

WHEN I GOT HOME FROM FRIDAY HARBOR, I GAVE Olive the cat my vibrator.

"I won't be needing this anymore," I told her. She seemed distinctly less interested in it, now that it wasn't taboo. Still, she carried it off. I wasn't certain that Lillian would be thrilled with her new toy.

Thanks to the arrival of Gavin's parents, who had come by ferry, we'd been able to swap modes of transportation. It had taken us longer to get home in Richard's Land Rover. But, at least, I wasn't going to spend the whole evening throwing up. His parents planned to fly home later this week. I made them promise to tell me as soon as they had made the journey safely. Richard had just laughed, with a questioning look in his eyes. Apparently, I was the only one who had a healthy fear of small aircraft.

It was late, so I didn't bother to call the girls with an update. I was ready for my bed. Gavin had hinted at me coming over to spend the night at his place, but this weekend had been emotionally overwhelming—in the best possible way.

Still, I needed time to process what had happened between us. I suspected that a night apart now might be one of the last I spent alone. Our relationship wasn't about to slow down. So, knowing that, and with the Majestic Theatre presentation in the morning, I'd chosen my place. I told him that I wanted to pour over my notes. Part of me felt guilty for not thinking about the presentation much while we were gone. Maybe Gavin and I would be good for each other— save one another from our workaholic tendencies.

But when I finally conceded that I couldn't be anymore ready, I found it was hard to sleep without him. Between that and the looming presentation, I tossed and turned all night. I decided I'd take him up on spending the night in the future.

The next morning I chose an ivory wrap dress that was polished, but not too professional, since I tended to feel over-dressed in the office. I gave my reflection a pep talk as I finished my makeup. Dusting on the slightest bit of bronzer, I told myself, "You've got this. You're a badass. No one is more prepared than you."

I wished I believed any of it.

Danny, who remembered I had a presentation, ran out after me on my way to the building and handed me my coffee. "Good luck!"

I made it a few steps away before I remembered the last time I had seen him. "Did you ask her?" I called to him.

"She said yes!" He practically bounced back into Sound Coffee.

That was a promising omen.

The second good sign was waiting for me inside the lobby in a charcoal gray suit and a blue tie that brought out his eyes. I resisted the urge to walk over, grab hold of it and drag him into a dark corner.

George shot me a knowing look as Gavin greeted me. I hadn't told my office friend about my romance, but it was clear he had guessed something was going on. I winked at him as Gavin and I walked toward the elevator, still carefully keeping a professional distance between us. I'd asked him to keep us hush-hush until I felt ready to share. With the presentation today and my intern status, now didn't seem like a good time to let everyone know that we were romantically involved. No matter what his dad said. We'd deal with it later.

"Are you nervous?" he whispered as the elevator arrived. The doors slid open and we stepped inside.

"No," I lied.

Gavin punched the button impatiently as we waited for the doors to close. Once they did, I was in his arms. It was a short elevator ride, which made the urgency of the kiss even more pronounced. I almost wished he'd hit the emergency stop. Gavin stepped away as a chime announced that we had arrived on our floor.

"I missed you," he said with a quick squeeze of my hand before the doors reopened and deposited us onto a chaotic, office floor. Everyone who worked for the company seemed to be here. Some I'd never seen before.

"That's the rest of the preservation committee," Gavin said in a low voice as we walked toward our workspaces. I considered following him into his office, but the presentation was in less than an hour and while the distraction was tempting, I needed to focus. Gavin seemed to understand. He ducked down into my cubicle, where no one could see, and gave me one more swift kiss. "I'll see you in there."

The hour passed like someone had sped up the clocks. Before I knew it, I was standing in the conference room, which was packed full of people, and nervously preparing my PowerPoint. Gavin sat on one side of the table and Imogen on the other. I recognized most of the people sitting next to Gavin and the ones crowded behind him. Most of the people that were with Imogen were strangers. They had to be the rest of the preservation committee. It was like a really tense wedding where people were actually taking sides. Some of Imogen's contingent looked a bit grouchy, but she gave me a bright smile. I wasn't certain if that was to encourage me or because her parents had told her that the weekend had gone well. This weekend I would see if she wanted to go to Skee-Ball just the three of us. I assumed the presentation would go well enough that would be a good idea. I'd definitely be ready to blow off some steam either way.

Since both Trevor and I were preparing project proposals, all questions were saved until the end. I walked the audience through my carefully thought out proposal.

"The Majestic Theater is a Capitol Hill landmark," I began. "NorthWest Investments wants it to continue to be for a long time." I hadn't bothered to go into the state of disrepair the building was in or the squatters who'd occupied it until we took possession. Instead, I focused on everything it had to offer the neighborhood already. "Our vision is a theater that will serve as a community gathering place, not just for classic films like *Bringing Up Baby*," I couldn't help but shoot Gavin a glance. He grinned, "but also for community events, concerts, graduations." I clicked through a variety of stock images that I had gathered for the presentation before pausing on one of our architectural renderings of the restored space. "Concerns that the restoration process will be a burden on the community *should* be taken seriously. It's our goal to work *with* the people who live in the surrounding areas during that time to make the process not only seamless but fun. We want the Capitol Hill community to know that we are part of their family."

This part of the pitch had come to me late in the night, inspired by my time spent with the Sounds. "We'll be hosting a variety of movie nights and community events. There will be fundraisers, which aren't necessary to our budgets. Instead, they will foster a communal sense of ownership— that sense of unity is what we hope to achieve with the newly-restored Majestic Theater throughout are very long relationship with the theater and its patrons, past, present, and future."

More than a few people clapped when I wrapped up. Since there were no questions, I grabbed my stuff to get out of the way so that Trevor could make his presentation. Gavin gave me a discreet thumbs up as I squeezed past him. I found a spot toward the back of the room, more than a few people scooting out of the way to give me some space.

"Great job," the guy next to me said. A few others smiled. Until the question and answers portion allowed the preservation committee to respond, I wouldn't know how everyone felt. Right now, I was soaring though. Not in a terrible, stomach-turning Cessna way, but rather I felt lighter than air. There had been a lot of great nonverbal feedback from the audience during the presentation. People were smiling and nodding. I had to take that as a good sign. Past any of that, it was over.

The room fell silent as Trevor began his presentation. He hadn't opted for a simple PowerPoint like me. Instead, he had come up with some type of strange, movie-style trailer. It flashed images of the theater in its current state of disrepair while playing ominous music.

"The restoration of the Majestic Theater shouldn't be seen as a blight on the community," he said, and I cringed. He already sounded hostile. "Instead, it should be seen as what it is: the gentrification of a dying landmark. NorthWest Investments is its savior."

Even from the back of the room, I saw Gavin's shoulders go rigid. I was going to have to give him a back rub later. He might have to give me one, too. This was getting intense.

Trevor's presentation didn't get better from there. Somehow, he managed to insult our company, the preservation committee, the neighborhood, even the historic trust that oversaw many of the nation's landmarks. He ended with, "This isn't a question of if, but when. Without us, the Majestic Theater will be nothing more than a memory."

So, he wasn't wrong exactly, he'd just missed the point about soothing the preservation committee's anxieties—the public relations part.

When Trevor was finished, Gavin got to his feet, with a blank expression on his face.

"Thank you for that." He didn't sound grateful at all,

but he kept his opinions to himself. "As we said earlier, we're now going to open the floor to questions. Please address your questions to the entire group, and whoever is best suited to answer them will jump in."

He looked to Imogen, who still seemed confused by the final presentation. That didn't stop a flurry of questions from erupting from her entire group. Some of them were easy to answer. What did our timeline look like? One year. Others were a little harder. How could it be a restoration if we were gutting the building? Answer: we didn't have a choice given its condition. I jumped in whenever possible to answer questions, but more often than not, Trevor beat me to the punch, displaying his keen *lack* of tact. We weren't the experts here, but that was PR, organizing all the concerns of an entire company and succinctly coming up with a response on the spot. A few of the engineers I'd consulted, nodded enthusiastically whenever I spoke about the construction process. They weren't the types to speak publicly, I was their mouthpiece. For the first time, I felt like I really knew what I was doing. All those years in classes had paid off.

When it was all finished, everyone looked to Imogen, the spearhead of the organization, for her comments. "First, I'd like to thank you all for taking our concerns so seriously." Her eyes flashed to Trevor as if to warn him to stay silent. "We see the Majestic Theater as a historical landmark and we want it to continue to be a point of pride for the neighborhood. I think I speak for all of us in saying that Cassie's plan understands the spirit of what this theater means to the community. With open communication and a clear vision, we're excited to see what NorthWest Investments can do for our neighborhood."

This time it wasn't a smattering of claps, everyone around me broke into applause. The people standing next to me congratulated me and patted me on the back. Trevor had pushed himself farther back into the corner, as though he was trying to fade from sight. It felt good to have it over with and even better that I managed to build a bridge between these two organizations.

Gavin stood and waited for the applause and chatter to die down. "Amazing job. Let's hope that we don't screw up Cassie's plan while she's off finishing college." Almost everyone laughed. A few of the preservation committee members looked around in surprise. "I wanted to take a moment to speak with you, because it's pretty hard to get us all in one place at the same time in the summer."

From the back someone yelled, "We need a bigger office."

"I'll keep that in mind," Gavin said dryly. "This actually isn't about the restoration, so my apologies to our guests. Although, it somewhat concerns them, too." He cleared his throat as if needing a second to collect his thoughts. What was he up to? "I unexpectedly spent the weekend with my father."

"Did he finally convince you to take over his company?" Agnes called from the end of the table.

There was a round of nervous laughter and some shifty-eyed glances. No one wanted to lose Gavin to Sound Coffee, but they seemed to realize that it was a possibility. I hadn't known until then, how many people knew about his dad, but Gavin believed in transparency. He might have taken his mom's name to put on a business card, but he hadn't hidden who he was. That would have been impossible.

"No, but he did remind me of a few things." The seriousness of his voice instantly quieted the room again. "He reminded me that a good boss is transparent. *Honest.*"

Gavin looked directly at me in the same moment that I realized what he was about to do. It was like the seconds before a crash. I could see it coming, but I was powerless to stop it from happening. All I could do was watch.

"So, in the spirit of that, I wanted to tell you that I'm seeing someone in the office."

This was met with a buzz of conversation, people began whispering under their breath and scouting the room as if they were looking for a suspect. No one looked upset. I didn't expect anyone to get out the pitchforks and form a lynching mob. Still, silently I prayed that he didn't name me. I thought he'd understood that I wasn't ready to be in the spotlight in that way.

"It's serious," he continued.

Oh no. No. No.

"How long have you been seeing her?" someone asked before quickly adding, "or him."

Either things weren't as transparent as Gavin thought, or he really dated so little that no one knew for sure if he was straight.

Gavin only smiled. "Her. Not that long. I wanted to be sure before I said anything. Because I think there's an office pool going around about whether or not I would die a bachelor. I didn't want to screw up the stakes."

"It's up to $200!" Agnes quipped from the back.

Imogen was trying to hide a smirk as all this unfolded. She dared a peek at me and it fell from her face. Her lips parted like she might leap in and stop this runaway train before he wrecked everything, but she didn't speak. Her eyes closed as if bracing herself as he continued.

At least, someone in the room was on my side when Gavin looked directly at me and ended the suspense. "I know that we all respect each other's personal lives here and that this isn't a big deal, but I wanted to be honest about it, and tell you that I'm dating Cassie Hart."

Every eye in the room swiveled around to stare at me.

Twenty-Two

I MADE IT TO MY DESK BEFORE I STARTED TO CRY. I'd left my cell phone there, afraid it would ring in the middle of my presentation. Picking it up now, I saw that my best friends had texted me a half-dozen good luck messages and inquiries about the weekend. I couldn't bring myself to respond. It had taken all of my strength to keep a smile on my face as I maneuvered my way out of that conference room. Most people wanted to congratulate me on a job well done. Only a few mentioned my new relationship with Gavin. To his credit, no one seemed angry. He'd told me that no one would mind.

That wasn't the point.

I felt a presence looming behind me and I spun around in my chair ready to face him. But it was only Trevor.

"Come to gloat?" I asked him.

"I came to tell you that your presentation was great." He shoved his hands in his pant pockets and leaned against the cubicle opening.

"Sure," I said flatly.

"No!" He shook his head with earnest sincerity. "You really seem to know what they want. You're really special, Cassie. I should have told you that before."

I blinked, trying to help my brain process what was happening. Trevor was *complimenting* me. This couldn't be good.

"I know what Gavin said back there. But you can't have been seeing each other that long." He straightened up and took a step closer to me. "What we had was special. I didn't see that before."

We'd bypassed not good and headed directly for very, very bad.

"Because you weren't looking." This was unbelievable. Another man had just laid claim to me. Now my ex-boyfriend had decided that we should get back together. Apparently, they'd missed the memo that this vagina was owned by no man. I didn't let him continue. "If you think you can just decide what's best for me— for our relationship, which is *soooo* over—then you're wrong. I'm not just sitting around here waiting for you to come around. I have plans and hopes and goals. I deserve someone who respects me all the time. Not just when it's convenient for him."

"Cassie, I—"

I cut him off. "Goodbye, Trevor."

He stalked away, muttering under his breath. Gavin had been standing behind him, watching the whole thing.

"Can I talk to you?" he asked softly. He'd overheard. He knew that my rant hadn't been directed entirely at Trevor.

"Do I have a choice?" I shot back.

"My office?"

I wanted to say no—that whatever he had to say to me he could say in front of the entire office, because apparently, we had *no* secrets from them. But I still had a measure of dignity left inside me. It was getting smaller by the second and probably couldn't handle a very public argument, so I stood up and marched towards his office. He followed me inside and shut the door. I cringed, wondering what everyone would make out of that.

"Did Trevor—" he began.

"I don't care about Trevor," I interrupted.

"You're upset," he said.

"Hell yes, I am. You made a promise to me." He needed to know how bad it hurt me that he'd made such an important announcement without my consent. "This was a big decision. It took me a long time to convince myself that there wasn't anything wrong with seeing you. I needed a little longer to prepare to face everyone in the office every day as not just their colleague but your girlfriend."

"I understand that," he said, spreading his hands in surrender.

"Obviously, you don't, or you wouldn't have told everyone, including the preservation committee that you were banging your intern."

Gavin winced as though I'd thrown a rock at him. "That's not what this is between us. We both know that. You think I would have told them about you if it was just about sex?"

"I think that if it was more—like you claim it is—you would've respected me enough to give me the time I needed before we told the world. I mean, first your parents and now the office."

"I thought you had a good time with my parents." His voice was so quiet that it sent a shiver rippling through me.

I'd hit my mark. I wanted to wound him, throw him off balance, like he had done to me. I didn't mean half of what I was saying, but that was the thing about fighting. It was dirty and there were no rules. Somewhere a small voice warned me that I was taking things too far. Still, I continued, "I didn't really have a choice, did I? It seems like I don't have a lot of choices around you. I mean, are we going to move in together? Are we getting married? When would you like your first baby? Just give me a timeline."

"That's not fair." The words rumbled through him like the first roll of thunder before the rain began. I'd pushed us past heated discussion into our first real argument.

There was a knock on the door. We both glared at it as though the significance of it being closed had been ignored.

"Give me a few minutes," Gavin yelled out.

"I understand that I blindsided you," he started, keeping his voice low enough that whoever was standing outside the door wouldn't hear us fighting. "I have to think not only about our relationship but my relationship with all of these people as well. I didn't want to hide my feelings for you. I'm not ashamed of them."

"You think I'm ashamed?"

"I don't know what's up with you," he admitted.

Oh, that was the final straw. I exploded, like an undetonated landmine that he'd accidentally stepped on. "I told you I wasn't seeing anyone, and you finagled your way into a date!

I mentioned that I had a habit of moving too fast, and you step on the gas! I've barely processed how I feel about you and you're shouting it from the rooftops."

"I thought we were on the same page." Now Gavin didn't look wounded, he looked devastated.

I hadn't just hurt him, I found the one thing that might destroy us. He'd taken steps during our entire courtship to make sure he wasn't crossing a line. At every turn he'd given me a chance to say what I wanted and he always made sure it was okay before he took the next step. Had he pursued me? Yes. Had I allowed that? Yes. I was every bit as culpable regarding what had happened between us. But that was the thing about lovers' quarrels, it was much easier to overlook the facts in favor of wallowing in my feelings.

The door to the office opened and Imogen peeked inside. "I'm sorry to interrupt, but I need to be going. I just wanted to say goodbye."

She looked between us nervously. Either we weren't being as quiet as we thought or she'd known this was coming. She'd picked up on my mood when we were in the conference room.

"It's okay," I told her. "We were just finishing up here. I had to tell Gavin that I was reconsidering my relationship with NorthWest Investments."

"Cassie," Gavin said, taking a step toward me. "Don't."

"I'll finish out my internship," I said to him before turning to her. "I'll make certain that whoever takes over the Majestic Theater project is well prepared."

I strode past both of them, bypassing my desk, and making a beeline for the bathroom. The first tears hit my cheeks as soon as the door swung shut behind me. I locked it, thankful that there was one place where I wouldn't be interrupted. A few minutes later there was a gentle knock on the door.

"Cassie?" Imogen's voice called through the door.

I swiped at my tears, but there was no way to hide my blotchy face. I cracked open the door and peered out. That was all she needed. She pushed inside and locked it behind us.

"Are you okay?" she asked.

"Did he send you?"

She shook her head. "I'm here on my own. No agenda. Although, he is pretty upset. It reminds me of the day our dog died."

That wasn't making me feel any better. I couldn't explain it to her. Imogen and I were the same age. We might have been friends. However, this was something only Gavin and me could work through. "I'm not ready to talk about it."

"I understand." She handed me a slip of paper. "That's my number. I wanted you to have it. Look, Gavin can be a pain in the ass. Believe me, I know. But he loves you."

"I'm getting really sick of everyone saying that like it makes it okay." The fact was Gavin hadn't even said it to me yet. She didn't know that. But, if it was going to be everyone's excuse for him acting in my best interest without my consent, that was going to be a problem.

"It doesn't excuse him," she agreed, "but you should know it all the same."

"I do know, but I'm not sure if I can get past this." That was the truth. I was too close to the anger and hurt to see whatever might be on the other side for us. If there was anything at all.

"Call me if you want to get a drink," she said with genuine concern.

I finished out the day, able to get away with making small talk with a few people. I refused to cry any time someone made a joke about my relationship with Gavin, even though my heart broke a little more each time.

I had no doubt the news of Gavin's announcement had filtered down to the receptionist's desk, so I practically ran out of the building as soon as five o'clock hit. At least, the apartment would be a sanctuary. Lillian would be at work. When I got home, it was blessedly quiet. Olive was batting around her new purple friend and she looked up when I came inside. I shut the door and collapsed against it as the tears began to flow. Other than my cry in the bathroom, I hadn't given in to this pain inside me. Now it consumed me.

"Cassie? Is that you?" A concerned voice called from the couch and I nearly jumped out of my skin. Walking the few steps into the living room, I found the last person I expected to see and the best friend I needed to talk to the most.

Twenty-Three

JESS WAS HOME FROM MEXICO, TANNED AND freckled. She hadn't told me, thinking it would be a fun surprise, and I'd met her in tears.

"I hope those are happy tears," she said as I rushed to give her a hug.

"I wish," I croaked, my throat swollen and raw.

She didn't push me for details, she just let me cry on her shoulder for who knows how long before I finally sat back, feeling completely drained, and ready to spill my guts.

"Pizza?" she asked, but it wasn't really a question. She ordered while I went to the bathroom and cleaned up.

Looking into the mirror, I discovered I was a hot mess with raccoon eyes and mascara streaks down my cheeks. My hair had gone flat as though the day's events had deflated it, too. I washed off all my makeup, put my hair into a bun, and slipped into my bedroom to find something more comfortable to wear. When I reemerged in my pajama pants, Jess had changed into hers.

"Where's your husband?" I asked her, looking around as though Roman might appear at any moment.

"He headed back to Olympic Falls. I told him I would take the ferry tonight," she said, quickly tacking on, "or tomorrow."

"Tomorrow," I confirmed. I was going to need a few hours to work through this and I'd rather face it with her.

Of my two best friends, Jess was the reasonable one. It was the reason why it had been such a shock when I found her hooking up with our former professor. She was living proof that love didn't always make sense. But while she might have taken a gamble on love, she knew how to keep a cool head. She planned to become a doctor, which meant she knew how to listen and then cut to the chase. It was exactly what I needed.

"Tell me what happened." She settled onto the couch, crossing her legs underneath her, and waited.

The story came out of me in fits and spurts. Some of it she already knew, but I repeated anyway. I needed to remind myself how I had gotten here. The pizza arrived about the time I got to his parents showing up at Friday Harbor. We took a short concessions break, grabbed some plates and she dug into a slice while I dug back into the story. When I got to today and Gavin's big announcement, she gasped.

"So, he told the entire office that you two were seeing each other?" She tossed her pizza on the plate as though she'd lost her appetite. "I can't imagine."

"You mean, you wouldn't have wanted Roman to announce to the entire faculty that you two were sleeping together?" I asked dryly.

"No, I wouldn't." She scooted closer to me and wrapped an arm around my shoulder. "But both Roman and I were kind of stupid about our relationship. Not being honest almost got us both in trouble. Remember?"

She had a point, one I didn't want to consider. Not while I wanted to be mad at Gavin.

"When the school found out, the disciplinary committee considered kicking me out. His department head spoke to him. It could've been really bad."

I read between the lines. "So, you're saying I should understand why he told everyone?"

She was the rational one. I knew she was right. That's why I was confiding in her now. That didn't change that I didn't like her response.

"He should have talked to you about it first," she conceded, "and he definitely shouldn't have agreed to keep it a secret and then told everyone anyway."

"Agreed! What is up with that?" At least we were on the same page there.

"Did you ask him why he chose today to tell everyone?"

She'd made another excellent point. I remembered for a second that she had considered being a lawyer like her sister before settling on medical school. She would've made a damn fine attorney. She could really cross examine any situation.

"I didn't," I admitted in a small voice.

"So, I guess you didn't give him a chance to explain why he thought it was really important for everyone to know?" she pressed.

"No." Now she really had me.

"Look, I understand why you're upset. I would be, too.

He blindsided you. But I think one of the reasons you're so angry is that things are just moving really fast. Somewhere deep down, I think you wanted to put the brakes on. You just have to figure out why that is."

"I love him," I said in a soft voice. It was the first time I'd said the words out loud.

"I know," Jess said soothingly. She hugged me close to her. "Don't freak on me, but I think that scares you."

"I'm going to say something really stupid now," I warned her.

"Judgment free zone," she promised.

"I don't think I've ever really been in love before. There I said it. I, Cassie Hart, the girl who is always in love, didn't really known what I was talking about for the last, oh, ten years of my life. I've been perpetually in love with someone since puberty, building futures in my head, and planning my life with a host of Mr. Wrongs. Why am I so afraid to do that now that I've found Mr. Right?"

"Because now you actually have something to lose." Jess had always been the wise one. Jillian was good for being angry and burning things down with, but Jess was the one you wanted when it was time to face facts. Now that she'd found her own happily ever after, she had more insight than ever.

"Do you think I've lost him?"

She shook her head with a smile. "It's not that easy. Love is actually hard. Love is sacrifices and compromises. Love is work. It's being angry and storming out of the room and then walking right back into it. So, no, I think that what you two have is real. Right now, things suck between you two.

But, in my experience, once you've found the one you'd go to hell and back to stay with them."

"I didn't find him," I whispered, "I reached him."

"It will work out." There was no doubt in her words.

How had I come this far? How had Gavin come into my life and I'd already tried to ruin things between us. "I'm not ready yet."

She seemed to understand what I meant. I wasn't ready to face Gavin. I needed to get a hold of myself. I needed to understand and except that this was frightening and fresh and raw—and I needed to have faith—or learn to have faith —that he would still be there no matter how crazy I got.

Because I might have reached Gavin, but I needed time to accept that I deserved him.

I CALLED in sick to work the next day. It wasn't the most mature move, but I justified it because Jess had returned. I hadn't taken a single sick day all summer and I'd worked overtime, I could have one day to clear my head. Gavin called about an hour after I was supposed to be in, but I let it go to voicemail. I would talk to him. Soon. But not yet.

The fact was, that I didn't trust myself yet. I needed to be clearheaded. While I was ready to accept that our relationship was going to take some work, I needed to find the right words to let him know where my lines were. I had no reason to suspect that he wouldn't respect them. Yes, he had expressly gone against my wishes. With a good night sleep, I could see why he had done it. I didn't agree with him, but I understood. That one lapse in judgment didn't erase all of the times he'd shown an exceptional magnitude for thought-fulness and respect.

Jess and I stayed in bed until an embarrassingly late hour, only getting up to grab food or go to the bathroom. We watched bad TV and she told me about her summer.

It was hard not to be in a good mood when you were around someone who was so in love. Even that gave me hope. Jess and Roman had faced their own obstacles and they'd found a way around them together. She was right, all of the hard stuff was what made love great.

We'd just begun to debate whether we should go out for take-out or order pizza again, when Jillian called us. The second we answered the video chat, I could see from her face something was really wrong.

"Guys," she said, her voice cracking.

Like that, all of my problems went out the window. Our best friend was on the other side of the world and I wanted to be there hugging her immediately.

"I finally got to see that specialist," she said.

Both Jess and I went rigid. Jillian had early onset Parkinson's. One of the reasons she had gone to Scotland, was to try to see a renowned specialist in Edinburgh. It had been her boyfriend Liam's idea—and we thought a clever ploy on his part to get her to consider moving there after graduation. The two of them were pretty serious, but nothing had been decided yet—that we knew of. I wondered if that was about to change.

"What did he say?" Jess asked in a clipped tone. If Jillian was going to be upset, she would be all business. Our best friend's diagnosis had been what pushed her to go for med school. She'd been by Jillian's side through this whole roller coaster.

"It's bad," she said, starting to cry. "I thought I would have a little longer. Maybe Liam and I would have a chance for a normal life. Now, it all feels off the table."

Jess shook her head. "You should have at least 10 years until --"

"Try five," she interrupted her. "I wanted to go to grad school. I wanted to have kids. I wanted to have Liam's kids."

She was getting increasingly upset. We heard a shuffling behind her and suddenly Liam appeared on screen, he wrapped his arms around her shoulders and held her close. I heard him whisper, "We can still have all those things, chicken."

We let her cry for a minute, all of us silent, as I held back my own tears. Suddenly, my own relationship issues felt ridiculous. Love was messy and life wasn't guaranteed. Why was I trying so hard to control both?

"I just needed to tell you," she said finally. "I knew it wouldn't feel real until I did, and I need this to be real."

"When are you coming home?" I asked her, no longer able to keep the question at bay. I'd been avoiding it for months, afraid of her answer.

"I'll be back before the fall semester starts," she promised. "It looks like Liam might be able to extend his student visa."

None of us said what we were thinking. There was a really easy way for Liam to get his visa extended. I'd never made the suggestion before because, well, I suspected we might lose Jillian to Scotland if he ever asked her to marry him. But seeing them together now—having found my own other half—I couldn't imagine how hard it would be if they were separated. He was her rock. She was his light. They needed each other.

Liam promised to look after her and cheer her up until he got her back home in weeks. We promised to be waiting at the airport as soon as she arrived. Then we hung up.

"Wow," I breathed. "Perspective."

"Don't mix up her relationship with yours," Jess said.

"It just makes me feel a little silly for being so upset."

"You have a right to your feelings. But you know one thing that Jillian and Liam have learned to do really well?"

I shook my head. "Is it something dirty?"

Jess smirked. "Besides that. They learned to talk. They stopped running away from all the things that scared them. Remember how Jillian used to pretend she wasn't sick?"

"Yep." Jess had a point. If those two could face that, then I needed to woman up and confront my own fears. I just had to have faith that Gavin would be there facing them beside me.

Twenty-Four

THE NEXT DAY GAVIN DIDN'T COME TO WORK. I gave him space. I'd accused him of a lot of things and then I've refused to answer his phone calls. If he was going to play hooky, then I could respect that. When he didn't come to work on Thursday, I began to worry. By Friday, I was a disaster.

Since I hadn't wanted to be the subject of office gossip, I tried to act like nothing was wrong. I kept up my running jokes with George and got us coffee each day. I chatted with people and endured the good-natured ribbing about my new relationship. I continued my work on the Majestic Theater project.

Now, however, after our big fight, I had to wonder if I wouldn't be seeing this through. I had been the one to say I wouldn't come back for a job here. I had promised Imogen to leave everything in good hands, though, and I would do that. There was plenty of work to keep me busy, but nothing could keep me from being distracted.

Through it all, I checked my phone religiously. I'd sent Gavin one text. A peace offering of sorts. A digital olive branch that simply read 'ready to talk' and nothing else. I left the punctuation off the end on purpose. I figured if he wanted to see it as a command and come running, that was fine. If he needed to see it as a question, then I would give him space to respond when he was ready to talk. The trouble was, that he was taking too long to decide. I was going crazy.

Jess had returned to Olympic Falls and her husband, which gave me a whole lot of time to overanalyze the situation. Because I didn't want to add to Jillian's already full emotional plate, we hadn't been discussing it over text. Jess seemed to feel that'd she helped me as much as she possibly could, even though, she continually offered to listen. I knew this was something I had to do alone. If I continue to analyze it, I'd wind myself so tightly that I might never get myself untangled from this situation.

Instead, I went through the motions. I went to work, I ate, I showered, I slept. Well, I actually didn't sleep. That was pretty impossible, since the bed was the place I missed having Gavin the most. We'd only spent a couple nights together and somehow my body already saw him as home. Without him next to me, I didn't feel as safe. I didn't feel as comfortable. I wanted his warmth. I wanted his arms. I wanted him.

I left work on Friday and headed home, wondering what to do. I was going nuts. So, I did the only thing I could think of, I called his sister.

"Hello?" she answered cautiously, and I realized I probably didn't show up on her caller ID. Thank God, she'd answered. I wouldn't have had the nerve to leave a voicemail.

"Hey Imogen, it's Cassie."

"Cassie!" She sounded genuinely overjoyed to hear from me. Maybe she was home babysitting her sad sack of a brother. Or was that too much to hope for? That he had been as miserable without me this week as I had been without him? "I was hoping you'd call."

"Yes, but it's for a pathetic reason," I warned her.

"You're looking for Gavin," she guessed.

"He hasn't been into work all week. I was pretty mad at him."

"That I know," she said. "It's been like a morgue here. I had to force him to eat and shower."

"Really?" Okay, so I sounded a little too excited about that. It was just good to know that he hadn't run off to marry a Las Vegas showgirl or something.

"I think he's on his way to Friday Harbor," she told me. "He said he just needed to get away and think and he took a bag. I could check to see if he filed a flight plan."

"When did he leave?" I forced myself to ask.

"About ten minutes ago."

There wouldn't be time to wait for her to call. He'd be on his way to the airfield. My stomach sank, but I realized that I still stood a chance if I left right now. "Do you think I could catch him?"

"Traffic's murder down here. If you run, you might make the plane."

I hung up with a quick goodbye and a promise to go out for drinks soon. Gavin was leaving—flying. My stomach did a nose dive, but I ignored it. I didn't have time to let my nerves get the best of me. If he was going to Friday Harbor, I would go with him. I'd go wherever he went, so long as we could finally talk.

Gavin was a little bit closer to the airfield than I was, since I was coming from the east. I was still in my work clothes and heels, and I had maybe a quarter of a tank of gas left. Friday night traffic would slow him down. Plus, there was the fact that Gavin was a cautious driver. I drove like a bat out of hell. The odds weren't in my favor, but it wasn't a lost cause.

Traffic was as terrible as I expected. My filter wasn't working, so I was well aware of the terrible things I was yelling at other drivers as I tried to manipulate my way through the gridlock. It was a little less than 8 miles from the condo to the private airfield. In Seattle driving conditions, it would take me approximately the rest of my life to get there.

I laid on the horn, flipped on my turn signal, and darted over into another lane that was moving faster. Gavin only had to go from his apartment downtown to the airfield, which according to my GPS was less than 2 miles. Still, Imogen had said the traffic was terrible in her part of town. It was the only hope I had and I clung to it like a life raft.

Given the later hour, the airfield was mostly deserted, except for some flight crews, who glared at me as I flew past them in my Toyota and drove toward the hangers.

I spotted Sound One waiting for her turn to taxi down the runway.

Jumping out, I didn't bother to turn off the car, only then realizing I hadn't changed out of my heels. I kicked them off and started to run. I made it to the plane as the propeller started to rotate. Yanking open the passenger door,

I hauled my ass inside. Gavin's hands rested on the controls and he whipped around in surprise. I couldn't hear him, even though his lips were moving. A few seconds later, the engines began to die, and I realized he wasn't going to take off. That was a relief. If I'd had to make the flight in my bare feet with no barf bag, I would have. But it wouldn't have been my first choice.

Gavin unbuckled and jumped out of the plane, tossing his headphones onto the seat. I opened the door and realized how hard it was going to be to get out with no shoes on, when he appeared on my side of the plane.

"What the hell are you doing?" he demanded.

I had no idea how many safety regulations private pilots had to follow, but I got the sense I'd just broken every one of them.

"I don't want you to leave." I said. "Not just because I don't want to have to stay in this plane and fly with you to have this conversation, but because I miss you. And I need you. And I love you."

Gavin's head fell forward, obscuring his face momentarily before he reached up, his lips twitching slightly, and lifted me out of the plane.

"Is that so?" he asked, as he set me on my feet. Frowning at my lack of shoes, he lifted me again slightly so that my feet were on his and not the hot tarmac.

"I love you," I repeated. It seemed like the most important part right now. Not my shoeless state or that I'd nearly caused him to crash on the runway. None of it seemed to matter as much.

"I knew that the second you got on the plane," he

murmured. He still wasn't looking at me, but his hands held my hips tightly as if he wouldn't—couldn't—let me go.

"I understand if you have to go think about things," I said in a small voice. "But I couldn't let you leave without you knowing how I felt."

"What do you want?" he asked.

"You," I said without question.

"Are you sure? You didn't seem like you wanted me the other day." He looked up, his blue eyes shining with pain. He was still hurt, despite my declaration. I couldn't blame him for that. I'd put him through the wringer. We'd put each other through it.

"This is new," I said slowly as I gained confidence. "It scares me a little. I didn't want people to think that the reason I got a job was because I was seeing you. I wanted to feel like my accomplishments were my own."

"Cassie," he said, shutting his eyes for a moment, as if he was shouldering a heavy burden. When he reopened them his gaze locked on mine. "Let me make something clear to you. I built NorthWest Investments. It means the world to me. *You mean more*. I would rather have you. If you want to leave your own mark, then I'll be by your side while you do it. If you want to do it together, then we can start something new. But you can't sabotage us. You can't second-guess us. Have faith in us."

He added softly, "I do."

"Sometimes I'm a neurotic, crazy bitch," I confessed to him. He started to shake his head, an involuntary, instinctive reaction to hearing a woman say that about herself, no doubt. "Seriously, if you understood the amount of analysis and self-doubt I deal with every day, you wouldn't be surprised when I did something completely insane, like trying to wreck the best thing that ever happened to me. I promise that I'll try to do better if you promise to have a little patience with me when I falter. Oh, and also, to let me know before you make major life decisions for us."

"Telling everyone that we're together is a joint life decision?" he asked. I thought I saw a smile creeping onto his lips.

"Hell yes, it—" I began, but his mouth was on mine before I could continue my tirade. He kissed me deeply. It was full of longing and apology and hope and promise. All the doubts, all the fear, all the second-guessing vanished instantly. In his arms, I had my answer.

When we finally broke apart, Gavin's eyes searched mine. "Then I guess I better tell you this."

I raised a questioning eyebrow. Whatever it was I could handle it as long as I was here in his arms.

"I love you, Cassie Hart. I'm not going anywhere. I want you. I don't want easy. I want crazy and neurotic and brilliant and clever and kind. I want *you*."

"I want you, too," I whispered.

He kissed me again, more softly this time. I knew it would be the first kiss of a lifetime shared together, so when he took my hands and glanced at the plane, I wasn't scared when he asked, "Where do you want to go?"

Because I'd reached my decision. "With you."

Epilogue

May

"Cassandra Marie Hart."

I walked up the stairs toward the stage, hoping I didn't step on my graduation gown. Why had I chosen such impractical shoes? It was a serious character flaw. I paused as the Dean handed me my diploma, looking out into the crowd I spotted my family. They weren't hard to find, because despite the admonishment at the beginning of the ceremony to wait for applause until everyone had walked, they were screaming and cheering. Gavin was smashed into a seat beside my dad and my mom. He wasn't cheering—following rules—but he didn't have to, his face was filled with pride. I gave them an embarrassed wave and trekked down to the other side of the makeshift platform.

The rest of the ceremony passed in a blur. Jillian received her diploma a few dozen people later. She stopped and did the rock 'n roll sign to her people, probably in a move to see if she could ruffle her mother's feathers. Jess was the last of us to officially graduate, since she'd hyphenated her name. I cheered for each of them. We'd gotten through this.

Together.

My girls joined me in the waiting area off the stage as the rest of the class was called. I wrapped my arms around each of them, giving them a big hug. In some ways this with the end of an era. We'd all be going off to do our own thing soon. Jess was headed off to Oregon to medical school at a university that had a position available for Roman. Jillian was going even farther. I didn't want to think about the distance that would soon be between the three of us. Or how I wouldn't be able to see them every day. Our lives were starting. It was exciting and terrifying at the same time. But I knew that no matter what, they would be a phone call or a plane ride away.

"We did it," Jess said with a shriek. It was uncharacteristically giddy of her. I knew how she felt.

"And I didn't fall on my face," I told them.

"And I didn't throw up!" Jillian said, equally excited.

Jess looked back at the stage and out to the quad where the ceremony had taken place. She smiled softly and said so only we could hear, "We survived."

WHEN GAVIN HAD TOLD me that he had planned a graduation party, I hadn't expected this. Neither had Jillian parents, judging from the grim look on Tara's face. Of course, that might have something to do with Jillian's other bit of news. My own parents had already come and gone, tired from their red eye flight into town this morning. Cheesy Pete's was only for the intrepid adult on a weekend night.

"I'm going to get another pitcher," Roman announced, getting up from the table.

"Will you get me a water?" Jillian asked him.

It wasn't even a question. We were all fawning over her at the moment.

Liam stood up to join him. "I'll come and help."

"How many men does it take to get a pitcher of beer?" Jess joked.

"I miss beer," Jillian grumbled and I gave her a sympathetic frown.

Gavin was off somewhere, too. Probably paying the obscene bill for the insane amount of food our party had scarfed down. He'd rented out the entire arcade. Somehow spending the evening with my best friends and my family together, drinking beer, and playing Skee-Ball was the perfect way to wrap up my college life and start my adult one.

"Is that what Roman gave you for graduation?" Jillian craned to see the locket that Jess was wearing. She nodded and held it away from her neck so that we could inspect it. "It was his grandmother's."

"That's so sweet," Jillian said. With a sigh, she patted her stomach. "All Liam gave me was this."

I stuck my tongue out at her. "Don't pretend like you didn't have something to do with that."

"Oh, I did," she said smugly.

"How did Tara handle the news?" Jess asked, glancing over her shoulder as if Tara might appear like Bloody Mary when her name was mentioned.

"She turned ten shades of red." Jillian smiled, as if this memory pleased her.

"She turned purple," Liam corrected her, taking the chair next to his fiancée. "I thought she might have had an aneurism."

"She's upset that we aren't married," Jillian explained. "It doesn't matter that I decided to have a baby while my body still could. Nope, it's more important that she gets to plan a wedding."

"Hey, I asked you to marry me," Liam said defensively.

"And I said yes!" Jillian laughed and leaned over to kiss him, wiping the disgruntled look from his face instantly.

"You still haven't done it," he said, as he took the hand that wore his ring.

"I'm not getting married while I'm fat."

"You aren't fat, you're pregnant," Jess and I said at the same time.

"The wedding can wait until after the baby," she said, putting an end to the matter. "We're just going to be nontraditional. Jess could deliver the baby!"

"Medical school is a bit longer than nine months," Jess said dryly. She elbowed me in the side. "What did Gavin get you?"

I bit my lip, my cheeks flushing. "A key to his place."

The unofficial proclamation was met with ohhhhs!

It had kind of been an expectation at this point. I'd spent the last year finishing up my classwork in Olympic Falls and spending my weekends with him in the city. In fact, almost every Friday night we'd been here, blowing off steam, playing

Skee-Ball, and getting reacquainted with each other after a long week of work and school. I'd been nervous to bring up what would happen after graduation, all the same. I hadn't wanted to assume that he wanted me to move in with him, even after I took the job in the PR department at NorthWest Investments.

"She couldn't afford a place of her own," Gavin said, joining us with a wink. "Not with what her terrible boss pays her."

"It's more than I made last year," I joked.

"Last year, you only made him," Jillian pointed out. I threw a wadded up napkin at her.

Our families didn't last as long as we did. Probably because none of us were quite ready to leave. Not just this place, but this part of our lives. As the evening wore on, our group dwindled. Jillian was the first victim. Her ankles had swollen during the graduation ceremony and despite the fact that she was barely showing, she found it hard to play most of the games.

"I'm taking you home to bed," Liam said finally, when she began to stretch her arms over her head and yawn.

"I thought you'd never ask," she said coyly.

"I didn't ask, chicken," he said mischievously. He was on his feet, helping her out of her chair a moment later. We all stood to give her hugs goodbye.

"Call me tomorrow," she whispered in my ear.

I still had so much to talk about with her before she left for Scotland next week. I couldn't believe that she'd chosen there. The selfish part of me had hoped that Liam and her would choose to live in Washington, but I knew they had their reasons for going to Scotland. I hugged her extra tightly and promised I would call.

They'd made it halfway to the entrance before Liam stopped and scooped her up into his arms. She rested her head on his shoulder, obviously too tired to even make it to the parking lot.

"I think that's our cue," Jess said apologetically as she and Roman gathered their things. He'd won her a large, stuffed chili pepper out of a claw machine.

I jumped up and caught her in a giant hug. She pulled back, laughing. "I don't leave for another month."

"And we'll only be three hours away," Roman reminded me. "Plus, I promise to take good care of her."

"Don't let her work too hard," I said, afraid that at any moment I would start to cry.

"I'll try, but no promises." Roman reached out to take his wife's hand and she pressed herself against him, giving him a swift kiss on the lips. They were like night and day, her blonde with skin pale from being back under Washington's lack of sun, and him dark-haired and olive-skinned—complete opposites and a perfect match.

"Call me tomorrow," Jess said with a wicked smile. Apparently, my best friends wanted to make sure that we spent as much time as possible together before we all went our separate ways.

"And then there were two," I said to Gavin, as we looked down at our empty table, cluttered with plates and cups.

The bartender that had been slinging drinks for our party appeared and grabbed an empty pitcher. "Last call."

"I think we're good," Gavin told him. Turning to me, he

held up his gameplay card. "Up for one final game of Skee-Ball."

"I'll kick your butt," I promised him.

"Of that, I have no doubt."

Since we spent so much time here, my game had gotten even better. Even Gavin couldn't pretend to hold a candle to my mad Skee-Ball skills. We each took a spot at our favorite machines and Gavin swiped the cards. The balls rolled down the chute, racking in a familiar, comforting way.

"I bet you that I can get you a top shelf prize," he said, recalling the deal we'd made during our first, unofficial date.

My lips twisted into a smirk. "You never learn."

It was my highest-scoring game ever. I didn't even pay attention to what Gavin was hitting, but given the number of hundred pointers I racked up, I knew there was no way he could keep up. When the final ball dropped into the fifty-point rung, I jumped back and looked up to check my score.,

Except there was no score. Had the stupid machine not been tracking my all-time greatest-ever Skee-Ball round? Then I realized the scoreboard was scrolling a message, not a score.

Will...

You...

Marry...

Me?

The question continued to scroll across the board and I continued to stare at it. After I regained my motor functions from the shock, I looked to Gavin. He was on one knee with a plastic prize capsule in his palm.

"Is that a top shelf prize?" I asked weakly.

"Open it find out," he suggested, his eyes as bright blue as a clear day.

I took the prize from him and popped off the plastic lid with shaking hands. Inside, tucked into a flimsy piece of foam, was a brilliant diamond solitaire. I looked down at him, my eyes shining with tears.

"Will you marry me, Cassie?" he asked, his own voice rough with emotion.

"Yes," I said breathlessly.

Gavin stood and took the ring, sliding it on to my finger. It fit perfectly.

Reaching for him, I took his face in my hands and drew it down to mine. Our lips sealed the commitment we just made to one another, our bodies beginning to press urgently together. I finally remembered where we were and pulled away. "Ever done it on a Skee-Ball machine?"

I was only half joking. I wanted to get him alone—quickly. Then, I glanced around and realized we were already completely alone. "You planned all of this," I accused him. Now I knew why my friends expected phone calls in the morning. "How did you get everyone out of here?"

He looked down at his shoes like he'd developed a sudden interest in footwear before sheepishly admitting, "I own the place."

"And I've been paying my tab for the last year." I smacked him on the shoulder playfully.

"So, if you are serious about the Skee-Ball machine," he said in deadpan tone.

"Too hard." I took his hand and tugged him toward the door.

"Where to then?" he asked.

"Take me home," I told him, "to our bed."

He caught me around the waist and brought me back in for one more kiss. When our lips broke apart, he pressed his forehead to mine and I marveled at how lucky I was. This man who had taught me that I could be loved just the way I was, who had shown me some things were worth fighting for, who I felt like I'd been looking for my whole life—I had finally reached him.

Acknowledgments

It's hard to believe that this is the last book with these characters. Jillian, Jess, and Cassie have become my friends over the years, and I'm so happy to see them off on their happily ever afters!

So many people helped this book into the world. A huge thank you to my agent, Louise Fury, who puts up with me, encourages me, gets me lost in the South of France-you are my spirit animal. Thank you for your patience and support. To the entire team at The Bent Agency, thank you for always being on the ball and keeping me together.

Thank you to my foreign teams who have helped my books reach a worldwide audience. For a girl who loves to travel, it's a dream come true.

Huge thanks to the team at Blanvalet, especially Wiebke Rossa, editor extraordinaire, and my friend Berit Boehm.

Thank you to Leonie Schoebel at the Meller Agency for your tireless work on behalf of my own.

Thank you to Kristin Gumpert for coming out of 'retirement' to edit this book. You're not only a great editor, you're a better friend.

To my readers, who've waited a really long time for this book, thank you! Your stories have inspired mine. Your photos and messages, meeting you —I couldn't do this without your support and love.

Thanks to the home team. Elise, for her enthusiasm (kid, this is your book), my kids for accepting mom's crazy career, my whole big wild family, Olive, our newest cat, who inspired me, and of course to Josh. You've taught me what love is. Every love story I've ever written is a piece of ours. I'm so thankful I *reached* you.